THEY MOSTLY COME OUT AT NIGHT

BENEDICT PATRICK

Published by One More Page Publishing

ISBN: 1530640105
ISBN-13: 978-1530640102

CONTENTS

ACKNOWLEDGEMENTS

If you found me a few years ago, you would have met a slightly less grey-haired writer who believed he could do this writing thing all by himself, with as little input from anyone else as possible.

Yes, I was that stupid.

My ongoing, immeasurable thanks to:

All of my early readers, for invaluable feedback. To Edingell, for being there from the beginning. To Craig and Graham, for your speed and honesty. To Mark, Sean and Rory, for getting there eventually! And finally to Kat, for making me laugh and cry more than I thought I ever would when reading my own book.

Laura and Jenny for their professional polish, for helping to make this story into something I am proud to publish.

The Writers of All The Things, for being my constant companions on this journey (and long may we continue!).

Also to The Plotting Telltalers for being writing buddies, to the handful of people on Kboards who helped throughout the process (and to everyone else on there for all the valuable info you give to everyone, everyday), and to Bryan Cohen and his Facebook group for their help with the book description.

And finally, to Adele. Thank you because I promised I would, and thank you because you make all of this worthwhile.

CHAPTER

ONE

Splintered wood, teeth and claws, blood in the night. Lonan had seen these events so many times before. He knew exactly what was coming.

"Can't you get him to shut up?" The voice belonged to Lonan's father. This was a dream about that horrible night eight years ago, and back then, Lonan had been unable to stop screaming.

His father grabbed him roughly by the shoulders. "Boy, you have to stop. They are above us, we can hear them through the floor. You will lead them straight to us."

Lonan was a young man now, but could not help the guilt he still felt about that night. He had known that to survive the dark, he should be silent. If a child needed to cry, they did so with their head tucked under their pillow. But Lonan also knew that back then, back eight years ago, he was desperately trying to tell them all something.

Nobody had listened.

"I don't want to do this," his father said, before slapping young Lonan across the face with the back of his hand.

That was the last exchange that took place between Lonan and his father before the cellar door cracked open and the creatures took his father's life.

1

As always, it was as those sinister clawed hands reached into the cellar that Lonan woke up. The dawn bell was ringing, signalling it was safe to go outside. Lonan knew he was going to be in a foul mood after his dream, so he chose to slink out of the cellar and make his way into the forest without having to speak to anyone.

Most of the village hated Lonan. Even now, years later, they blamed him for the events of that awful night, for the multiple breaches and the lives that had been lost. It had easily been the worst night in Smithsdown's history. The villagers were right about one thing - there was somebody to blame for those events, but it was not Lonan. However, back then, nobody had wanted to listen to the boy who they believed had led the monsters to their doors, and now nobody wanted to listen to the man he had become.

Lonan made his way into the forest because he had roots and herbs to gather for the village healer. However, as often happened after he dreamt of his father, Lonan instead wasted the day away dealing with his anger, taking it out on the forest so as not to mistreat the few in the village who still cared for him.

As the sun began to fall, Lonan returned home, eager to see the village buildings before the sky darkened. As he crossed the river that ran close to Smithsdown, he stopped, looking downstream. There in the distance was Branwen, the woman who used to be Lonan's closest friend.

On seeing her, Lonan quickly hid in the bushes. Branwen had not welcomed the sight of him for a long time. Out of all of the villagers, it was she who hated him the most.

What's she doing? It'll be dark soon, and they'll be coming. Why is she still here?

From his crouching position in the bushes, Lonan strained his neck upwards to look at the setting sun. In truth, it was still around two hours until nightfall, which gave her and him plenty of time to return to the village and to safety. However, like many of those who lived in the forest, the hairs on the back of Lonan's neck always stood on end when the sun began to fall. Worried, he turned to look at the young woman he was hiding from.

When they were children, they had spent as much time together as possible, playing on the village green or in the wild of the woods. But now...

Now, Branwen despised Lonan most of all. He knew they could never have a future together anymore, all because Lonan

2

had been blamed for a crime committed by another.

Worst of all, Lonan's boyish affections for Branwen had changed too. His memories of his childhood friendship with her were precious to him, and as he had grown into a man, his feelings of affection towards her had deepened. This was why her attitude towards him hurt so much.

He gave a small breath of relief when he saw Branwen finally gather her washing, adjust the small bundle she held swaddled to her chest, and left for home. Once she had disappeared from sight, Lonan stood, stretching his thin legs and ruffling his scruffy, dark hair to loose any brambles that had become tangled in it. It had been a number of weeks since he had last seen Branwen. Even now, he dared not get too close. His battered heart could not cope with the inevitable look of loathing she would give him. Worse still were the recent changes in Branwen's life. Lonan had been actively avoiding seeing her because he feared that the sight of Branwen and her newborn baby would finally convince his heart to give up on the chance of ever being able to be in her life again.

His journey back home after a day foraging in the woods brought him past families whose talents contributed to the endurance of the village as a whole - seamstresses, tinkers, fishermen, pottery makers - and all gave Lonan dark looks as he walked, some opting to include a sneer or a whispered comment to their companions at the sight of him.

The village itself was unremarkable. It was made up of a selection of about a dozen stone, wood and thatch buildings, home to as many families. The most prominent building in the village was its titular smith, and as always Lonan gave it a wide berth. He travelled west of the main buildings of the village, doing his best to avoid the busier central area.

Dragging his heels, he finally made his way to his mother's cottage. He gave himself a few moments at the doorway, pulling in a deep breath before entering.

The cottage was dark, lit only by the small tease of natural light that made its way into the building via two windows set into the east and west walls, and by the coals in the fireplace opposite the doorway. The stone walls provided the family with only one room, as was common in Smithsdown, and as a result the room was very busy. It was dominated by the large table in the centre of it, currently covered in a number of pots and plates that his mother was using to prepare dinner over the fire. These would soon be cleared away in time for the meal, and as usual Lonan would uninvite himself. Lonan's mother kept her back to him, not acknowledging his entrance. He was used to this response, and instead turned to the owner of the blonde curls whom he spied crouching behind some grain sacks off to his left.

As he made his way over to see his sister, Lonan dropped a hemp bag onto the kitchen table with a small thud. "Found a family of mushrooms. Thought they might be different for you both."

His mother's head turned slightly to glance at the parcel, but otherwise she did not respond.

Lonan tossed a smaller bag to his sister. "Here you are, don't gobble them all in one go."

"Berries?" Aileen asked, wrinkling up her nose as she picked up one of the small fruits and squashed it between her fingers, letting the purple juice dribble down her sleeve.

Lonan put his hand on her head and gave his sister a playful push, just enough to force her off her knees and onto her bottom. "Blueberries, stupid. Good for eating, and for making a mess." He pointed a finger at her face to suggest he was getting her into trouble, but the playfulness in his eyes betrayed his true intent. "And I gave you them for eating, so no messing, you hear?"

His sister giggled in reply, plunging her fingers into the bag and squashing a sticky mass into her mouth, prompting her to let out a large chortle.

Like a mother hen suddenly alerted to her brood's peril, Aileen's laughs prompted Lonan's mother's immediate reaction. She dropped the copper ladle that she was stirring her stew with, allowing it to tip up in the pot, sending it and a generous amount of food careening to the floor. With a stern face she rushed over to her daughter, shoving Lonan out of her path.

"What is that?" she barked at Lonan, her eyes never leaving her daughter's mouth, which was now pinched between a calloused forefinger and thumb. "What have you given her now?"

"Poison, of course. Thought it was about time we got rid of her." Lonan's reply was laced with spite, but he made sure to catch Aileen's eye so she knew he was not serious. He should not have worried - his sister was used to how the rest of her family interacted by now.

His mother gathered a lick of purple juice on her finger and placed it on her tongue, sneering her lips in response to the sharp sweetness of the fruit. She chose this moment to finally look at her son, the glower in her eyes showing that she was clearly unimpressed with his gift.

Lonan's lips pursed at his mother's disapproving gaze. The blood boiling behind his eyes urged him to say something to her, to invite her into an argument. History had shown him that his mother was more than willing to fight. But Lonan had long since learnt the cost of these arguments, how hollow and alone they made him feel afterwards, so he bit his tongue and said nothing. Lonan still loved his mother even if she was unable to love him back.

His mother swiftly gathered the remaining fruit into the pouch and hurried back to repair the damage left at the abandoned cooking pot.

"Don't you have somewhere else to be?" Again, this was uttered without looking at her son. Instead, her eyes were focussed on the meal.

"You know I've nothing better to do than enjoy our witty banter," Lonan shot back, regretting the harshness of his reply instantly. He had never heard a kind word from his mother, never even seen her smile, since the night that his father had been killed. Her love for Lonan had died that night too, and Lonan struggled to remind himself that this was not truly her fault. She believed that Lonan had been responsible for the death of the man that she loved, a lie that the rest of the village was also guilty of believing.

Before leaving, he knelt down to Aileen again, giving her a heartfelt hug, enjoying the feel of her blonde curls tickling his ears. "Magpie King protect you," he whispered into her ear.

He pulled back to look at his sister and was greeted by a face full of curiosity. "What's up, spud?"

"Is he real? Really? Niall Tumulty says there's no such thing, like bears and dragons."

Lonan gave a knowing grin. "The Tumulty boys know nothing. 'Course he's real. Who else looks after us at night?"

This was the response his sister was looking for and she gave her brother a stronger hug before he got up to leave. By now, a bowl of stew was waiting for him on the table. He picked it up and left the cottage without further disturbing his mother, fearful of further darkening her mood.

Once outside, Lonan's eyes went immediately to the sky. It was getting darker - he gave it less than an hour before nightfall. He trudged slowly down the village paths, gathering big chunks of stew onto his spoon before gulping it down his throat. It was mostly grain, but a mix of carrot, trace amounts of bacon and a healthy assortment of herbs served to turn it into an interesting meal. Lonan's mother no longer loved him, but he could still enjoy the benefits of her Knack for cooking. It was a good skill to have in the family, but unfortunately it did not provide them much to barter with. His mother was certainly not the only cooking Knack in the village.

He marched in a circle around the village, giving the Tumulty boys an exaggerated nod as he passed by them coming back from the day's harvest.

"Knackless," Callum muttered in return, a clear insult.

Otherwise, they ignored him, which was probably the best response Lonan could have hoped for. They were a family of farming Knacks, experts in sowing and reaping, and this made them indispensable for life in the village. They did not let their importance go to their heads and had the reputation of being a friendly, generous bunch. Lonan was the exception to this rule.

Giving himself time to finish his meal, Lonan quietly settled outside the north window of the Hammer household. Smithsdown had no storytelling Knacks, not any more, but Grandfather Hammer still knew a fine selection of tales and, best of all, he was loud. It was not uncommon for him to recount one to his grandchildren before they locked down for the night, and as luck would have it, he was beginning a tale right now. It was the story of Wishpoosh, the giant beaver. Not one of Lonan's favourites, he had heard it so many times before, but one of the young Hammers often requested it. However, it did have Artemis in it, and it was tales of Artemis that Lonan preferred. That sly man was ever the outsider, yet never let anyone talk down to him or deny him anything. Lonan rolled his eyes at the screams of the Hammer grandchildren as Artemis yet again tricked Wishpoosh into swallowing him whole. Lonan chose this moment to take his final walk of the evening, not needing to stick around to hear the end of the tale.

He paused briefly outside the blacksmiths. This was a building he dare not look at directly for fear of his own reactions to the sight of it. So many of Lonan's formative years had been spent inside it, watching his father beat metal into pots, cauldrons, weapons and decorative items. The sounds of the smithy - the clang of hammer onto anvil-pressed iron, the hissing protest of water as angry metal was lowered into it, the crackling of coal in the forge - had been a balm to Lonan as he had watched his father's powerful Knack at work. When he had been truly focussed, Lonan had seen his father's eyes turn amber and sparks fly from them to mirror those he crafted by the beating of his hammer, the sign of a truly potent Knack. The other families of Smithsdown provided for all of the inhabitants of the village, but it was Lonan's father's skill, and the skill of his father before him, that had made Smithsdown just as important to all of the Corvae people, or so Mother Ogma often told Lonan. In the days when people had moved more freely throughout the forest, other villages had sent envoys on day-long treks to place an order with the Anvil family. It was said that the Magpie King himself had regularly sent his people from the Eyrie to claim Lonan's grandfather's taxes in the form of wrought-iron decorations or weaponry, but the last contact with the Eyrie had been made before Lonan's lifetime.

His father's Knack and his smithy should have been Lonan's inheritance. Instead, Lonan had to settle for standing outside this building and listening to the fumbling crashing of a hammer being slapped against abused copper, the resulting tune a bastardisation of the skillful notes his father used to play. Knowing it was a foolish act, Lonan could not help but turn his head to catch sight of Jarleth Quarry, wearing Lonan's father's leather apron, pummelling away in the workshop. The curly-haired young man looked up, caught Lonan's eye and flashed him a knowing, taunting grin.

Lonan snapped his gaze away from the smithy, spat the remnants of his stew onto the muddy path, and took off. His fists were tight and shaking, and as Lonan focussed on the path in front of him, he had to will his rage to dissipate before he entered Mother Ogma's house. She could not abide his fits of anger.

Quarry had no Knack for metalwork. Neither did Lonan, for that matter. He had always hoped that time would allow the Knack to develop, someday giving him ammunition to claim his father's legacy back, but long before his twentieth birthday Lonan had given up the hope of any Knack materialising for him, let alone the potent one that his father had possessed. There was a lot of debate in the village about where Knacks came from. Most believed that they were inherited, passed down from father to son by blood. Lonan believed differently. He believed that a Knack was earned, that it was a type of magic that somebody developed by applying themselves to a certain task with dedication and pride. After his father's death, Lonan had been denied the chance to practice blacksmithing, and as such had been denied the opportunity to develop his family's Knack.

It was clear to Lonan and to anyone else with experience of what a decent smithy could produce that Jarleth Quarry had never developed this Knack either. However, Lonan knew all too well that Quarry did have a Knack of his own, one that Lonan could not hope to combat or expose, and these facts made any attempt to reclaim the forge futile.

Wrapped up in his angry thoughts, Lonan was not paying attention to his surroundings. It was for this reason that he walked right up to Branwen Quarry, Jarleth's wife, just as she was leaving Mother Ogma's cottage. Lonan froze when he saw her so close. As much as his interactions with his mother pained him, this was the woman in the village who held the secret to hurting Lonan.

Branwen's scarred face - the entire right hand side of it had been mutilated - was as ugly as the emotions that she held towards Lonan, and was a constant reminder of the crime that she blamed him for. What he had feared seeing for the past few weeks, however, was now right in front of him. Swaddled to Branwen's chest was her newborn daughter, still unnamed for the first month, as was the village's custom. Lonan's eyes fell upon the babe, the child of the man that he hated and the woman that he loved, and he froze.

Branwen paused too when she sighted Lonan and her eyes narrowed to slits. She clutched her baby tighter to her chest.

"Anvil," was her only acknowledgement of him. The hate in Branwen's voice stabbed directly at Lonan's heart. He felt his anger force its way towards his throat again, threatening to come up with a retort to hide his pain. Lonan quickly quelled this urge, instead remaining silent as she stormed past.

As Branwen hurried away, she turned her head from him, to hide her face. Since her scarring, Branwen had done her best to avoid having to socialise with the rest of the village, doing what she could to conceal her face when she had no choice but to go outside. When Lonan looked at her, he often forgot that Branwen's injury even existed. All he saw was the girl that should have been his wife. Another part of his future that Jarleth had stolen from him.

What shocked Lonan now was his reaction to the sight of the child. He had been so certain that seeing the baby - finally coming face to face with the reality that Branwen's life was attached to another - would let him give up on her. He had experienced the same fear after Branwen and Jarleth had been married. However, just as he had felt on that unhappy day two years ago, Lonan now realised that his heart was not ready to give up.

He knew that Branwen was not happy. Few people could be, Lonan was sure, sharing a life with Jarleth Quarry, but it was painfully obvious to Lonan that she hated her existence. She never smiled, she still spent most of her day down by the river, away from people. This was not the Branwen that Lonan had grown up with. Even the arrival of her daughter had done nothing to remove the scowl from her face. Deep within his heart, hiding but not forgotten, Lonan still held the belief that Branwen would have a much happier life if she was sharing it with him.

Lonan gave a small smile. *When will I learn? Why won't I let myself stop hoping?*

And then he thought for a moment, letting his smile fade from his face. *Or... maybe I should finally do something about these feelings. If my heart won't give up on the idea of a life with Branwen in it, can I do anything to make that life happen?*

He turned to look at Branwen, but she had already entered her own home.

First things first. I will get you to stop hating me. Somehow.

With that promise to himself, Lonan opened the door of Mother Ogma's cottage.

This cottage was similar in structure to Lonan's family home, but the interior decor was completely different. Where Lonan's mother had cooking utensils and furs hanging from the rafters - practical items for the daily life of a family - Mother Ogma's cottage had shelves of ointment pots and some rare glass jars filled with unusual substances gathered from the forest over the years. She had a few kitchen items close to her fireplace as well, but the majority of the roof space was dedicated to the hanging of a wide variety of drying or dried plants, most of which had been gathered by Lonan over the years. Because of this unusual garden, Mother Ogma's cottage was overwhelmingly aromatic, with dozens of differing scents vying for the attention of a visitor's nostrils.

"Nice day, dear?" Mother Ogma questioned, cheerfully arranging some dying marigolds in a vase by one of her windows.

"Oh yes, fantastic," Lonan replied dryly. "I do so love my work."

Mother Ogma rewarded Lonan's sarcasm with a friendly tutting. "Did you manage to find me some evening primrose?"

Lonan responded by taking a bunch of long stems with dainty blue petals and placing them on the kitchen table, before moving over to Harlow's chair. Although he was technically not a permanent resident of the cottage, Harlow had lived here since before Lonan could remember. Most of the children in the village assumed that Harlow was Mother Ogma's husband, but after spending time with her, Lonan found out that her husband had died many years ago. Mother Ogma had a Knack for healing, and nobody in the village had ever heard Harlow utter a single sound, or perform any kind of action without assistance. Mother Ogma had told Lonan that when she was younger, she had found the old man wandering alone in the forest, and has cared for him ever since. His groomed, long grey beard could not hide the mess of scars that made up his face, and only one lifeless eye remained to stare blankly at the flames licking up from the dying fire.

"Dearie," Mother Ogma said hesitantly, probing at the flowers that Lonan had brought her, "these aren't primroses, Lonan. I asked for yellow petals, not blue. Mother Cutter has a bad chest again, and these won't do anything to ease it for her."

Lonan sighed. "I'll get them tomorrow. Or do you want me to head back now?" He gave her a cheeky grin as he said this.

"We can try again tomorrow," she responded diplomatically. "Right now, I need your help to get everything below. The sun is setting."

Together they moved the kitchen table to the wall and pulled aside the aging deerskin that was covering the floor underneath. This unveiled a sturdy oak door set into the floor, reinforced heavily with iron supports. Bolted firmly to the door was a worn metal ring, which Lonan fed a rope into and, setting up a basic pulley system using a hook embedded into the eastern wall, he pulled the great door open. This granted them the familiar sight of the cellar, where three beds greeted them. Working together, Lonan and Mother Ogma helped to guide Harlow down the wooden staircase that Eamon Cutter's father had fitted years ago. Most families chose to use ladders to get into and out of their cellars to conserve space below, but some opted for the staircase to help those who could not cope with the physical strain. Mother Ogma had had the wooden stairs fitted for Harlow before Lonan was born, but they both knew that she benefited from them just as much now.

As they tucked him into bed, Harlow let out a low moan, and Lonan flinched backwards. That was the first sound he had ever heard the old man utter, and Lonan had slept in the same room as him for the best part of the last five years.

"He's been doing that all day," Mother Ogma explained as she pulled the woollen blanket up to the old man's neck, running a soothing hand over his forehead. "It used to happen a lot when he first came to me, but he grew out of it when I still had fire in my hair. Very strange."

Lonan glanced uneasily at the thick beams above him, and at the same moment he heard the bell ring out across the village to signal five minutes before sunset. "I suppose you're going to tell me that it means something?" he said, attempting to hide from the squirming sensation that the bells often initiated in the pit of his stomach.

Mother Ogma smiled, turned to Lonan and now stroked his face reassuringly. "Mean something?"

Lonan shrugged her hand away from him, turning back towards the cellar stairs.

"Yes, I suspect it does. It means that those berries that you brought me yesterday are far too sweet for poor Harlow's gut at his age. Back to porridge for him I'm afraid. Now, shut us up, will you, dear?"

Lonan walked up the stairs again and took a hold of the thick rope that was attached to the inside of the cellar door. With much effort he pulled the door closed on the cellar opening with a thud. Using the light from the candle that Mother Ogma had lit to guide him, Lonan proceeded to do up the many bolts that allowed them to lock the door from below. His job completed, Lonan prepared himself for bed, mumbled good night and crept under his covers. With everyone in place, Mother Ogma blew out the candle, plunging them all into darkness.

His eyes now useless, Lonan used his ears to reassure himself that everything outside was normal. The first few minutes were interrupted by two large thuds, which experience told Lonan were other homes in the village shutting their own cellar doors a little later than was recommended. Lonan knew that his mother's door would not be one of these - she always made sure that Aileen was secreted away well before the sunset bell. A steady wind was blowing and Lonan could hear the soothing rustling of it weaving through the thatch high above them, its constant whistling punctuated only by the occasional unusual grunt or moan from Harlow.

And then, suddenly, ears trained by a lifetime of listening for noises in the night, Lonan picked out a crunch of straw. The saliva dried up instantly in his mouth and he stopped breathing, doing all that he could to pick up anything further from the cottage roof. Sure enough, the first noise of impact was followed by three further crunching sounds, which Lonan knew was the straw that roofed the building snapping under the weight of something heavy walking across it. Lonan's heart screamed at every step, waiting in dread for any changes in noise that might signify the inside of the cottage being entered, but no more sounds came at all. After what seemed like an hour of tense silence, he heard Mother Ogma exhale in relief.

"They're out there, aren't they?" he asked her, already knowing the answer.

"Oh dearie, they're always out there. But the Magpie King protects us, so we need not fear."

Harlow gave another moan, and Lonan heard rustling which signified Mother Ogma moving over to the old man's bed to comfort him. Lonan turned around onto his side and shut his eyes to do his best to force sleep to come.

"He doesn't always protect us," he whispered to nobody in particular, and then his exhausted mind descended into darkness.

Adahy watched the shadows slink like poison through the streets.

From his position high above the village, and with the training that he had already received from his father, he clearly marked their movements as they did their best to merge with the pools of darkness cast by the moonlight. Every now and again, one of them would leap on top of one of the crude homes of the villagers, scurrying around on the rooftop for moments before rejoining its brothers on the streets. Adahy had been taught that such activities were meant to breed fear, and from fear generate the chaos of panic, which would make the shadows' task all the easier.

All of the tribes that Adahy's people had contact with worshipped a different totem animal - the Leone worshipped the lion, the Tytonidae the owl. However, the Wolves were more than just another tribe who had picked a particularly vicious animal to associate themselves with. Even from this distance, Adahy could make out that the Wolves were not quite human. Sometimes they walked on two legs, sometimes running on all fours. Despite the clear humanoid shape of their limbs, they acted more like animals as they prowled through the village below, scratching at doors and sniffing for food, doing what they could to gain entry into the guarded homes.

The villagers of the forest had long ago learnt how to protect themselves from the Wolves, locking themselves away beneath the earth when darkness fell. Further trickery had been added to their tactics across the years, and often some homes would be abandoned altogether, or offerings of fresh meat were left for the Wolves to sate their hunger. Alas, it was not mere hunger for food that led the Wolves to hunt. It was the hunt itself, and the thrill of the kill. A child's scream would be all that it would take to direct this band to an individual house, and then it would become a war between Wolf claws and the carpenter's door. Adahy was to defend these people. It was his calling to hunt the hunters, to be the thing that the beasts that stalked the darkness feared. This was Adahy's first time outside at night, and he was terrified.

Down below, the shadows continued to roam the streets, but Adahy was beginning to see a pattern form in their movements. All dwellings were getting attention from the Wolves, but more and more of them paused to sniff and claw at the cottage beside the blacksmiths. Adahy tutted again at the fact that the smithy's chimney was still coughing forth smoke from the dying embers of its forge. Did they not know that such a signal would surely draw attention to their home? He would have to have an envoy sent to the village in the morning to chastise them for their slovenliness.

"Where iz he? I see no one," came the frustrated call of Celso Dulio, an envoy from the Muridae people from the grasslands to the south of the forest.

The two guardsmen who were assigned to him motioned for silence.

"I want to know where 'e iz," the little man continued in his strong, buzzing accent. "Why elze would I be freezing my balls off out 'ere except to see thiz great god in action."

This further outburst only awarded him with a thump from one of the guards' spear shafts, which he wisely did not respond to.

"He's no god," Adahy muttered under his breath, turning again to look down at the ant-like shadows. "He's a king. And a hero."

Celso's people worshipped the mouse, and as such, Celso was clothed in grey furs and a ceremonial hood that was shaped to look like his people's totem animal. Maedoc, Adahy's whipping boy and closest friend, joked that the diplomat must have had a thousand mice killed to make his clothing for this journey. Adahy suspected that moles were actually the unwilling donors. His own people, the Corvae, were fortunate their totem animal, the magpie, left plenty of feathers on the forest floor. Looking around him now, he felt proud at the sight of his Magpie Guard in their long black and white feathered cloaks, matching his own, and their dull black helms.

Only Maedoc stood out, wrapped in a thin grey woollen cloak, with a basic tunic on underneath, as befitted his lower-born station. The scrawny, wild-eyed young man had grown up with Adahy at the Eyrie, yet Maedoc was not of noble blood. It would not have been fitting for a prince of the Eyrie to be beaten when he misbehaved, so instead Adahy had been allowed to befriend this young orphan, and it was Maedoc who had been punished when Adahy did something wrong. Many years had passed since Maedoc had last suffered because of Adahy's actions - both because of their age, and Adahy's fearful obedience to his father - yet Maedoc remained a constant presence at the young prince's side.

"Damned Mouse is going to get us all killed," Maedoc confided with Adahy, rubbing his arms in a vain attempt to generate heat inside his cloak.

Adahy could not disagree with his childhood friend. Today was to be an important part of his own training, to witness what he would eventually be called upon to do. It was unfortunate that the visiting Muridae had caught wind of what was afoot in the Eyrie and had pressed to be allowed to attend.

Those who are not of the forest cannot understand the dangers that night holds here. The Mouse thinks of its squabbles with the Serpent and the Owl and assumes that their conflicts are mirrored the world over. The Wolves are different. They are not human, they cannot be reasoned with, and they have very good hearing.

The Magpie Guard stiffened, snapping Adahy out of his thoughts and drawing attention to the distant scene. The Wolves were clearly converging on the blacksmith's hut now, with a number of them prowling on the roof and the rest scratching at the walls on the streets below. By Adahy's count, there were about a dozen of them down there, but their frenzied movement made it hard to track them with complete success. However, what had generated a response from the guardsmen was the appearance of another shadow, this time on the roof of a building to the north of the small village. This figure moved slowly, more precisely, and by its careful steps made it clear that it wanted to remain hidden from the violent throng. Furthermore, this shadow was considerably larger than those cast by the individual Wolves, and seemed to ripple in the breeze.

"By Alfrond's whiskers, what in the hells iz he doing?" Celso gasped, completely abandoning his composure in the tension of the moment. "He iz down there alone? Those things will tear him apart."

A guardsman gripped the Mouse by the throat and thrust him to the earth. "You speak again and I put this through you," he thumped the butt of his spear onto the earth in front of Celso. "Get yourself killed in your own time, we will not let you endanger the young prince."

Adahy, however, was not interested in what was happening up on the ridge, his eyes were fixed on the village, hands clenched tight on his clammy skin.

As the large shadow jumped to another rooftop, attempting to get closer to the cottage, which was now under clear assault, it was evident from the reaction of the Wolves that they had spotted the newcomer. Like a wasp swarm, they moved as one towards the cottage the intruder was currently on top of. Realising that he had no other choice, the shadow that was Adahy's father raised his weapons and jumped into the oncoming mob.

At this moment, the moon was shrouded by a cloud.

All hope of continuing to watch the village scene was hopeless, as without the moonlight only the whitewash of the distant cottage walls was vaguely visible. Worse still was the fact that the Muridae diplomat began to scream.

"'E is dead, 'e is dead - flee while you can!'"

The Mouse had clearly escaped from his captor, as evidenced by the cursing of the guardsmen as they stumbled about in the starlight.

"Artemis take you, put a damned spear into the Mouse's throat before he gives us away."

Adahy ignored the commotion, instead straining his eyes towards the spot where he last saw his father alive. Taking pity on him, the moon unveiled herself again, gifting Adahy sight of the devastation down at the village. Black shadows, unmoving, littered the muddy streets, and only two figures remained, one clearly Adahy's father, the Magpie King. The last remaining Wolf was on the other side of the settlement from his pursuer, but made the fatal error of turning to cast a growl back at the assassin before melting into the forest. In the time it took Adahy to gasp, the Magpie King was beside his foe. A sharp flicking movement caused the top of the Wolf's shadow to fall to the streets below, quickly followed by the rest of its body.

"I don't believe it. One dozen of them and he bested them in zeconds. The man is incredible, he..." The rest of Celso's sentence of praise died in his throat as it was opened up by the point of a Magpie Guard spear. In death, the diplomat was finally silent.

"Count the bodies. I can only find ten. I read twelve before the clouds came. Can anyone see the others?"

"Are you certain? I thought there were only eleven."

"There are still only ten bodies, damn it. Take the prince and flee."

The warning came too late as a dark, hulking mass of fur and fangs leapt from the foliage, disembowelling the guard captain with a single swipe.

Adahy had never seen a Wolf up close before. The creature's body was roughly humanoid, but it seemed disproportionately muscular, with every sinew of gristle standing out and flexing on the thin leather of its belly. The rest of the creature was covered in dark, thick fur which sprouted from it like legs from a spider. Adahy faced the harbinger of his death with a detached curiosity, all at once wanting to take in as much information about this nightmarish figure, but also keenly aware of his impending and violent demise.

As the captain's body slowly fell, steam rising from his freed warm innards, Adahy peered into the face of the beast, grey eyes and dark fangs reflecting the now-menacing moonlight. It flexed its fingers and lowered its gaze to regard Adahy, emitting a grunting laugh. It knew who Adahy was.

The prince closed his eyes, waiting for the end.

A boyish scream pierced Adahy's serenity. He opened his eyes to the sight of Maedoc falling to the ground, having intercepted a killing blow that was meant for the prince. A thud to his right signified the arrival of a second Wolf who began to tear apart the remainder of the guard. The first creature moved closer, its lethal grin betraying the pleasure that it took in stalking the young prince.

Magpie Spirit, give me the strength to die with fight in my heart, Adahy prayed, yet he remained rooted to the spot. A spreading warmth in his undergarments alerted him to the fact that he had just soiled himself. He was going to die a coward.

And then the Magpie King was there. Adahy's father was just a man, but in the dark with his feathered cloak swirling about him, he seemed like a giant. In each hand he wielded two giant black iron sickles, a single one too heavy for Adahy to hold aloft for any length of time. His key distinguishing feature, however, was the mask that he wore to cover his face. The decorative iron helm protruded forward and down, mimicking the beak of a Magpie, and was connected to the king's cloak by a matching mane of black and white Magpie feathers. When he wore it Adahy's father stopped being human and took on the mantle of his ancestors, pledged to protect the Corvae and the forest.

The Wolf moved too slowly, and in a graceful dance the Magpie King breezed past it, moving to intercept the second while the first Wolf's torso slid into two halves. The last remaining guardsmen had managed to keep the final Wolf at bay with their spears and the sacrifice of two of their number. In a smooth movement, the King reached his sickle forward and opened the beast up.

Then the Magpie King was at his son's side. "Are you hurt?"

The uncanny utterance of those tender words from such an imposing figure was ignored due to how welcome they were.

"Father," Adahy began, and then to his shame he embraced the Magpie King and sobbed openly.

"My lord..." This spluttered address came from Maedoc, who miraculously had survived the Wolf's blow, but his torn face would never recover.

"Quick, boy," the Magpie King commanded, "see to my son. There will be more on their way, and our numbers are much depleted."

Maedoc looked briefly at his master in shock at being asked to continue his duties with half of his face hanging off, but with a muttered, "Yes sire," he thrust himself under the shoulder of a still-sobbing Adahy and limped his way in the direction of the Eyrie.

"What happened here?" Adahy could hear his father query in the direction of Celso's corpse.

"Mouse wouldn't shut up, led the Wolves right to us," came the reply.

"What a shame," the Magpie King's gravelled tones continued, "that the Wolves took him first."

A pregnant pause was followed by the remaining guardsmen's affirmations, but Adahy was already miles away. He was a coward, and he would have died a coward tonight. Even poor Maedoc, a slave boy, had more courage than the young prince.

I will never be worthy of taking the mantle of the Magpie King when my father is gone.

ARTEMIS
AND THE
THREE DAUGHTERS

A tale from the fireplaces of the Low Corvae.

Many seasons ago, seasons more than any in this village have seen, there lived an old pig farmer. He was a kind man whose wife had passed on many years ago through a sickness in her lungs, yet before she left she had gifted him with three beautiful daughters. These fine girls were the sole source of the farmer's happiness, and he guarded them jealously from the outside world. In turn, the farmer's daughters loved the old man more than life itself. They would tend to the pigs for him, prepare his food, tidy his home and sew his clothes, all to provide joy in the old man's world. But often, the girls would stare wistfully at the forest path that wound its way beside the fences of the pig farm, their minds filled with desire for the life that might exist for them outside of caring for their old father. This pang of curiosity would go unsatisfied until the youngest of the girls reached her sixteenth birthday.

When the autumn leaves laid a rust-strewn blanket throughout the dark forest, they brought trouble with them. This was not the evil of wolves or of birds, but instead was an untrustworthy, handsome smile and hard leathered feet, for the leaf fall brought sly Artemis with it. An apple in hand, travel sack thrown across his back and a patched cloak sheltering him from the misty winds, the trickster walked and skipped his way towards the farm. Indeed, he may very well have continued past it if the old farmer's youngest daughter had not decided to take that very moment to lean over the fencing of the pig sty to throw out the muck that the animals had produced for her on that day. Artemis took a greedy bite from his apple and decided he was hungrier than an apple would satisfy, so took it upon himself to go knock, knock, knocking on the old farmer's door.

The old man himself answered, and his eyes narrowed at the sight of handsome Artemis. The farmer did not like this confident stranger turning up on his doorstep, but could not ignore the responsibilities of hospitality so he reluctantly invited sly Artemis into his home.

Artemis relished the reveal of the second and third daughters, both hard at work preparing supper for that night.

"You are welcome to sit and eat with us, of course," the farmer offered the stranger, "but I will ask my daughters to stand and watch us eat. They shall not feed until we have finished and you have left our table. These three girls are the only joy left to me in the world, and it would break my heart if a strange man stole them away from me under my own roof."

Artemis agreed wholeheartedly with the farmer's suggestion, and bowed to each of the daughters in turn, begging their forgiveness for delaying their meals. The girls smiled back at the stranger, causing a knot of dread to form in the farmer's gut.

After Artemis had dined, he rose from the table to allow the daughters to sate their hunger. As was custom, Artemis enquired for a basin so he could wash himself after a day of travelling. The farmer nodded, and ushered his girls to boil water for the stranger, filling a basin in front of the stove.

"However," the farmer warned, "whilst you bathe I shall ask my girls to leave the house and wait outside for you to finish. Their eyes have never before beheld another man's body, and they shall not do so tonight. These three girls are the only joy left to me in the world, and it would break my heart if a strange man stole them away from me under my own roof."

Artemis thanked the kind old man warmly, and apologised again to each of the daughters as they wrapped their shawls around their shoulders to help them brave the bite of the evening air while Artemis bathed. The girls smiled back at the stranger, forcing the knot in the farmer's gut to writhe like a starved rat.

The girls returned inside after Artemis had bathed and clothed himself again. Being as close as it was to moon rise at that time, the old farmer was obliged to offer Artemis lodgings for the night.

"However," the old farmer warned, "I can only offer you my barn for your rest this evening. There are two beds in this house, one for myself and the other for my daughters. I cannot trust another man to be under the same roof as my girls during the night. These three girls are the only joy left to me in the world, and it would break my heart if a strange man stole them away from me under my own roof."

Artemis was in complete agreement with the farmer, and thanked him humbly for the straw and roof to sleep under. As each daughter made her way to bed, Artemis gave them a kiss on the hand to wish them goodnight. In turn, each daughter again smiled at the stranger. The knot in the farmer's gut threatened to crawl up his gullet, leap out of his mouth and strangle the stranger where he stood, but the old man was satisfied to see the handsome man finally leave his home.

However, every smile that the farmer's daughters had given Artemis had just made the stranger want them more, and the final wanton glance from the youngest daughter as she closed the bedroom door behind her had made Artemis' mind up for him. As soon as the farmer had shut Artemis outside in the cold, the trickster began to hatch a plot. During his time in the old man's house, Artemis had noticed that the farmer's eyesight was very poor, and often asked his daughters to clarify what he was looking at. This gave Artemis an idea.

After a smoke on his pipe and a stiff drink, the farmer decided to turn himself in for bed. As was his routine, the farmer lit a candle and crept into his daughters' bedroom to kiss them goodnight. His girls were sleeping restlessly that night, shuffling and squirming under the covers. A result of this evening's intrusion, the farmer decided. He moved across the head of the bed, planting a soft kiss on the pink skin of each of his daughters in turn. Confident that his girls were safe under his roof, the farmer slept peacefully that night.

The daughters were not, of course, safe under his roof. While the old man had been smoking his pipe, Artemis had secreted the girls one after the other out of their bedroom window, replacing each in their bed with a piglet from the farmer's own herd. It would only be in the morning that the farmer would realise he had not kissed any of his daughters goodnight at all. While the piglets rested, the daughters were being seeded by Artemis in the barn, having their eyes opened to the life that existed beyond the pig farm fences.

By morning, the stranger was gone, leaving behind him only an old man's broken heart, three awakened appetites and three well-rested pigs.

CHAPTER TWO

Lonan awoke with a start. Wide eyed, he looked around the room, expecting to see Magpie Kings and wolf men jumping out at him from the shadows.

What a dream. He shook his head, doing his best to sort out reality from the vivid fiction of last night. *Normally my dreams are about my past. Where did all of that come from, then?*

Lonan blinked, willing himself to deal with the real world, and looked around the cellar. The ceiling door was already open, and Mother Ogma had already helped Harlow upstairs.

How long have I slept in? He pulled himself out of bed, still wearing his clothes from the night before, and marched upstairs.

En route Lonan pondered the strange characters that had appeared to him last night. What kind of names were Adahy, Maedoc and Celso? They were nothing like the names of the villagers, who took their names from their people's history before they hid in the forest. Mother Ogma had said once that dreams were your brain's way of sorting out the information that got jumbled up in your head throughout the day. That would explain the presence of the Magpie King and the monsters - those figures were an aspect of daily life for the villagers - but the images that his brain had summoned to represent those mythical figures made Lonan shudder involuntarily. It was not uncommon for village children to wake up screaming at the nightmares that their brains conjure during the night, but never had Lonan experienced anything so real. He allowed his mind to wander back to the night he lost his father. Did the shadowy image of his father's killer match the Wolves from last night?

"Good morning, Lonan," Mother Ogma cheerily welcomed him, already working away at the fire. "Sleep well?"

Lonan glanced over at Harlow in his chair, who had already fallen back asleep. "You shouldn't have taken him up by yourself," he reprimanded, "I should have been awake ages ago."

"You won't catch me disagreeing with you there, but everyone needs a little treat now and again. You were so unsettled last night, I thought you might need the extra rest."

Unsettled? Lonan did his best to blink the sleep away, opening his eyes up wide to drink in the reality of the cottage interior. His dream last night had been strange. So violent. "Thanks," he mumbled. "So, yellow flowers?"

"That would be nice, yes. Oh, and we're low on agaric toadstools if you happen by any."

"I'll grab them if I see them, but I'm heading up the ridge today. Don't catch many agarics up there."

Mother Ogma shot him a curious glance. "Anything I should know about?"

Lonan shook his head dismissively. "Just planning a little jump to see if I can fly."

Mother Ogma grinned. "You can't scare me that easily, dearie. A few years ago perhaps, yes, but not any more. Too much fire in you now to give in like that."

"How was last night? The roof looking okay?"

"I had a quick peek and couldn't spot anything, but you know what my eyes are like. Take a look for me when you go out, won't you?" She waited for him to respond and then added, "The village seems peaceful enough."

"Good for them," Lonan muttered under his breath, grabbing an apple from a small bowl of fruit and making his way towards the doorway.

Blinking to adjust to the daylight, Lonan took a quick turn around the cottage to survey the roof. No new marks seemed to have been added to the doors or window covers, but he did notice some deep indents in the straw roof that he would have to reshape later. It confirmed what he thought he had heard - something had definitely been up there last night. This was not an unusual occurrence in Smithsdown. The villagers hid themselves in the cellars because the dark of night was almost guaranteed to bring the monsters. Most of the time, locked doors and windows were enough to dissuade the invaders from bothering the village any further, although a keen eye could always find evidence of their prying. Indents in the thatching of roofs, scratches on window frames or signs of burrowing at front doors.

It had been a few years since a Smithsdown cottage had been broken into after nightfall, and the night that Lonan's father was killed was the only time in Lonan's life that any cellar doors had actually been breached - his family's and Branwen's. But even though the possibility of an attack was low, there were enough signs every morning to remind the village that danger was always very, very close.

As was his ritual, Lonan walked in the direction of his mother's house to catch a glimpse of his sister before heading off to forage. He gave a grin as a giggle signified his sister's safety from inside the cottage. After confirming Aileen was in good health, he walked around the outside of the settlement, continuing to ponder what he had seen last night.

It had been Smithsdown that was being attacked in his dream, he was sure, right down to the fact that Quarry would be fool enough to leave the forge fires running. And he knew that something had definitely been on Mother Ogma's roof last night, but that was not unusual. He imagined that most homes in the village were disturbed in some small way at least once a week.

The villagers never knew exactly what threatened them at night. They simply referred to them as 'the monsters'. Only a small handful in Smithsdown had ever caught a glimpse of the creatures and survived, and none of those survivors were left in a sound enough state of mind to recall an accurate image of their attacker. Lonan wrinkled up his nose and tried to remember what he had seen on the night that his own cellar had been breached, the night his father had been killed. Could that dark shape have been some kind of wolf man? The memory of that time had been so twisted within Lonan's mind that he could not really trust it.

Lonan stopped and blinked. *Am I really trying to find evidence that the dream last night was real? A dream that had the Magpie King in it?*

He allowed himself a chuckle at that thought. He had long ago decided that the Magpie King was a myth, a story tale figure like Artemis the trickster designed to make people feel safer in their beds while death stalked the streets.

If the Magpie King does exist, why can't I remember anyone from the Eyrie contacting the village? Lonan raised his gaze to the distant highlands in the north, to the sight of the ancient fortress that blended into the rock of the skyline. There were a number of villagers who had attempted the trip during Lonan's lifetime - the Eyrie was a day's worth of hard travel away, which made the risk of being caught in the forest at nightfall a real threat - but none of them had ever returned. The other Corvae villages were about the same distance away, and contact with them had been more fruitful, but the dangers of any travelling in the forest meant that contact with the villages remained sparse.

Despite Lonan's doubts, he could not help himself. The blacksmith's cottage was where most of the action would have been last night, where the Magpie King had attacked most of the Wolves. A quick peek at that part of the village would put his mind at rest, and then he could continue about his day as normal. He edged around to the south of the village to where his father's former forge lay. A quick scan of the area betrayed no sign of any conflict, although peering closer drew Lonan's attention to some grooves on the window frame that could have been claw marks…

Lonan swore at the sight of a scarred face at the window, which quickly vanished when it made eye contact with him.

"Time for me to get out of here," he muttered, but it was too late.

He heard the sound of the front door opening and angry footsteps pounding dirt, moving around the cottage.

"Artemis, give me strength."

"Lonan Anvil, you stay the hell away from my baby," came the angry shriek from Branwen. "Just stay the hell away from us."

Lonan bit back the retort that threatened to bark out in response, and instead waved his assailant off and attempted to move towards the forest.

Unfortunately, Branwen's cries had already attracted the attention of other members of the community, including her husband.

"Oh hells," Lonan swore.

Jarleth Quarry strutted out from behind his forge, leather apron and gloves still attached, and his puzzled face turned to a sly grin when he noted Lonan's presence.

"All right, forager, what have you done to upset my beautiful wife?"

Jarleth's snide comment seemed to have more of an effect on his spouse than Lonan, with Branwen flinching at the mention of the word 'beautiful', causing her to raise a hand to her afflicted face. Of course, Jarleth's irritation of his bride was all designed to make her angrier towards Lonan, who she blamed for scarring her.

Branwen took a step forward, pummelling her calloused hands onto a shocked Lonan's chest. "What did you do to us? Why did they come?"

Lonan stood stunned, taking the blows while puzzling through what was happening. *Is she talking about eight years ago? I know she still holds a grudge, but it's not like her to explode in public like this.*

More faces appeared as further villagers came to see what the commotion was all about. Branwen continued to beat Lonan.

Has Jarleth done something? Lonan raised his arms to fend off Branwen's fists as he puzzled the source of her rage. *Maybe that 'beautiful' was the last in a string of insults? I wouldn't put it past the man at all.*

"Just what is going on here?" a gruff voice from the gathering crowd addressed the trio. Old Man Tumulty emerged from the growing throng, his thick white beard and bald pate announcing his identity. "Branwen, this rascal bothering you?"

"Oh, nothing to worry about, Mr Tumulty," Jarleth responded, arms open wide in a welcoming gesture at the sight of the village elder. "We're used to this one by now." He turned to regard Lonan, but also to hide the spark in his eye caused by his Knack being brought into play. "It's just that poor Branwen is more tired than usual with the wee 'un, and after everything last night."

"Wait, what?" Lonan said immediately. "Something happened last night?"

"Now listen here, you... rogue. Why can't you leave this family alone?"

"Did anyone else notice she came over to me? No, anyone?" Without waiting for a response to his question Lonan continued, pointing his finger at Jarleth. "Now, what the hell happened last night?"

"I said leave them alone, dammit." The rebuke from Tumulty was accompanied by a slap to Lonan's hand. "What happened to ye, Lonan? I remember such a nice little boy from my visits to yer father's forge. Why'd ye have te change?"

"Well, you are getting pretty old. Maybe your memory isn't as good as it used to be." Lonan could not help but lash out as he rubbed his stinging fingers, but catching Jarleth's wicked grin moments later made him instantly regret it.

This is exactly what that bastard wants - more reasons for the village to hate me.

"I knew your father well, you little pissant, and I can tell you one thing - he'd be ashamed to see you here today."

Lonan looked Jarleth in the eye as he answered Tumulty's retort. "Well, finally we found something we both agree on." He turned to Branwen again and did his best to be as sincere and to sound as commanding as possible. "What happened last night?" *Please, you used to trust me. Just answer my question. Magpie Spirit, let her hear me.* For the first time in many years, Lonan looked Branwen directly in the eye.

She gasped slightly, and Lonan hoped that this meant she had realised that he had no clue about what had happened last night. However, it was her husband that responded.

"We were breached last night. Only the house, not the cellar of course, but it brought up… bad memories. You know what I'm talking about, right? Well, Branwen has been suggesting all morning that you might have had something to do with it - why would that be? I've been doing my best to calm her down. Guess you chose the wrong time to go sneaking up behind our cottage."

All the while during this speech, Lonan could see amber glints in Jarleth's eyes telling him his Knack was in play. Branwen seemed to remain unaffected this time, her face displaying confusion and guilt more than anything else. Lonan could not help the small grin that crept across his own face at the realisation that he was winning over Jarleth's Knack. For the first time in eight years, Branwen was listening to him instead of the man who stole her away.

You've made a mistake, Lonan wanted to say, forgetting all about the dream last night. *For so long, you've made a mistake. It's me you should be with, me you loved.*

However, at this moment Lonan became aware of aggressive changes in the body language of many of the surrounding villagers.

The larger male villagers. This is what Jarleth did, he changed people's minds, this was his Knack. The worst thing is that Lonan was the only one who knew. Every other deluded soul in the village was convinced that Jarleth had developed a metal-working Knack. Convinced by Jarleth, of course.

Time to cut and run. "I'm sorry to hear about last night," Lonan responded, looking straight into Branwen's eyes again. "I'm glad you're all right."

I have to leave now, but I won't give up on you again. It should be my hand that comforts you, not his.

"Well, I appreciate the sentiment, forager," came the reply from Jarleth, Branwen too conflicted to make any response. "Just as much as I'll appreciate you staying away from my family in these difficult times."

Lonan gave Branwen a final nod, turned, and walked towards the forest. As he disappeared into the trees, the gossip mongers began their work.

Breached? That was the word that rang through Lonan's head as he plodded deeper into the forest, climbing up the wooded hills that lay to the south of Smithsdown. His thoughts turned back to the coincidences that existed between the dream last night and the state of the village this morning.

Had the blacksmith's cottage been breached in my dream? None of the characters mentioned it, but they were really more focussed on saving their own skins. Except for the Magpie King, of course. By Artemis, if I believed in an all-powerful protector that watched over the villagers and kept us safe, then I'd want it to look like that guy. He was immense, so fast, and in the end he was really damned scary. Definitely the most terrifying thing about that dream.

There had been evidence of commotion around Quarry's cottage, of course, but nothing that had given Lonan the impression that anything had gotten inside.

But it wasn't really me watching the events last night. It was the prince, Adahy. Adahy hadn't noticed a breach, but maybe he wouldn't have. Would a prince notice if one or two villagers got caught up in a struggle? He certainly didn't have much of a reaction to those guardsmen that died protecting his life. Or the whipping boy, Maedoc, who lost his face to give the prince some extra time to shit himself. The forest was in trouble if this guy is going to end up looking after it.

Lonan chuckled as he caught himself thinking of the figments of his imagination as real people. The more he thought about it, the more he was able to tie the elements of his dream to aspects of his waking life. The assault on the cottage was obviously a mental reaction to seeing Jarleth working his father's forge yesterday evening. And the whipping boy's face was clearly to mirror the damage caused to Branwen when she had been attacked as a child. The attack Lonan had caused, as far as the rest of the village was concerned.

Lonan had not always been hated. As the son of the local blacksmith, he had been well received by all in the village, even as a young boy. In fact, the only person who had ever held any spite for him had been Jarleth, but since Quarry had never strayed far from his mother's arms, Lonan had never felt any threat from one boy's jealous looks.

This changed on the night Lonan had turned to wave goodbye to Branwen as her family locked up for the night. Lonan had spotted Jarleth turning a key in her house's lock. He was unlocking the door. Lonan had let out a cry to alert someone, but his father misunderstood and had dragged his son into the cellar, worried about a twelve year old's screaming attracting too much attention as night fell. Jarleth had seen, however. He had been terrified when he met Lonan's eyes across the village centre, but had scuttled off all the same, leaving Branwen's door open. The open door served as an invitation for the monsters, and that night her cellar was breached and her mother and face were taken. Worse still, Lonan could not rest knowing that something was wrong, and down in his family's cellar he had continued to scream out of panic and frustration. This brought the wrong sort of attention, and that was also the night that Lonan's father was killed.

Lonan never found out why Jarleth had done it. He had always assumed Jarleth had decided that if he could not have Branwen, then nobody was going to have her. The motives did not matter though. In the morning, when the village rose to the massacre, Lonan found himself accused of foul play. This was the first time he realised what Jarleth's Knack was. All those years of convincing his mother to do his bidding had brought it out in him - Jarleth had a Knack for making people believe him. They believed it was Lonan who unlocked the Dripper door as the sun went down. Nobody, not Branwen nor his mother, had ever treated him the same again.

With these foul thoughts polluting his mind, Lonan found

29

himself unable to locate the ridge that Adahy had stood upon in his dream last night. He did not find this surprising at all, as Lonan was now fully convinced those events were all figments of his imagination. What he did find surprising, however, was how much he had allowed himself to care when he did think that an attack might have taken place last night. He meant those last words that he had spoken to Branwen - his heart felt considerably lighter knowing she was all right. Lonan's brow creased in confusion at these thoughts. How could he feel that about somebody who hated him so much? Somebody who had let him down. She should have never believed Lonan would ever have put her or her family in danger, Jarleth's Knack be damned. What good would it be now if she finally decided that Lonan was innocent? She was a Quarry now, with a Quarry child. Any hope that the earlier encounter with his former love had given Lonan was slowly drowned in these dark thoughts as he stumbled about the hillside.

Lonan shook his head to urge these thoughts to leave him. *I have to get out of Smithsdown, go somewhere that's not been poisoned against me. Magpie King forbid I allow any feelings for that ruined woman to hold me back.*

He found the rest of the day to be unproductive, and returned to Mother Ogma as nightfall beckoned, shrugging off her soft reproaches at the continued lack of evening primroses for her medicine cabinet. He curled up in bed in a black mood, craving the oblivion sleep would give him.

Adahy felt terrible. Ever since last night, he had remained in his room, staring out of the glass window to gaze at the dark forest that sprawled out beneath the Eyrie. His father had not spoken to him since their embrace last night. Poor Maedoc had been taken away to the healers and Adahy had not seen him since. All that the young prince was left with was the shame of his lack of action when the moment had called for a hero. He had always fancied himself to be a great warrior in the making. The tales of former Magpie Kings were his stories of choice from his nanny, fuelled by the promise of becoming a legend when he reached adulthood. He hated that child now, sitting upright in his bed with his optimistic, feckless grin.

He clutched at a small portrait of his mother, her tumbling white hair framing her young face. Adahy missed her so much at moments like this. He wanted to bury his head in her arms, for her to stroke his hair and to tell him that everything would be better soon. Adahy's father was not capable of replacing the tenderness of her touch.

There was a knock on the door. After waiting for a few moments, a voice from behind it queried, "Adahy? It's me."

Maedoc. Adahy ran across his chamber, opened the door and embraced his wincing friend. The prince did not care that tears ran freely down his face - he just wanted to feel comfort from somewhere.

"Argh, no, not so tight," Maedoc begged.

Sniffing, Adahy backed away, beckoning the whipping boy into the room. Head lowered, he took this time to glance at Maedoc's wounds. The entire right side of his friend's face was bound by wine-stained linen, tied to his head by a bandage that wound diagonally across his face. He walked with a limp and cradled his right arm horizontally at his waist.

"By the Great Spirit, Maedoc, your face..."

"I know," Maedoc replied, his lip wavering between a sneer and a grin. "The eye's gone." He sat on a stool, tapping the table top rhythmically with his good arm. "And when this comes off, I'll look like a monster."

"Gods..." Adahy's' voice wavered off. "You saved my life."

"Hmm..." Maedoc continued his tapping. "What did your father say?"

"He hasn't spoken to me."

Maedoc raised his remaining eye.

"I imagine he hates me right now."

"Nah, you'll be all right. He won't abandon his son." Maedoc did his best to worm his fingers under his bandage at his ear, to scratch an itch. "Not sure what my prospects are now, though."

"Are you kidding? You saved my life. You're a hero."

Maedoc raised his eyebrow. "The Magpie King didn't seem to notice last night. Reckon he thinks it's about time to get rid of me. Guess you're too old to be spending so much time with servants, now."

Adahy fell to his knees in front of the servant, grabbing the lower-born boy's tapping hand. "Never. I'll never let it happen. I wouldn't be here without you, I won't abandon you."

Maedoc gave the prince a weak grin. "You gonna argue with him?"

Adahy's heart sank. Both of them knew that his father's word was law.

As if their combined thoughts summoned him, a black shape appeared in the doorway, regarding the kneeling prince with a stern gaze.

"My son?"

Maedoc was the first to react, going to his knee and bowing his head. "M'lord."

"Leave us."

Maedoc grunted as he stood, and Adahy felt a silence rush into the room as the whipping boy left, leaving the prince with the stifling sensation that the air in the room had already been breathed by a crowd of people.

"I've shamed you, Father," Adahy finally uttered, hanging his head as befitted those words. "I am not fit to carry the legacy of our people." He looked up to find his father regarding him dispassionately, cradling the cowl of his station with one arm.

"Follow me," came the command. With that, Adahy's father fitted the mask on his head, and to Adahy's eyes he almost doubled in size as he became the Magpie King. The creature walked to the window overlooking the forest, pushed the glass pane open and stepped outside.

Adahy allowed himself time to blink and take in what had just happened. *There is no balcony to my room - where has he gone?*

The prince rushed to the open portal and thrust his head into the darkness, spitting rain peppering his face. Adahy's window was cut into the slate roof of the Eyrie, and a few feet away was a sheer drop down the side of the castle and the mountain it was built on top of. The forest floor, which Adahy knew was below him, was invisible in the dark. Adahy's eyes found his father hunched like a gargoyle on the edge of the roof, a brooding sentinel keeping watch over his forest kingdom.

It became clear Adahy would receive no help in making his way across the rooftop, and it would be foolish of him to wait until the Magpie King had to reissue his order. Gingerly, Adahy stepped out onto the wet slope. In all the years he had lived in his room, this was something he had never contemplated, let alone actually done.

Getting the second foot onto the roof was considerably more difficult, as if his brain's survival instincts were actively fighting the danger that he was placing his body in. Hands gripping the edge of his window frame, he swung his legs outside and painfully inched along the roof. The last stretch towards his father involved having to let go of the bay window and trusting to the grip between his bare feet and the ancient rooftops. With his heart feeling like it would leap out of his mouth with every frantic beat, Adahy slowly slid his hands and feet across the slate until his father's cloak was in reach, and then he threw himself towards it, panting with relief at reaching safety.

"Hold on tight," was his father's only acknowledgement of Adahy's accomplishment, before grabbing him tightly by his collar and leaping off the parapet towards the valley below.

Despite his fear at what should be a fatal fall, Adahy was oddly confident his father would keep him safe. The young prince pulled himself into the Magpie King's cloak, taking comfort in the feathers' soft embrace. His father was controlling their decent by aiming himself at protrusions from the fortress and the cliff, using the momentum of their fall to propel them to the next available outcrop. This was a technique that many Magpie Kings used in the old stories, but Adahy had never heard of it being performed whilst carrying a passenger. It would be an impressive sight to behold if the young prince didn't have his eyes closed the whole time.

A rush of leaves and the lurching sensation of a sudden upwards motion told Adahy they had reached the forest, his father presumably using the tree branches to swing them, quelling the speed of their fall. After a rough bump and a gruff, "We are here," Adahy opened his eyes to find himself at the Corvae shrine.

As the main religious site of his people, Adahy had been to this building many times before. The shrine lacked the solid stone structure of the Eyrie, borrowing more from the cob and brick village houses, but used those materials in a much more ambitious construction. The main wing of the building was three times the height of a home in most Corvae villages, and it was roofed with slate instead of thatch. Several smaller constructions that bore more resemblance to the traditional cottage were connected to the main hall, presumably living quarters for the priests. His father walked past the guards at the main entrance, expecting Adahy to follow at his heels.

The interior of the shrine was dark. The light of the many candles cast shadows from the sculptures that littered the hall. Incense soaked the air, giving the empty space in the room a heavy feel. Habitually, Adahy's eyes were drawn to the wooden carvings that dominated the walls of the shrine, each showing a separate tale of the Magpie King's past exploits. How the first Magpie King had chosen the forest for his people's home. The deceit of Artemis causing the Magpie King to cast him out of the Eyrie. When the outsiders had come into the forest to hide from the horrors of the world, turning the Corvae from a family into a people. These were stories Adahy had grown up with, that his father had diligently relayed to him night after night, always checking that the young prince could remember and understand each tale. Adahy had loved the journey into these worlds of adventure, but had hated the pressure that had been put upon him to commit them to memory.

Three robed priests were kneeling before a wooden sculpture at the back of the hall, a pole consisting of Magpies standing atop of one another, reaching to the roof of the shrine. Up there in the darkness, black things shuffled in their sleep. The floors of the shrine had to be cleaned regularly.

"Leave us." This was aimed at the priests.

Taking a glance at their sovereign, they bowed and exited by one of the hall's side doors. When they were alone, the Magpie King took off his cowl, becoming Adahy's father again.

"I won't be able to do it, Father. You saw me last night. And, for the first time, I saw you. How can you expect someone who can shame themselves the way that I did to move and fight like you can?"

The large man did not walk to his son, but instead wandered around the shrine interior, gazing at the wooden carvings on the wall. "What do you know of the Magpie King's power? How can I do the things that I do?"

Adahy raised his eyes to the ceiling as he recalled the facts from the stories of his childhood. "Deep in the forest, when the first Magpie King was more in need of help than ever before, the Great Magpie came with a black flower in its beak. Consuming the flower blessed our line, giving us speed, strength, unnatural reflexes. None of which have passed on to me."

His father paused and turned to look at Adahy. "That is not the true story. That is the story all other Corvae are told, but our family has another version, the truth."

Adahy's brow creased in curiosity, but he did not interrupt the flow of his father's tale.

"Our line was blessed, this is true, but not with the power you speak of. We were given a resistance. A resistance to the poison of the flower." The king moved closer to his son now, his voice lowering to hide his words from surrounding ears. "I had the same fears as you, at your age. That is when my father told me that each Magpie King has to seek the flower for himself. Consuming it would turn any other man mad, its venom burning through their blood and their mind, but not our family. This is how I can do what I do when I walk the night. You too will find the flower to become king."

Adahy's mind was buzzing with this revelation. All those years he had spent feeling unworthy of his title because this final fact had been kept from him. "How... where is the flower?"

At this question, his father walked forward and clasped his son's head in his two great hands. "You already know where it is. The information is locked away in here. Your final test is to find that information, and then find the flower. Once you have done that, the two of us will walk the night together, and we can rid the forest of this plague of Wolves."

Keeping his grip on Adahy's head, the Magpie King lowered himself onto his knees, bringing himself to the prince's eye level. "Son, this is a quest for you, and you alone. You must do this by yourself, I cannot help. Do you understand?"

Adahy nodded his head dumbly.

Suddenly, the shrine door crashed open.

"Sire, they are here. The Eyrie is-"

The guard who uttered the warning disappeared back into the doorway from which he had come, pulled by an unseen force. Then the door burst open, a flood of Wolves rushing through it.

"Artemis' bones," swore Adahy's father, in one movement mounting his cowl and pulling his son to him.

The first Wolf leapt at the Magpie King, blood-stained claws flashing to catch him whilst he was vulnerable, without his sickles. The man grabbed the monster by its throat, and with a noise similar to the tearing of wet fabric he used both hands to pull its neck free from its body. Throwing the animal down, Adahy could see his father calculating the severity of their situation. There were about a dozen more Wolves in the building now, some advancing at the pair directly, but others skulking around the hall, looking to cut off all possibility of escape. Without his son to protect, Adahy was confident that his father would have faced these monsters head on, but would he be able to fight them and ensure that Adahy came to no harm? Screams from outside told the prince they would receive no aid from the shrine's guards, and also that more enemies were close by. He could see no chance of escape.

Grabbing Adahy by his collar, the Magpie King leapt once again, this time upwards into the blackness of the rafters. Naturally, the Corvae shrine was home to a tiding of magpies, encouraged and cultured by generations of priests. As much kinship as the Corvae felt with the animals, the black and white birds remained wild and could not cope with the presence of two humans in their nest. With a cacophony of squawks and screams the birds flew forth, some making for holes in the rooftop, but most rushing towards the largest exit they could find - the front door. As the Magpie King had planned, he leapt down with the swarm of blackness, sheltered from his predators by the shock of an avian exodus. Adahy marvelled at his father's ingenuity, wondering if that too was a gift from the flower that had turned him into the Magpie King.

Once outside, his father leapt towards the trees, his monochrome cloak billowing out behind him as they escaped the frustrated howls of the Wolves. The Magpie King's speed was more than a match for his enemies now that he was in the treetops, and soon Adahy felt that immediate danger was behind them.

"Father, the priests. Should we not head back to help them?"

The Magpie King's metal beak turned to regard his son, the black iron glinting in the moonlight. "We both know they are already dead. You saw how many Wolves there were. Our guard was not prepared to defend against such numbers."

Adahy could only agree. "The guard, the first one, he spoke of the Eyrie. Do you think they could be in danger?"

His father raised his head to regard the fortress on the cliffs high above them. "If I was to attack my enemy, I would strike at the heart of their operations before taking out outlying fortifications. We can only assume the Eyrie has already fallen."

The prince did his best to quell his rising panic, steeling himself to think like a leader. "But will the Wolves be thinking like that? I did not think that there was much planning behind their attacks."

His father nodded in approval at Adahy's statement. "An hour ago, I would have agreed with you. But we have already seen more organisation from them than I ever thought was possible."

As his father took his first leap towards the cliffs, Adahy could only hope that the Eyrie and his family and friends could hold off attack better than the shrine did. After all, they did have more soldiers up there.

Clinging to his father's back, Adahy's heart was in his throat as the Magpie King bounded upwards, his massive hands finding purchase in what appeared to be a sheer cliff face. The knowledge that his father's physical attributes were not natural had somehow lessened Adahy's fear of his own inadequacies. He no longer expected himself to be capable of the feats he had seen his father perform, confident in the knowledge that he would inherit them when he solved the riddle of the flower. Adahy's fear now came from what he expected to find when he reached home, from the fates of his household. He may not have the body of a Magpie King yet, but Adahy was now determined to face his fear of conflict head on, and vowed to do all he could to help liberate his home.

Upon reaching the castle foundations, the Magpie King took several more bounds to bring them both to the roof. The Wolves were not unaware of their enemy's capabilities, and three of them were prowling in the area that Adahy's father landed on. The first was easily dealt with, as the Magpie King grabbed it by the scruff of its neck and hurled it into the abyss behind them. Unfortunately, the monster's screams alerted its remaining companions to the fact that they were no longer alone. These two posed more of a problem, quickly moving to circle the Magpie King and his son, making sure to remain at opposite sides of the King. The animals had realised Adahy's vulnerability, forcing his father to stay his hand from an attack that would leave Adahy open to the remaining Wolf.

The two animals howled, presumably to attract reinforcements. With time not on their side, Adahy cursed the fact that his own uselessness would be their undoing. In fact…

If my father does not need to protect me, then their advantage is lost. The young prince took a deep breath, furrowed his brow and ran directly at one of the Wolves. The Wolf's animalistic instincts came into play and it leapt towards the oncoming prey. Unfortunately for it, the Magpie King was faster, and he bounded over his son, in one movement turning to face the other Wolf behind him whilst breaking his son's assailant's neck with a wet crunch. The remaining animal turned to flee, but only made a few feet before it was caught too, silently dispatched by the Magpie King's brutal hands.

"That was well done," his father commented without turning his mask towards Adahy, but the boy could hear the smile in the Magpie King's voice.

His heart, previously doing its best to escape from his rib cage due to panic and fear, now felt twice its size. *I will do whatever possible to take back this castle*, Adahy vowed silently.

They moved along in the darkness, coming into contact with no others on the roof. His father made Adahy wait for a few agonising seconds whilst he entered the window to his own chambers. Adahy spent most of that time spinning his head wildly, fully expecting to have a Wolf lunge at him at any moment. The Magpie King emerged shortly with his twin sickles, now properly armed for battle.

"The throne room," he said in a gravelly voice. "We shall find the strongest resistance there, if any are left."

They crept across the slates again, Adahy amazed at how difficult traversing this environment had been only hours ago. They came to a pair of ornate ceiling windows. These looked down onto the Magpie King's throne room, where Adahy and his father could see a huddled mass of nobles and soldiers. All eyes in the room were on the great doors that were the main entranceway into the chamber. They had been barricaded by tables and chairs, and the wooden mass in front of the doors was shuddering under what Adahy assumed were the Wolves trying to get through from the other side.

"They live," Adahy exclaimed, stating the obvious in his excitement at sighting more of his people.

"Indeed. Now there is hope," his father replied. The dark figure paused, then continued, "My son, I need you to do something for me."

"Anything, Father."

Another pause, and this time the Magpie King chose to remove his helmet to look the boy in his eyes. "You saw how my worry for your safety nearly undid us both? I cannot risk you like that a second time."

"Father?"

"I go now to save our people, but I cannot do so and worry about my only son. You must stay here -"

"No."

The Magpie King put out his hand to stop his son's outburst. "You have done me proud this night. You have proven you have our family's gift, and you shall be a great warrior, in time. Do not waste that gift by walking into death now. Men will die tonight, and their loss will be great, but not as great as the loss of our next Magpie King."

Soberly, Adahy nodded his agreement.

"Now I must go to make *you* proud." And with that, Adahy's father opened one of the window panes and dropped down to his people below.

The Magpie King's arrival was met by great cheers from the survivors, and Adahy felt a pang of jealousy that he was not also receiving those cries. From the body language of the commanding officer's explanation of the situation and his father's subsequent commands, Adahy gathered that the men and women in this room were barricaded in, and as far as they were aware no other survivors remained. The Magpie King ordered the soldiers to flank the barricaded doorway, but he alone stood in the middle of the room, twin sickles held menacingly in a ready position.

"Open the doors." His father's command rang loud enough for it to clearly reach Adahy's ears. Men at arms quickly pulled aside the furniture and the pounding of the Wolves did the rest. The doors splintered open and a wave of fur and teeth poured in. A few of the beasts sidestepped out of the doorway, assuming to slink off down the sides of the room to flank their main opponent. This was why the soldiers had been positioned there. Not expecting as much resistance, these Wolves were quickly cut down by the spearmen working in unison.

The majority of the horde flew at the Magpie King, who stood between the animals and the cowering nobles sheltered at the back. Adahy's father flashed his sickles, conducting a symphony of death as animal after relentless animal fell before him. Adahy found himself unable to follow any individual movements. Only the bodies that began to pile up at his father's feet gave any indication of the king's success. Every now and again a Wolf did break free. These monsters made straight for the women and children at the back of the room. A few guards remained stationed there for such an event, but these mere men could only cope with so much. Soon the human bodies began to pile up.

Then the attack stopped. The exhausted cheering from the survivors below echoed the relief in Adahy's heart, but this relief proved to be short lived. The cheering was quickly overshadowed by a deathly groaning noise, which Adahy eventually realised to be a howl. This noise was unlike anything that any of the Wolves had emitted.

Adahy found himself straining over the edge of the room to get a look at the scene below. The unnatural howl had caused panic among the few surviving nobles, and many of the guardsmen joined the craven lords in scrabbling at the window openings set in the stone walls, clearly too narrow for any human to feasibly fit through. Only Adahy's father stood firm in the centre, using his commanding voice to shout orders to the remaining soldiers at the door. However, even he took a step backwards when the creature that emitted that awful sound finally stepped into the room.

It was a Wolf, clearly, but unlike any Adahy had seen so far. Such was its enormity, it entered through the throne room doorway on all fours, but rose to its full height once inside. The beast was twice as tall as any of the other Wolves, and eight distended teats hanging from its chest told Adahy this was a female. A mother. The remaining Wolves followed the mother, using the distraction of her monstrous appearance to quickly overpower the soldiers at the door, diving onto them and feeding in an orgy of blood and gristle. With their way now clear, the horde began to move around the walls of the room, but with a grating growl the mother seemed to warn them to stop. Either she did not want to lose any more of her children to the Magpie King, or she wanted this fight for herself. She hunched down, back on all fours, and growled a challenge to Adahy's father.

The Magpie King was first to strike. At her invitation he leapt forward, using his supernatural speed to dip under the Wolf mother's massive arms and cut a messy red line across her torso. However, he was unprepared for her survival of the attack, and the speed of her reprisal. She caught the Magpie King with a backhand blow, dislodging his mask from his head and sent the man tumbling into the throng of creatures that now surrounded the combat. Where he landed, a frenzy of activity sparked, the animals rushing forward to claim a piece of their most hated foe. The mother barked at her children to move away from her prey, and they grudgingly obeyed, but Adahy could already see the damage had been done. Through some miracle, his father remained standing, but his face was now a mess of blood, running from innumerable wounds on his head and into his eyes. Both sickles remained in his hands, but his right arm hung weakly at his side, reminding Adahy of how he felt when trying to heft one of those great weapons. The young prince wanted to scream, to do something to help his father, but no actions came to him, other than the salty tears that streamed down his face.

The Wolf mother slowly approached, and when she was within reach, the Magpie King gave a desperate swipe of the sickle in his left hand. The monster easily caught the man's wrist, and with a flick of her own snapped the bones in his arm in two. The sickle dropped to the floor, the clang of iron meeting stone drowned out by the scream of pain from Adahy's father. The Wolf mother lifted her own head, accompanying the man's shouts with a victory howl of her own, and then snapped her jaws shut on the man's neck, severing skin, sinew and bone.

The Magpie King was dead.

THE MAGPIE KING
AND THE
BLACK SQUIRREL

An extract from the teachings of the High Corvae.

It was in the early days of the forest, long before the outsiders arrived. The world was still new, and would look strange to your eyes if you saw it now. Cat and mouse would walk together through the leaves, chatting about a joke a human had told them earlier that morning. Rabbits sneered rudely at passersby, concerned that everyone was after their patches of clover. Strange creatures that you cannot imagine shared these trees as their home, such as mammoths, bears and dragons.

The Magpie King was young, and was still becoming accustomed to his power. He viewed every feature of his forest with wonder and delight, and found great joy in taking the opportunity to pass the time of day with every deer, leopard or wolf.

This idyllic paradise was shattered when a great darkness enveloped the sky above the forest. Man, woman, fox and frog alike threw themselves to the dirt and wailed for the Magpie King to protect them.

"What is causing this?" the Magpie King demanded of his subjects. "What is happening to the sun?"

"It is Mikweh, the black squirrel," they responded, writhing in unison into the dirt at the thought of the world ending. "He is eating the sun to teach us a lesson."

The Magpie King shielded his eyes with his hand and raised them up to the sun. Sure enough, there was Mikweh, balancing high on a fir tree, with the sun in his paws and daylight dripping like syrup from his mouth.

I should tell you now that squirrels back then were not like squirrels are now. For a start, there was only one of them - Mikweh

- and he was in a permanent state of anger, for he believed that the other animals were constantly laughing at his bushy tail. Our squirrels in the forest, when they appear, are small and weak, and frightened of their own shadows. Not so was Mikweh, in the dawn of the world. He was huge - taller than three stags perched atop one another - and incredibly strong. The Magpie King was still learning about his own abilities, but even then he knew he was no match for Mikweh, at least physically. Unlike the fiery red coats of the squirrels of our forest, Mikweh's coat was a wiry black. Black as the anger that gnawed at his soul.

"Raise yourselves, gentle creatures," the Magpie King bade the mourning animals. "I shall seek an audience with our friend squirrel and see if he cannot be appeased." So the Magpie King set off to meet with Mikweh, the black squirrel.

It was a journey that itself is worth many stories. Mikweh had made his home deep in the forest, at the top of the tallest tree. It took many years for the Magpie King to find and reach his quarry. In that time, he learnt how to sing, found and then lost a dear friend, and forgot how to smile. The dark figure who finally reached the top of that fir tree was an uncanny shade of the man he had been when his journey had begun.

"Mikweh," the Magpie King bellowed, a cloak of black and white feathers that had been gifted to him by the Great Magpie during the previous winter flowing behind him in the strong wind. "Put down the sun and speak with me."

Mikweh still had the sun in his grasp, but that once-fiery orb had diminished greatly in size and its juices stained the squirrel's maw. The black squirrel turned to the Magpie King to regard him with its red eyes, and the creature simply opened its jaw to scream at the man who had dared to disturb him.

"Mine. Sun belongs to Mikweh. Animals not laugh at Mikweh any more. Too busy screaming."

The Magpie King's lip curled and he took a leap closer to his target. He nodded in agreement with the squirrel. "Yes, oh great squirrel, you have truly shown us the error of our ways. Won't you come down to the forest with me so that all creatures can beg your forgiveness?"

The beast snarled again at the Magpie King, and turned back to the sun to sink his teeth into it once more. The sun did its best to pull away from its attacker, straining to lift itself back onto its celestial path, but the muscles in the squirrel's forearms bulged and the sun was held firm.

An almighty rumbling grew the Magpie King's attention to its source, and as his eyes fell upon Mikweh's distended belly, a plan formed in his mind.

"Oh, great Mikweh," he began humbly, "it pains me you have dedicated yourself so passionately to our deserved education that you have neglected your own needs. We all know that feasting only on the sun for the past year and five days will not have satisfied your hunger. A sun is composed of warmth and light, and not much else - hardly a fitting meal for one of your stature. Please, allow me to seek out more adequate food for one such as yourself while you continue to chastise the rest of the forest."

The black squirrel turned to snarl again at the Magpie King, and returned to gnaw on his sun. But the creature's belly rumbled and its red eyes darted to regard the Magpie King, and as they did so a flicker of hope rippled through them. A smile threatened to break on the Magpie King's lips at that moment, but he forced it into hiding and disappeared back down the fir tree.

The Magpie King's journey to locate food for Mikweh would take more time than we have now to recount. Save to say it was a perilous one, taking him to depths of the forest he had never ventured into before. He lost the ring finger of his left hand to an army of red ants. He found a wooden earring he would treasure forever, and he awoke a new enemy that would eventually be his bloodline's doom. Finally, he was able to return to Mikweh with an armful of red berries he had found within sight of the Lion's mountains, each fruit as large as a man's head, each containing a stone that was the size of a clenched fist.

"Here, good Mikweh. I have brought nourishment to fuel your great endeavours."

On sight of the red bounty the black squirrel leapt from its perch, dragging the mutilated sun with him. He slavered over the gifts from the Magpie King, sucking on the red flesh of the berries and crunching into the stones until all were gone, and his belly gave a soft rumble of contentment. The squirrel lay there for a moment in front of the Magpie King, one hand still clutching the dying star to his breast and the other cradling his satisfied gut. With a trembling hand, the Magpie King reached forth and patted Mikweh on his head. As he did so, the squirrel gave a whimper of contentment, shuddered, and then visibly reduced in size. The Magpie King smiled as this happened, and at that moment, the sun made another pull away from its captor's claws, but to no avail. The squirrel remained the size of a large horse, and anger still fuelled its powerful claws.

"You are much stronger now," the Magpie King complimented Mikweh, "yet I feel I have not been equal to the task I had set myself. Forgive me, almighty black squirrel, I shall away to find more to sustain you with." With that, the Magpie King leapt from the top of the fir. Once again, the details of his journey could entertain a mind for a lifetime. He stepped on a snake and had his face spat in. He met an owl and fell painfully in love. He was watched the whole time by a single mouse, but failed to pay it any attention.

Finally, the Magpie King returned with a single branch of blue flowers. Each flower was closed tight, as the petals were holding jealously to the rich nectar that was within. At the sight of the food, the black squirrel leapt down again, taking care to pull the sun with him, and gorged himself on the Magpie King's find. He burst through the cocoon of leaves to the amber liquid contained within, and the Magpie King could clearly hear the splash of the nectar hitting the walls of the squirrel's gut. Once again, the squirrel curled up in contentment, and once again, the Magpie King gave Mikweh a pat on the head. Anger draining out of him, the black squirrel diminished once more, down to the size of a wolf. However, it still snarled mightily at the Magpie King when it regained its senses, and quickly took up position again gnawing on the sun.

And so the Magpie King took a final journey down the fir tree. No records exist of what took place during this final trip. All that is known is that the journey took exactly three months and a day, and that when the Magpie King returned to the top of the tree once more, his hair was shaved off and he wept openly.

"Here, great Mikweh," the Magpie King offered, bringing forth a tiny golden egg for the squirrel. The black creature scurried down from his perch, forcing the sun to follow, and eyed the egg greedily. With great reluctance, the Magpie King passed it to the beast, who cracked it open and gorged on the purple contents within. The Magpie King could not bear to watch this sight, but closed his eyes and reached out his hand to pat Mikweh one last time on the head. When the Magpie King opened his eyes, the squirrel was finally diminished to the size we know today. Indeed, so drained of anger and strength was Mikweh that he could no longer hold on to the sun, and it returned to the sky. In time, the sun regained its health and brought heat and light to the forest once more.

The black squirrel withdrew to the high branches of his tree and propagated more of his kind. The Magpie King had drained the squirrel of the rage that had allowed him to pluck the sun from the sky, but those flames came from a fire that can never be extinguished. To this day, when we meet Mikweh's children in the forest, they shake their fists at us and chatter angrily, giving voice to their irritation. Dimly they recall their original greatness, and until they fade from the forest they will blame people for taking it from them.

CHAPTER THREE

"For Artemis' sake, Lonan, will you just shut up already?"

"Now, Mrs Anvil, perhaps you would like to step back and let me take a look?"

"No, I certainly would not. You don't think I can deal with my own son?"

"I really do think you should let me see him. I am good with this sort of thing. Happens with my wife a lot, you see."

"I don't... yes, yes I see. Go ahead."

As Lonan regained consciousness, the first sensation that came to him was that of being grabbed by the collar and being raised roughly out of bed. His blurry eyes came into focus and he was met with the face of Jarleth Quarry. The blond man's serious face broke into a wicked grin at seeing Lonan awake, and he jerked Lonan roughly to the side so he could not see anyone else in the room.

"You see," the blacksmith continued, "I've found that the only way to wake them up once they get like this is a short, sharp slap." The word 'slap' was accompanied by the back of Jarleth's hand making contact with Lonan's face.

Lonan leapt up with an angry shout, bellowing incoherently and reaching his hands for his assaulter's throat. He did not make it that far, however, as he found himself being held back by two of the Tumulty boys.

"See," the grinning bastard continued, slipping to the back of the cellar, "works every time."

"What the hell's going on?" Lonan questioned groggily, still struggling against the Tumultys.

As his eyes became accustomed to being awake, it was quickly obvious that something was wrong. He was down in Mother Ogma's cellar, exactly where he had gone to sleep last night, but there were a lot of unfamiliar faces down here with him now. The Tumulty boys, as well as Old Man Tumulty, Lonan's mother and of course Jarleth was there too.

Fear struck at Lonan. "What's happened? Where's Aileen? Is she all right?"

Old Man Tumulty walked across to him and stared at his face. "Seems all right now, doesn't he? Got a sore voice, have ye son?"

"Damn your sore voice, is my sister safe?" Lonan shouted back at the elder. Funnily enough, a grating pain shot down his throat as he yelled.

A commotion from upstairs let Lonan know there were more bodies in the building.

"...my own house. I should be down there too - healing is *my* Knack, as you are all well aware."

The furious face of Mother Ogma trotted down the cellar steps, followed by a protesting young man. Mother Ogma spun and pointed her finger at him, "Ciaran Dripper, you let her through now or I personally will guarantee those sores on your pecker will not heal by the end of the winter." She turned to look at Lonan again. "You back to us, boy?"

"Where else would I go?"

Mother Ogma muttered, "We'll find out about that later," before addressing somebody up the stairs again. "He's fine, come and take a look."

"Lonan?" With that innocent question, Lonan was greeted by the sight of his sister running into the cellar, pushing past the crowd in the safe room and embracing her brother in a tight hug. "Don't do that to us again, you scared me."

Lonan hugged his sister back, carrying her as he stood up from his bed. "Well, now I've got the girl, would someone mind telling me what in the Magpie's name is going on here?"

"You were screaming," his sister responded, her head nuzzling his chest, "and you wouldn't stop."

"Is that it?"

"You've been doing it for the best part of an hour now, lad."

Lonan looked in shock at the collection of faces before him, the pieces of the puzzle all falling into place now. Of course such a long period of shouting would attract attention in a community such as Smithsdown. That did not explain the unusual assortment of faces he woke to though.

"I wouldn't wake?" he questioned dumbly.

Jarleth stepped smugly to the fore. "No amount of shaking or pinching seemed to do it. We decided your mother would be the best person to make a decision about what should be done if you were indeed going mad. My expertise in these matters made me a natural fit to advise." Lonan ignored the telltale flare of Quarry's Knack in action.

"Well, I am touched that you all care so deeply," Lonan addressed the room with a distinct lack of sincerity, "but I do hope you all understand I have better things to do than sit around and chat all day. Does no one else have somewhere to be?"

Tumulty grunted, "Comon boys, we're already behind with today's harvest."

"I preferred him when he was screeching his throat out," Callum said to his brother as they followed their father, emptying the cellar.

"Anytime, old sport," Jarleth playfully pinched Lonan's face where his hand had made contact minutes earlier, highlighting to Lonan how tender that area was now. "I'm starting to get quite good at this kind of thing." He left too, swiftly followed by Lonan's own mother, who whisked Aileen away without ceremony.

Ten minutes later, Lonan found himself upstairs, sitting at the table in a room whose general untidiness betrayed the gathering of people that had occupied it until recently. Only Harlow remained now, rocking mindlessly on his chair by the fire as if nothing unusual had occurred.

"Bet you loved having someone else to chat to," Lonan addressed the old man, not expecting any kind of response.

Mother Ogma busied herself around the room, sweeping up the dirt brought in by half the village and rearranging the many aspects of her pharmacy that had been upset by the bodies.

"I don't suppose you'd like to talk about it, dearie?" she said as she worked.

It was a good question. Uncharacteristically, Lonan did not respond with a barbed comment and instead mulled over his dramatic dream as the porridge cooled on his spoon. *Is it normal for a dream to continue the story from the night before? Maybe it's because I spent so much time yesterday thinking about it? It would just be natural for my mind to try to continue the story, I guess. But last night's vision was brutal. Adahy's life was cut down just as he was given hope of a better future. It must take a sick mind to come up with a situation like that.*

Lonan could not help giving a sly grin at that thought.

"Well, things can't be that bad if we can still manage one of those once in a while."

Lonan nodded at Mother Ogma, his grin continuing. "Just a dream. A mad, out-there dream. Had it last night too."

"I would ask if there was anything exciting in it, but I dare say I already know the answer to that one."

"Heh. Well, you know, just doing what I can to keep you on your toes."

"You'll be all right, though?"

"Just my mind using the worst bits in there against me. I probably should have warned you a while ago that I'm a right fountain of craziness, me."

Mother Ogma raised her eyebrows. "I don't suppose somewhere in there is the type of craziness that would finally be able to pick me some evening primrose today?"

Lonan threw his hands into the air in mock frustration, warding off the guilt that his repeated failure at this task was making him feel. "Artemis' beard, fine."

He grabbed his bag and made towards the door, but paused just before he left. "Mother Ogma, you've been around for a while."

"Thank you for noticing, dearie."

"I mean, I know people say the attacks weren't always as bad as they are now. Is that true?"

The old woman turned to her young charge, studying him quizzically. "I suppose not. They still came though, but I guess we got more visitors, dearie. Got a chance to see a bit more of the forest myself too."

"Did you ever get the chance to see the Eyrie?"

She barked a laugh in response. "Oh no, not me, dearie. A fine

50

palace like that, they wouldn't let me close enough to smell it. Nearest I ever got to the Magpie King was when we went to visit the temple when my mammy and pappy died."

Lonan's blood stopped running. "Temple?"

"Well, I guess so. Or a shrine, I can't really remember what we were supposed to call it. Used to be tradition for a family to take a trip there every few years, to honour the Great Magpie or to pay respect to the dead. And pay taxes, of course, some stupid tax or other."

"You went to the shrine?"

"Oh, yes, dearie." She visibly shuddered. "Twice, I think. Scared me silly too, if I remember rightly."

"What was it like? Inside, I mean."

"Oh, dark I suppose. Dark, and lots of bird poo. But I do remember this big pole at the back. Magpies standing on magpies, all made out of wood, reaching to the top of the rafters. Silly, but those birds terrified me."

Lonan did not respond.

Mother Ogma returned from her deep thoughts. "Are you all right?"

Without saying a word, Lonan turned and left.

Emerging into the daylight, Lonan fell into a full sprint and headed straight into the forest. *The totem pole? How in Artemis' name did she know about that?* His foot snagged on a rotting branch, sending him briefly to the ground but he hardly seemed to notice. *Damn it, this was supposed to have been just a crazy coincidence. It couldn't actually be true.* He dropped to his knees and screamed into the wild.

Lonan spent the majority of the day wandering around the greenery, puzzling over things in his mind. By chance, as he was doing so, his eyes caught a glimpse of yellow, and he recalled Mother Cutter's primroses. The guilt from earlier that morning came back, and Lonan spent the rest of the day ensuring he had enough of the weed in his gathering pouch before he considered heading back to Mother Ogma's. He also managed to find some weaselwort, which he knew helped with pain. Perhaps that might make up for the extra days of discomfort he had caused.

As he searched, he started to consider Adahy, and how terrible things would be right now for the prince if he actually did exist. *To watch his father being ripped to pieces like that, to have his whole life taken away from him.* Lonan shuddered at the thought, as if someone had been walking across his own grave. After that, his mind began to consider what was going to happen next. If the Magpie King was gone…

If the Magpie King is gone, then there is nobody left to protect the villages. Things have been bad enough with the King looking out for us, but now that the Wolves have free reign over the forest, what's to stop them beating at cellar doors until the wood finally gives?

Lonan sat down at the thought, his heart beating rapidly in his chest. *It's not real though, is it?* He thought he had convinced himself with his theory about dreams being byproducts of waking thoughts, but how could that have explained the coincidence of the breech at the Quarry cottage last night? And the continuation of his dream? There was no way Mother Ogma's description of the temple was a coincidence.

Why me, the Knackless man from Smithsdown? Why should I be the one to see these things? Is it some kind of warning? Because if the dreams are real, then we're all in a lot of trouble.

Lonan took a few moments to ponder these last thoughts, and then sat up straight, mind now resolute. He felt like a madman, but he could not take the chance that these were all just figments of his imagination. *If I'm going to treat these dreams like some kind of warning, what can I do about it?* After a moment of quiet contemplation, Lonan picked himself up and ran home.

The sun was setting when Lonan huffed into the village again, and he made straight for his mother's house and banged on the door. Her hard face regarded him through the half open portal.

"Yes?" she queried bluntly.

"I'm coming here tonight."

She physically jerked her head back, lips curling. "Won't Ogma miss you?"

"Nope. She's coming too."

"No. Not in my house-" his mother began to respond sharply, but Lonan cut her off by grabbing at her blouse and pulling her close to his face.

"Listen to me now, you will need me tonight. It's going to be bad. You heard my screaming this morning? It is going to be bad." He let go off her, sending a shocked woman staggering back into the cottage. "Get Aileen downstairs and take any weapons and as much oil as you can, understand?"

Without waiting for any kind of response Lonan took off again, this time to Mother Ogma's. It took a short amount of time for him to convince her to take part in his scheme, mostly achieved by Lonan picking Harlow up and dragging him to the doorway by himself. When the three of them made their way back to Lonan's mother's house, it was empty.

"Aileen?" Lonan's shout echoed down into the vacant cellar. "Aileen?"

"What's going on, dearie?"

The sunset bell began to chime outside. Lonan ran out onto the village green and shouted at the top of his lungs, "Aileen. Aileen. Where is my sister, her home is empty? Aileen."

No heads popped out at this time of night, as darkness threatened to fall. His only responses were shouts of abuse from nearby buildings, or the thuds of cellars being sealed shut.

"I'll stand here shouting until I have my sister, and dammit if I won't lead the Wolves right to one of your doors if you leave me outside."

"She's with me, Anvil. Get to bed." Lonan's heart sank as he turned to see Quarry in his doorway. Was his sister's life really going to be in the hands of this idiot tonight?

Lonan ran to Quarry's cottage door and shouted past the blacksmith, "Mother, come to me. It's going to be bad tonight. I can protect you."

"Like you looked after daddy?" Jarleth jibed spitefully. "Or Branwen?"

"Go hang yourself," Lonan spat back. Tears were running down his face by this point, and only then did he catch the glowing embers from the forge that Jarleth had stolen from him. Lonan's gut curdled at that sight, and at what it meant for tonight. "He's even left the damned forge fires going again. The smoke'll lead them straight to you."

Jarleth rolled his eyes, shrugged and closed his cottage door. A thick thud moments later signified Lonan's family being taken away from him.

"Lonan. Quickly, into the cellar." The sound came from Mother Ogma, leaning nervously from Lonan's mother's doorway. "I have never been out this late in all my years."

"The Magpie King is dead." Lonan stood with his arms outstretched, shouting across the silent village, tears running freely down his face. "Dammit all, he's dead, they got him. There's nobody out there looking out for us now. They will come for us tonight."

"Lonan. The sun has gone. I'm shutting the door now."

Sobbing, Lonan followed Mother Ogma's voice, tripping down the steps and collapsing into the bedsit as the cellar door slammed shut.

"Now then, dearie, what's this all about?" she murmured comfortingly, moving over to stroke Lonan's head. "What is this about the Magpie King?"

Lonan let everything spill forth, about the Magpie King, Adahy and the fall of the Eyrie.

Afterwards, Mother Ogma regarded him silently. "That is some story you have there, dearie. You might almost be able to convince me it was true."

"You don't believe that it is?"

"Do you?"

Lonan thought again about this. *There are too many coincidences for me not to believe it, now. Mother Ogma's description of the totem pole, the scratch marks on Branwen's cottage. And then there's Adahy. I've been inside his mind twice now, and it felt too... real. This isn't a little offset of my own mind that feels sorry for itself and needs a hug. I've been feeling the emotions and hearing the thoughts of a real person.* Lonan simply nodded his head.

"If it's true, if the Magpie King has been watching us for all of this time and he's now dead, then there are dark times ahead."

Lonan looked up and gave a desperate little grin. "But things were going so well."

She chuckled at that. Moving to Harlow's side to ensure he was tucked in, she changed the conversation topic. "So, it seems that young mister Quarry has a bit of a talent for making people do what he wants."

Lonan raised his eyebrows at this. "You noticed?"

"I've had my suspicions for a while, but this morning confirmed it."

"Took you long enough." Lonan sniffed and rubbed his nose. "Thought I'd always be the only one. That maybe that was my Knack or something..."

"No, your Knack should have been your father's. The village sorely needs a proper smith. That young fool certainly doesn't have the Knack for it, despite what he's convinced us all for so long. How long has he been able to do that, exactly?"

Lonan looked her in the eyes. "Since the night my father died."

That was when Aileen started to scream.

There was no mistaking it was Lonan's sister as she was screaming for her brother at the top of her voice. It pierced the night like a knife.

"No," was all that Mother Ogma could manage.

Panic welled within Lonan. His first reaction was to shout and scream for his sister, but he fought himself and brought those instincts under control. They had not served him well in the past. More voices joined Aileen's now. Lonan was fairly certain they were those of his mother and Branwen. He scanned the cellar madly, hungry for a way to move forward. His eyes landed on the oil lamp. He leapt up the cellar stairs and put his ear to the door.

"Can't you hear them well enough already?" Mother Ogma fretted, but Lonan waved her silent. After a few moments he jumped down, grabbed the oil lamp and jumped back up the steps again.

He turned to the old woman. "I'm pretty sure there's nothing upstairs. As soon as I'm out, close the door again, quietly."

Mother Ogma, eyes wide, looked confused for brief moments before she realised what Lonan was proposing. "No. You can't do this. What exactly do you think you are going to do up there?"

Lonan shrugged. "Save my sister? Kill a few Wolves? At the very least, offer them an easier target? It's not as if I was looking to amount to much anyway." With that, he pushed open the heavy cellar door, shuttered the oil lamp and slipped out into the dark cottage.

He blinked hard, forcing his eyes to adjust to the moonlight as quickly as possible. Every muscle was screaming for him to scramble back to the trapdoor in the floor and beat his hands bloody on it until he was safe underground. The only thing goading him forward was the continued wailing of the women in his life.

He scanned his mother's cottage, his breathing coming sharply, his eyes frantically searching for anything out of the ordinary. He had left the front door of his mother's cottage slightly ajar, and now inched himself towards it, his fear of the night forcing him to scuttle along the floor like a wounded spider.

Upon reaching the open portal, he peered outside and gasped at the white light of the night. Lonan had always pictured night time as blackness, with the moon painting a blue hue across the landscape. But the light from the moon was a brilliant white, perfectly illuminating the white washed walls of the village cottages. Other than the unnaturalness of this time of day, Lonan's eyes could not spot anything unusual in the village.

Going out of the front door seemed like madness, so Lonan turned himself around and pushed himself through one of the side windows. Laying low to the grass, one arm cradling the shuttered lamp, Lonan urged himself across the green towards the Dripper cottage, still a few buildings away from where all the screaming was coming from. Reaching the cottage he huddled into the corner between the wall and the ground, fully expecting to hear the noise of pursuit after his panicked dash. Lonan moved from cottage to cottage like this, at every advancement counting his blessings that he was undiscovered and steeling himself for the next small stage in his journey. As he moved closer to the Quarry household, other noises began to mix with the screaming. The sound of wood being chipped away at. Growling. What Lonan was sure was snarling.

Finally he was there, outside of Quarry's house. Lonan had not actually expected to get this far, and now found himself slightly unsure of how to proceed. The noises from the animals inside were overpowering, inhuman groans that Lonan was convinced could not actually be a form of even basic communication.

He edged himself along the wall towards a window and urged his body to look inside. It refused. Lonan, panting, was dumbfounded. He had never before found it so hard to perform such a basic function, to have his own body fight against him. He forced himself again, pushing his head inch by inch towards the glass. The thatched roof came into view, then the rafters, the whitewashed walls and then the monsters. He caught a glimpse of black, a single knotted limb lifted high in the air before descending on the cellar door with a thunk and a howl. Lonan's body took over and pulled him back from the window.

"Lonan!"

His sister's cry was the catalyst he needed. He took a breath, uncapped the flask of oil that he had clasped to his belt, ran to the front door and threw it into the blackness inside, closely followed by the naked flame of the lamp. The interior of the cottage erupted into a blaze of fire and inhuman howls. Lonan, however, had not stuck around to witness this. He had already made it most of the way to the forest bordering the village, his effortless sprint powered by the fear that he now allowed to overcome him.

He stumbled through the vegetation, the greenery taking on a completely different character in the moonlight. Not having time to appreciate the change, Lonan kept running. When he felt his legs and lungs were close to giving out, he cast his gaze upwards to the gnarled branches he so often climbed in search of fruit and seeds for Ogma's pharmacy. Bloodying his knuckles as he did so, Lonan pulled himself upwards until he was in the canopy. He found a nook to rest himself in, and studied the ground below intently. Any small movement, swaying of leaves or nocturnal animal wanderings caught Lonan's eye.

It was not long, however, before his pursuers made their appearance. He could make out the movement of two black masses on the ground below him, glimpses of darkness glaring at him through the autumn leaves. The sense of inevitability about his fate actually made it easier to bear, and he marvelled at the gliding motion of the evil below him, moving smoothly over the forest ground which Lonan had tripped and stumbled his way through. He was suddenly reminded of Adahy's similar reaction to impending death and a thin, begrudging smile played on his features.

Where was that boy now? Had he survived for much longer without his father? The shapes below moved directly towards him, and quickly disappeared from his line of vision because of the thick tree branches. They would be at the foot of the tree now and soon would have him. Lonan could not decide whether he would rather hear their approach, hear the crunching of claw embedding into wood whilst the Wolves made their climb, or would rather that they appeared at an unexpected moment, stealing away his life like rats in the night.

As the seconds turned into minutes, Lonan decided he would much rather hear them approaching. The length of this wait and the lack of information was agonising. He expected that they were toying with him now, the way that he had seen wild cats tease shrews moments before snapping their necks. He stared at the white moon that hung low over the forest, waiting for the snarl that would precede his end. His first moment of shock was when a large bird pierced the skyline that he was focussing on, breaking his tense meditation by hanging before the moon, its silhouette perfectly centred within the white orb, before disappearing back into the canopy.

His second moment of shock was when the sun rose.

When the horizon first started to turn blue, Lonan just assumed the end was about to come. The monsters had been playing him up until this point, letting him think he had survived the night, and then they would kill him just before the first rays of sunlight peeked out. When he actually saw the sun break the skyline, he gasped and looked around wildly. There was nothing there except for the branches of the oak he had sheltered in. Shaking, he clamoured down the tree, dropping the last few feet when his quivering arms gave out on him. Teeth chattering, Lonan stumbled back through the woodland. He had spent enough time with Mother Ogma to realise he was going into shock - a natural reaction to his body releasing all of the tension he had built up over the night - but all he wanted to know was what had happened at the village.

He could see from a distance that the green was busy, and a dark plume of smoke was still rising steadily from Quarry's house. Lonan rolled his eyes at the thought of the spin that Jarleth would put on that one. *If only someone had actually seen what I'd done.* Lonan shook his head. *As long as it worked, as long as they're all safe, I don't care what they think.*

"Aileen." Lonan croaked as he came within earshot of the crowd. He had not realised how dry his throat had been, and the shouting hurt.

People turned to look at the approaching figure and the crowd parted as he ran toward them. They eventually revealed an angry Jarleth Quarry, face blackened with ash.

"Lonan." The blessed figure of his sister pushed past the blacksmith, running into the arms of her brother.

Lonan fell to his knees, cradled the little girl, and wept in relief.

"You bastard," came the inevitable outburst from Quarry. "You destroyed my house."

Lonan raised his face from his sister's curls to regard the smoke-topped cottage. Indeed, the thatched roof had all but disappeared from it now. Without anyone in Smithsdown with a Knack for weaving new roofs, it would be some time before the home would be habitable again.

"You don't think it's an improvement?" Lonan responded weakly. "I thought it was getting a bit stuffy."

Jarleth moved with aggression towards Lonan, but Old Man

Tumulty interceded with a firm hand on his shoulder. "Seems to me a straw roof is a fine price to pay for your family's lives."

"What, you don't actually believe that drivel, do you?" Lonan could see the tell-tale sparks of the Knack in Jarleth's eyes and prepared himself for the sweetness of the moment turning bitter. "It was Anvil at our door all the time. He-"

Jarleth was interrupted by a loud clap.

"That's enough of that, thank you, dearie," Mother Ogma stated sharply, breaking Jarleth's spell and earning a sneer from him. "You lot were all screaming well before he left the cellar, and I would love you to explain how he could have made those claw marks by himself or those screaming sounds everyone heard."

Other villagers nodded. There was no chance that Quarry, Knack or no, could sway them now.

"You couldn't have come up with something that didn't involve burning my home down? Are you all telling me he shouldn't be held responsible for that?"

"I guess I'm just not that good at thinking on my feet," Lonan responded, standing, heady with the positive attention he was receiving from the villagers. "Why, what had you planned to do?"

Jarleth opened his mouth to speak but struggled to respond. This was all the space that the crowd needed to interject with some chuckles.

"Come on now, everyone," Old Tumulty bellowed, waving his arms to disperse the crowd, "we've got some work to do to be ready for tonight. Reinforce your cellars. Quarry, get that forge going."

The anxious onlookers trotted back to their cottages. Aileen gave her brother another hug and ran to her mother. Lonan's mother turned and left without looking her son in the eye. Other than Mother Ogma, only Branwen Quarry remained, clutching her sleeping baby to her chest. The young woman was staring right at Lonan, lip trembling.

"Branwen?" Lonan questioned.

She turned and trotted back home to her husband, wiping her face with her free hand as she walked.

Mother Ogma took Lonan's arm. "I think someone has done you a great wrong there, dearie."

"Huh," he replied. For the majority of Lonan's life, Branwen's ruined face had been a reminder of how hated he was in the village. It had been a long time since she had looked on him with anything other than disgust. For the second time in as many days, the thought of Branwen threatened to bring a smile to Lonan's face.

"Have you slept yet?" the old lady queried.

Lonan laughed. "Artemis' beard, no. I don't think anyone could have."

"Let's head back, dearie. I can tell you've got a story that I need to hear."

Lonan allowed himself to be led back to the healer's cottage, now feeling safe enough to let his exhaustion show. He mumbled his story to the old lady, certain that half of it did not make sense. Harlow was waiting for them in his sitting chair, staring glass-eyed at the cottage wall. Mother Ogma led Lonan down the cellar steps and tucked him into bed.

She stroked his forehead. "Dream of happier times, of a young girl running with you through the woods."

As Lonan slipped off into unconsciousness, his last thought was: *I hope not - there's someone else I want to dream about.*

The wind blew cold across the young prince's cheeks. Adahy was crouching in the bushes in front of the shrine. The building looked completely different in the midday greyness, the once-foreboding tall doors now pathetic as they hung from their hinges. Congealed pools and wet collections of tattered fabrics and bones signified where guardsmen had fallen and had been eaten. Adahy stared at those piles soullessly.

What do my father's remains look like now?

A figure emerged from the temple and waved. Adahy stood up, wrapped himself in his grey cloak and trotted forward.

"No sign of them, sire," Maedoc addressed him in a low tone.

"Don't call me that," Adahy replied as he walked past the whipping boy. "The king is dead."

Adahy had found Maedoc the morning after his father's murder. The prince had remained curled in a ball on the roof for the rest of the night, and it had been a miracle no other Wolves had ventured up there. At daybreak, he had spent the morning making his own way down the castle walls, unheeded by the invaders who avoided the daylight. Maedoc had spotted him during his descent. The whipping boy had been just outside of the castle, wandering in the forest, lamenting the loss of his face. As soon as the sound of battle had reached his ears, he had made for the nearby river, using it to hide his scent and hid far from the combat. Adahy should have chided him for abandoning the rest of the palace, but instead had hugged the boy and sobbed his heart out to him. The pair had fled upstream and had spent all of last night huddled in a cave, fully expecting to be found and gutted. It was Adahy who had had the idea of returning to the temple the next day. Action needed to be taken - they would not remain undiscovered forever.

"I still think we should be heading to one of the villages," Maedoc repeated for the third time that day. "They have defences built for this kind of thing, don't they?"

"The palace had defences too, and look how that helped us," Adahy countered. "We would only prolong the inevitable by heading there." He marched through the ruined hall, turning over wooden plaques that littered the room. "They won't survive long without protection. They need the Magpie King."

"Well, we're buggered then, aren't we?" Maedoc replied. "Do you think we could reach the Mice by nightfall? Or the Owls?"

Adahy ignored the slave. He was busy studying the wooden wall ornament that he had turned over.

"My father told me I already know everything I need to become the Magpie King," Adahy mused. "How was he so sure I had all the information that I needed?"

He looked over to his whipping boy who just shrugged his shoulders, absentmindedly rubbing the bandages that covered his mauled face.

The young prince eyed the plaque in front of him. It had been so damaged, he was unable to tell which story it was depicting. "When we were cowering in that cave last night, all I could think of was the story of Artemis hiding in a cave from the Web Mother."

"Yeah, I loved that one. How she hunted for him all night, and was so exhausted in the morning, he was able to nip out and open her egg sacs without her being able to lift any of her eight legs."

"Wasn't that strange? My father had been killed, we were almost certainly going to die, but all I could think of was a stupid story."

Maedoc shrugged again. "We do weird things under pressure, I guess? I was mostly worried about how bad I needed to piss, and if the Wolves would be able to smell it if I did."

"My father told me that story, you see. Since I began to speak, every night until my thirteenth birthday he would come to me before bed, tell me a story of The Magpie Kings, sometimes even about Artemis, and would make me repeat it before I could go to bed."

"My father told me stories too, I think. Pretty sure I didn't have to repeat them though."

"No. Looking back on it now, I don't think it was some sort of fatherly ritual he was taking part in. What if there was something important in those stories he wanted me to remember?"

"Riiiight," Maedoc replied, stalling. "Okay, how about this - why was he telling you about Artemis? I thought they were villager stories. We were always told that noble children had Magpie King fairy tales, and we had Artemis fairy tales."

"They aren't fairy tales, Maedoc. Artemis was a real person."

Maedoc looked sceptical at this, but let his master continue.

"The nobles, the original Corvae, are not fond of him, for obvious reasons, but he's still an important part of our history, and a key link between the nobles and the villagers." Adahy stopped over the wood carving of Artemis stealing the Magpie King's treasure. "Still," he continued, "you are correct. Most of us were not told tales of Artemis for entertainment. So, why did my father want me to know about him?"

"Do you know the stone soup one? That was always one of my favourites. Berty told it that one of the key ingredients was a virgin's first blood and Artemis convinced the carpenter's daughter to give it up to him over the pot, in front of the whole village. 'Course, that could just have been because Bert was a horny bugger."

Adahy smiled, despite himself. "No, my father did not tell that one." He nudged the carving again. "This one came often, though. Why was that?" His eyes narrowed. "Maedoc, when you were told this tale, what was the treasure that Artemis stole?"

"I don't know. I've got the picture of a gold chalice in my head, but I can't remember if that was what my pappy said or I added it myself. What about you?"

"My father always just used the word 'treasure'. He was very strict about that bit, actually. I said it was a crown when I first repeated it to him and he made me say the whole thing again, using the correct word." He indicated for his servant to have a closer look at the carving in front of them. "What do you think the treasure is here?"

The carving was very detailed. Set against a backdrop of tall oaks below the Eyrie, clearly identified by their thick trunks and the shape of their leaves, Artemis was shown running from the Magpie King. The Magpie King was flying in the treetops, wings spread wide and an angry look carved on his bird-face. Artemis was depicted with his traditional travelling cloak, sack on his back, and a sly grin on his face. His right arm was held forward as he ran, and in his open palm was a pile of...

"Coins? I guess, yeah. Must be, but they're a weird shape, squashed even. Bit of a shame really, because the rest of the carving is so good."

"If you did not know the story, what would you think he might have been holding?"

"Oh, well, leaves probably. Maybe petals, depending on the flower."

Adahy nodded slowly, pleased to have someone else confirm his suspicions. "Maedoc, I think Artemis stole the source of the Magpie King's power. I also think that these carvings might be able to lead us to it."

Maedoc cast him a disbelieving look. "Sorry, where the hell did that come from? Do you know something I don't?"

Adahy nodded. "It is something I cannot share. I am sorry, my friend."

Maedoc exhaled, looking back at the carving. "Fair enough. Don't see how it helps us, though. There's nothing else on this that could tell us where to go."

Adahy nodded, the whipping boy voicing his own frustration. "You are right. Perhaps one of the others?"

"Artemis' beard, we're not in a position to mess around right now. It'll be getting dark outside and we are right beside where those monsters are sleeping. Sorry, Adahy, but I think your idea is rubbish. The Artemis stories don't have any distinguishing features for their settings. It's always 'a village' he visits, or 'a noble' he tricks. That's one of the reasons villagers like them so much - they get to imagine it was their own village in the story, or one of their rivals that gets screwed over."

Adahy nodded in agreement, but then stopped. "Gallowglass." Maedoc looked up in puzzlement. "Artemis visited Gallowglass."

A grin spread over Maedoc's face. "The one with the pigs and the farmer's daughters? My pappy said it was Gallowglass too - I always just thought it was because he had a grudge against someone living there."

"No, my father was very clear about the village's name. The only time any of our settlements appeared, other than the Eyrie. Quick, find the carving."

They spent precious minutes scavenging through the rubble and broken wood. The carving for this story had been broken in two by the invaders, but luckily the pieces had landed close to one another. The boys pieced it together again and studied it in depth. The centrepiece of the carving focussed on the blind farmer kissing three pigs goodnight inside his farmhouse while Artemis enjoyed the daughters in the sty outside. Adahy had blushed madly when his father had told this unusually bawdy tale, and was even worse when made to repeat it himself. The backdrop of the carving was a strip of thin birch trees that ran in a line across the artwork. Except for a single oak that stood at the left hand border of the carving.

"Look." Maedoc exclaimed. "It joins with the first one." Sure enough, when placed beside the carving of The Theft it seemed as if the two belonged side by side. "And check it out, the coins." Maedoc pointed, and sure enough there was a pile of familiar items beside Artemis' belongings in the artwork.

"Petals," Adahy corrected, sharing a grin as well as his trust with his friend.

"Well, that's it then, Gallowglass." Maedoc stood up. "That's where the source of power must be kept, right? What are we waiting for?"

Adahy stood also, but pursed his lips. "I don't know," he mused. "That seems too easy. I can't imagine a village would be a good choice for hiding something like this."

As he spoke, his eyes continued to study the carving and the line of birch trees. The tree to the far right of the background tree line was bare, and the branches on it were considerably more gnarled than those of its neighbour. Adahy's heart sank.

"Find those trees," he commanded, pointing at the twisted growth.

The prince started making his way through the rubble, but Maedoc stared at the tree in brief confusion. After moments his features contorted to horror. "Oh gods, no..."

"Yes," Adahy replied, returning already with the exact carving that he knew to look for. Sure enough, the backdrop on this one consisted of a line of twisted, naked trees. There were no people on this carving, just a single wooden cottage with a crescent moon painted onto the doorway. The hairs on the back of Adahy's neck stood up when he realised that what he thought was a shapeless blob in the cottage's window was actually a female silhouette.

"The Lonely Cottage. The Pale Lady."

"No..." was Maedoc's repeated response.

Adahy put a gentle hand on his friend's shoulder and shot him a reassuring grin. "Fear not, my friend, this is not a quest for you. It was made very clear to me that when the time came to claim my birthright, I would have to do it by myself."

Maedoc's face was a mixture of relief and loss. "But... what am I to do then?"

"Survive," came the simple reply. "It could be that fleeing to one of our neighbours might be the best idea. Certainly, somebody needs to tell the Mice of their ambassador's fate."

Maedoc's face creased. "You can't seriously think you can do this all by yourself? A couple of days ago you peed yourself because your daddy didn't come quick enough."

Adahy's nose wrinkled at this insult, but it hit upon a nerve that he was desperately trying to avoid. *If father could not survive against the Wolves, what hope do I have?*

Sensing his prince's conflict, the whipping boy pressed his advantage. "I don't have to go all the way. Artemis knows I have no urge to go anywhere near the Lonely Cottage. Maybe just as far as Gallowglass? That's on the way to the Leone lands, isn't it?"

Perhaps this would be for the best. Abandoning a wounded subject would not be the best way for a king to begin his reign, and he could not argue with the fact that the company would be welcome.

"To Gallowglass, then. We move now, though. Darkness is almost here."

With that, the two boys exited the temple, heading towards the setting sun.

ARTEMIS
AND THE
MOUSE

A tale from the fireplaces of the Low Corvae.

It was a time of famine. A great heat had battered the land for many months and the people were suffering for it. Lakes and streams that had been reliable sources for lifetimes no longer existed. Fruit and berries were small and hard, if they grew at all. Grass was dry, brittle and often brown. During these times, people became desperate. One bad day could be the difference between living and dying.

Three months into the drought, two kings met on the borders of their kingdom. One was the King of the Grasslands, leader of the mouse folk. The other was King of the Forest, the Magpie King. These two men met by chance where the forest gave way to the waving plains, and both were immediately drawn to the body.

He had been an old man, this corpse. Despite the obvious age of the deceased, his head was still fully covered in hair, and was shot through with confident streaks of black among the predominant grey. It was not the man's hair colour that interested the two kings, however. In one hand, the dead man was holding a coin purse. The other lay close to a half-full water skin.

The King of the Forest licked his lips at the sight of the damp earth surrounding the water container. He had used the last of his supplies up on the previous day, and had ventured this close to the forest border in order to seek more of that precious liquid. He noticed that the King of the Grasslands had a similar air of desperation about him. Despite the king of the mouse folk's fine clothing - a silken black suit wrapped in a fine moleskin cloak, the royal crest clear on his breast and a golden crown on his head - the Mouse's eyes were wide and roving.

Only one of these men would walk away from the encounter satisfied, and the other may not live to see another sunrise. Luckily for the Magpie King, he walked into this situation with two secrets up his sleeve. The first was that, despite appearances, one of the two kings present at this scene was not a king at all. You see, the Magpie King had heard many tales of Francesco of the Muridae, and all accounts described him as an overweight, spoilt noble used to having servants fawning over him. There was no chance this was the same man. Also, as the King of the Grasslands had first stepped into the open, the Magpie King had spied a long, hairless tail curl up from behind the man and hide itself under the moleskin cloak. The people of the Grasslands may worship the mouse, but only one of them had a tail like their totem - that was Alfrond. Alfrond the trickster, Alfrond the liar, Alfrond the exiled.

The other secret the Magpie King entered this situation with was that the remaining king involved in this encounter was also not a king at all. You see, although it certainly seemed that the Magpie King had appeared on his own borders - after all, he was currently dressed in a fine black outfit, protected by a mantle of thick, black and white feathers, and had a crown of finely weaved bramble circling his head - the man who was currently posing as the Magpie King knew that all of these items had been stolen from the Eyrie only days ago. That was because it was Artemis who was currently representing the forest in this dispute, not the Magpie King at all. Artemis the trickster, Artemis the liar, Artemis the exiled.

"Well met," Alfrond greeted the Magpie King, bowing with all the trappings of nobility one would expect from someone of royal blood.

"And you, brother," Artemis replied to the King of the Grasslands, matching his rival's fine graces.

"It appears," Alfrond began, "we have a situation here before us. This poor soul has passed on, and I wish to have his remains returned to his suffering family. The black through this creature's hair is a trait of the Muridae. Your common folk have bushy brown hair that turns white and falls out when they are older, unlike this wretched man. That solves this mystery before it has even begun. Let me claim this body and its belongings and be on my way."

"Ah, brother," Artemis replied, "I do not believe we can solve this conundrum so quickly. It is true, as you say, that many of the Corvae have thick brown hair, but we also celebrate a great variety of peoples in our kingdom. It would be unwise of me to not allow this man to make his final rest in my kingdom simply based on the colour of his hair. Also, you fail to take notice of the garments this man wore," he continued, indicating the simple woollen tunic on the corpse. "This is the traditional clothing of my people, and does not match the fine silks that the mouse folk clothe themselves in. I shall take this man and his effects back to the forest, and shall not rest until his family have been reunited with him."

Alfrond tutted, allowing a shadow of anger to cross his face. "It seems we shall not come to an agreement over this matter. Such a shame that such a simple thing causes our great kingdoms to argue. I call into effect the ancient laws forged between our peoples when they first met. See here, the roots of this oak tree," and with his right hand Alfrond indicated the closest tree to the body. "This is the last tree before my grasslands. The laws of both of our kingdoms dictate that where the oak's roots end, so too does your domain. You can well observe that this man's feet lie at least a pace beyond the border. Thus, I claim this body for the Mice."

Lips pursed, Artemis studied the scene. "Very well," he eventually relented, "I cannot debate this matter further with you." Alfrond reached down to grab the water skin, but Artemis placed his foot on the precious artifact.

"Ah, I cannot allow that," Artemis chided apologetically. "You may observe that this water skin is carefully balanced between two knotted oak roots. That is, as you already clearly stated, well within the limits of my kingdom. Although I do regret that I shall not be able to return this body to his rightful home, I claim this skin and its contents for the Magpies."

With that, Artemis took the water skin from the dirt and emptied its contents into his stomach in front of vanquished Alfrond, who could only grit his teeth at the sight of the clear liquid splashing down his enemy's cheeks. The two of them bowed and went on their way, although only one had the promise of surviving for another day.

Alfrond did endure, although that is a story that I myself do not know. If you speak to any of the Muridae of this tale, they shall swear until their whiskers fall out that it was Alfrond who ultimately deceived Artemis, forcing him to slink back to the forest unsatisfied.

But now you know the truth.

CHAPTER FOUR

Lonan's eyes fluttered open. He sat up in bed, now fully convinced his dream visions were true. *There is hope, then, if we can just hold out until Adahy succeeds.* He glanced upwards at the cellar door, still ajar. He mounted the stairs to find Harlow rocking away by the fire, but Mother Ogma was nowhere to be seen. Peering out of the window, he saw an unusually large gathering of people on the village green.

Panicking about another attack tonight, as well they should. I wonder what kind of defences they came up with while I slept?

However, when he opened the door to go to join the crowd, he realised something was wrong. Most of the village was there, gathered to listen to the speaker who was standing elevated in the middle of the green. This was a common way for the villagers to commune together when the occasion demanded it. What was unusual about this particular gathering was that Lonan had never seen the speaker before in his life.

"...forty-three sheep and nine horses."

"We don't even keep any bloody horses anymore, damn you, how are we supposed to pay that?" one of the Tumulty boys bellowed at the speaker.

"Now Niall, calm down before you do yourself harm," came

Old Man Tumulty's gruff voice from below the speaker.

"I hope I do not need to remind you yet again the penalty that will result for interrupting me in my royal duties?" the stranger shot back at Niall. The speaker was in his late thirties, early forties, and had very little meat on his bones. The man's hair was smoothed close to his head, jet black except for a dusting of grey around his temples. His skin was an almost-unnatural white, clearly the result of very little contact with the sun. From this distance his eyes seemed to match his hair and skin colour - dark black dots framed by brilliant whites. His garment was a long, hooded purple robe with golden embroidering at the neck, wrists and hem. He spoke with a superior air, expelling his words almost violently towards their targets.

"Next, the Anvils. You have been sent a number of unfulfilled requests over the years, much to my Lord's displeasure. I have here a detailed list of his numerous orders, and a demand they be fulfilled."

"I'm sorry," Lonan raised his hand, shoving his way to the front of the crowd. "Sorry, only just got here. Needed a bit of a lie-in, my apologies."

Having made his way to the front, he pointed his finger firmly towards the visitor. "Now, just who in Artemis' name do you think you are?"

He had not meant to be as confrontational out of the gate, but Lonan knew that deep down, he was irritated by this man. Irritated by the fact that Lonan should currently be basking in the gratitude of the village, of Branwen, for his heroics last night. He was certain that his deeds would still have been the talk of the village if not for the arrival of this stranger, and part of him blamed this unusual man for taking his due away from him.

Also, Lonan could not help but feel a slow sense of dread building at the coincidence of an outsider arriving so soon after the previous night's incident.

As if by clockwork, Jarleth took this moment to step out of the crowd. "Watch your tongue, Anvil. Inteus here is from the Magpie King." Turning to the newcomer, Quarry continued, "You will have to forgive the man. He's something of an oddity around here, the closest we have to a village idiot. Also, your information is a bit out of date, I'm afraid. The Anvils have not been smiths in this village for quite a few years now. That would be my role," Jarleth continued, puffing his chest out in pride. "I'm sure you will agree I can't be expected to honour somebody else's debt." Lonan did not have to see Jarleth's eyes to realise his Knack was being brought into play. "But I'm certain we can come to some kind of arrangement."

Lonan had not really reacted to the 'village idiot' jibe. He was too busy reeling from the suggestion that this Inteus had come from the Eyrie. Lonan backed away from the centre, searching for a familiar face while Jarleth began negotiations. Lonan found Mother Ogma at the back of the circle of people, a look of bemusement playing on her face.

"With all of these friends you've been making recently, it's no wonder poor Mrs Cutter had to wait so long to get her medicine."

"You're going to have to fill me in. Where did this guy come from?"

Mother Ogma shrugged. "He turned up this afternoon. Just trotted in on a donkey, of all animals, and set up shop in the centre of the green, making all kinds of demands. You can imagine the commotion the sight of him caused."

"Demands?"

"Yes. We are all in very serious arrears, apparently. I myself owe several carts full of ointments and poultices." The smile on her face grew even bigger.

"Did he say when he left the Eyrie?" Lonan urged.

"Well, he'd have to have left this morning, wouldn't he? Otherwise he'd have been out in the dark, and I don't know any kind of fool who would spend the night under the stars." She cast her eyes pointedly at Lonan, who just flat ignored her.

"He's lying. The Magpie King is dead, Mother, I'm certain of it. Something is very wrong here."

If Mother Ogma was sceptical of Lonan's claims, she kept this to herself. "Well, he's certainly playing with us anyway. It must be obvious there is no way anyone here can fulfil the demands he is making. He's softening everyone up right now - we'll find out what he really wants soon enough."

Lonan watched as the messenger referred to a long scroll again, reading out another family's name and their dues. "He knows who we are?"

"He's from the Magpie King," was Mother Ogma's reply. "This is how we used to pay our taxes. They know our families and their trades."

Old Tumulty's voice rang out across the green, interrupting the multitude of hushed conversations that were taking place. "The sun is getting low, Mister Inteus. Might I suggest we get under cover for now, and continue this tomorrow?"

The tax man sharply nodded his approval.

"We'll take the ass in with the rest of our animals. Is there anyone with room for Mister Inteus tonight?"

Slowly, all eyes turned towards Mother Ogma and Lonan cursed softly under his breath. Mother Ogma had a reputation for taking in strays, currently evidenced by her housing of Harlow and Lonan. The only other stranger that Lonan had ever seen in his life, an escaped thief from a neighbouring town, had also housed with her for a number of weeks before it was decided to put him to death to honour the judgement of their neighbours. This had been shortly after Lonan had started to stay with Mother Ogma, and he had bonded with the witty young man, often chatting well past the bells in the darkness of the cellar. His loss had been a blow to the already angry boy, but he had appreciated Mother Ogma's kindness towards the man in the final days of his life. He only wished the rest of the village would not take advantage of that kindness, especially now when Lonan wished to speak with her in private.

"I have room," Mother Ogma relented to the accusing stares, "if you can stand the smell of dried herbs and flowers."

Inteus wrinkled his nose, but replied, "Well, it is better than the alternative." He picked up his small pieces of baggage and marched across to the building that Lonan had emerged from not minutes earlier. Disgruntled at having to return to the cellar after spending most of the day in it, Lonan hurried after Mother Ogma. He entered the cottage to find Inteus staring at Harlow.

"Had I not demanded that all villagers meet at the central green to share their skills with me? Is this another who seeks to avoid paying fealty to the Magpie King? And what is your trade, old man?"

"Unless the Magpie King is particularly interested in farts and dribbles, I think you could leave Harlow off of your list," Lonan said, helping Mother Ogma heft the old man down the stairs.

"He is an invalid?" Inteus queried.

"Either that or the best liar I've ever met."

"Your husband?"

"Ha," Mother Ogma grunted, lowering the old man into bed.

"Just a poor soul that needs someone to look after him."

"You have quite a collection of those already," the man shot back, eyes firmly fixed on Lonan.

"Do you need the candle on, or were you planning on sleeping straight away?" his host questioned, ignoring the inference in the previous statement.

Inteus was aghast at the question. "It must not even be eight o'clock. How could you possibly contemplate going to sleep now?"

"Life here is very different from what you're used to, I gather," Mother Ogma explained. "Our day starts and ends with the sun. It allows us to work and keeps us safe."

Inteus shook his head in disgust. "I understand the concept, but to lose so much of your day... Still, if it allows you to make best use of your talents for the kingdom. Healing and... foraging, was it?"

Lonan grimaced at the suggestion. "I've no Knack for it. I just do it to help out."

"Oh? Well, where do your talents lie then? Another healer?"

Lonan looked increasingly uncomfortable. Mother Ogma answered for him, "Lonan hasn't discovered his Knack yet. He is helping me in return for room and board."

Inteus scoffed in response. "Yet? Look at him - well past his twentieth year already, isn't he? No Knack will come to him now. That is what comes of laziness and lack of application."

These were all accusations Lonan had heard before. The development of a young person's Knack was cause for great celebration in the family, as this strong talent would support the future of that bloodline. Lonan's failure to develop his father's Knack for metalworking was seen as a lack of respect for his father, his father's ghost punishing him from beyond the grave, or Lonan just simply not working hard enough at it.

"Dreams," came the unexpected response from Mother Ogma. "I'm beginning to think that dreams are Lonan's Knack."

Lonan gave the old woman a warning look, but it was too late - the snake had bitten. At Mother Ogma's offhand remark, Inteus' head had shot up, fixing Lonan with a penetrating stare.

"Great, thanks," Lonan replied sarcastically to the old woman, attempting to put Inteus off his scent. "She's always accusing me of sitting and watching the clouds and day dreaming, instead of hunting out herbs and flowers for her."

"Well, how else do you explain my lack of damned primroses then? Poor Mrs Cutter is going to explode before I am able to unblock her innards, and all because you keep chasing squirrels in the sky." Luckily Mother Ogma had recognised Lonan's attempts to keep the dreams quiet.

"I suspect she is correct, young man," the messenger chided him, turning to his paper and ink quills. "Otherwise, you would have developed a Knack many years ago. Even the lowliest of talents let us provide for the kingdom. Excuse me while I put my own Knack to use." With that, the tax man turned his back on the others and began scribbling frantic notes on his parchment.

Lonan signalled his thanks to Mother Ogma by raising his eyebrows, a gesture that she wished away with a wave of her hands.

A thought came to him. "You know," he began, shooting a knowing glance at Mother Ogma, "you've got it wrong. I wasn't watching squirrels the other day. I was chasing stories."

"Oh, that is much more productive, I do apologise."

"I was following the Tumulty boys. They were telling each other tales while they worked the fields. I couldn't quite catch one of them that sounded particularly interesting. The Pale Lady - have you heard of her?"

Mother Ogma looked puzzled, throwing a questioning glance at Lonan. He simply shrugged his shoulders to indicate that it was a genuine question.

"Well," she began, still a bit unsure, "she does not really have much of a story attached to her, to be honest. She is old, I remember that. Been in the forest before any of us, before even the Magpie King, they say. There is a house, deep in the woods, where nobody else would be able to survive on their own. You shall know it is hers because of the crescent moon that hangs above it. Her power is of the moon. She is a woman, and thus lives in the moon's cycle. She is of the night, and her deeds are best performed in darkness. She is of changing mood, and just as the moon waxes and ebbs so does her hospitality. She is waiting for you, young Lonan. She stands forever at her window, awaiting her next visitor. Those who seek her out are always seeking aid. They are also desperate. If she chooses to help, then they will certainly succeed in their task, but not before leaving a piece of themselves behind with her. If her mood is not hospitable…" Mother Ogma ended the tale there, watching Lonan expectantly.

"Well?" he questioned after a few seconds had passed.

"I do not have the answer to that query, I am afraid, as none who have witnessed her displeasure have returned to tell that tale." She gave a grin of triumph as she finished on that line. Lonan gave a grin too, appreciating the trap that had been woven into the story.

"But, that's it?" he pressed. "No other stories? No other characters met her, like Artemis or the Magpie King?"

She shook her head. "That is all, I'm afraid. It is an odd one for you to ask for, if I'm being honest. Normally it is a tale for women. For girls, really. The only enquiries I have ever had after her have been from girls in trouble. Not much call for that recently."

He nodded, his brow creased. So he knew very little about what Adahy was walking into. What he did know did not suggest a situation Lonan was envious of. He bade the room goodnight and lay down on his bed, willing himself to slip back into sleep. He did not fear the Wolves at the village doors tonight, he knew they had more important prey to seek.

Gallowglass had been hit hard before Adahy and Maedoc had arrived there. They had spent most of the previous night running downstream, desperate to keep moving and not leave any tracks. Both of them were very aware that they had no chance of surviving any possible attacks, so their only option had been to keep moving. Morning had greeted them not with cockcrows and people rising peacefully from their beds, but with screams and lamenting wails. Three cellars in Gallowglass had been breached last night and the villagers were dealing with the loss in the way that villagers did - fear and anger. They were not at all interested in a young boy who claimed to be a son of the man who was supposed to stop all of this from happening, and when Adahy felt that this fear and anger was in danger of being directed at the two new faces, he suggested that Maedoc and himself should quickly continue on their journey. They had walked for half an hour more, with the Eyrie to their back at all times, as suggested by the woodcarving map in the shrine, and then they climbed a tree to get some sleep.

"The Lady is of the night," Adahy explained. "My father was

very clear about that fact. I would not want to wander right past her because we were travelling at the wrong time of day."

"All of this seems crazy," was Maedoc's reply, "but I'm not going to argue with the suggestion of sleep. Even if I have to do it up a tree, in the middle of the day."

When night fell, they continued, and it was not long before a clearing with a single cottage in it broke the monotony of the undergrowth they were stumbling through. The building was simple in its design, but a few key features made it stand out from those they had seen in Gallowglass earlier. Where the village buildings had been constructed of stone and thatch, this cottage was made entirely from wood, with cut planks forming the walls and in place of slates on the roof. This cottage was dominated by the gnarled tree that stood behind it, dead branches twisting like a clenched fist. From where he stood, Adahy could not tell if the tree was simply close to the house, or if the house was actually built into the thick trunk of the tree. The twin windows on the front of the building reached up high, arching at the top like those back at the shrine. The door seemed normal enough, but a simple crescent moon carved from wood hung over it. As expected, there was a pale face standing at one of the windows, waiting.

"This is where we part ways then," Adahy broke the silence, unable to hide the tremor in his voice.

"My Lord," Maedoc stammered, "perhaps I should-"

"Mind our bags," the prince interrupted, not giving the whipping boy time to make a suggestion his heart would not wish to follow through with, "I shall be back soon."

Adahy marched towards the house, not wanting to give Maedoc time to respond, but also not wanting to give himself the opportunity to change his own mind. As he moved into the clearing, the featureless pale face that had hung in the left window withdrew, disappearing. He arrived at the door and gave it a knock. He was rewarded by a breathy voice speaking to him from beyond the portal.

"Shall your young friend not be joining us?"

Adahy's eyes grew wide. Whatever he had been steeling himself for, it was not such a mundane conversation as this. "Um, no. He, uh, he's going to stay over there."

"But he has come so far to see me. It would be a shame for him to have to wait while we chat."

"He's, uh, he's fine. I have come for the Magpie King's flower.

It is a task I have to perform by myself."

A child-like tutting rang out from behind the door. "Oh dear. You have not performed this task alone though, have you? He has travelled across half the forest with you and you think these last few feet shall make any difference? Oh dear."

A shiver ran up Adahy's spine, but he persisted. "He is much happier over there. I will be entering by myself, if I am permitted."

"Oh, by all means, do come in," whispered the Pale Lady, the door opening at the sound of her invitation. Adahy caught a glimpse of a white robe drifting through a doorway at the back of the hall, and then stepped inside to follow her. The room was plain, the woodwork well finished, but left undecorated. A thin layer of dust coated the floor, enough to grey the strong oak brown. A glance upwards opened Adahy's eyes to a dense collection of cobwebs, in which the owners were particularly active, travelling along the slender threads to the struggling prey they had stored there.

Adahy walked down the hall and entered what was evidently the main chamber of the building. It maintained a similar finish and cleanliness as the hallway, with the exception of the back wall of the room, which appeared to be made of the exposed trunk of the dead tree that stood behind the Lonely House. He also noted an empty fireplace with a small potted black plant sitting on the mantelpiece. Adahy would have ran and grabbed the artifact there and then, if not for the figure that hung in the air beside his prize.

The Pale Lady was small, and from the features Adahy was able to discern he could swear that she was no more than a child, yet this fact did nothing to assuage his fear of her. She wore a long night gown, finely embroidered, that fell beyond her feet. Her oil-black hair hung across her face, hiding her features from the young prince. The skin on her bare arms matched the brilliant white of her simple garment. Most unsettling of all to Adahy was the fact that no feet emerged from the gown to touch the ground. Instead a mess of tree roots curled under that white gown, trailing across the floor of the room back to the exposed tree trunk wall. When travelling here, Adahy and Maedoc had been unable to determine what her mood might have been. The half-whispered stories they remembered about her suggested that her mood would have something to do with the phases of the moon, but that brilliant orb was currently halfway to waxing full - that meant nothing, surely?

Or ambivalence at best. Adahy had to be careful.

"My name is Adahy of the Corvae. My father was the Magpie King. I have come to claim my birthright and avenge his death."

The creature hung in the air for a moment and then responded with, "And why should I give you what you seek?" As the apparition in front of him spoke, she cocked her head slightly and gave an open gesture with her arms. Adahy's eyes widened as he realised the tree roots below her body were moving. He also noticed an uncanny rippling beneath her white skin, as if a family of snakes were writhing together just below the surface every time her body moved.

"It is my birthright," the prince repeated. "My father was the Magpie King, and his father before him. Our line goes back beyond our history, and I am next to shoulder this responsibility. You hold the power I require to protect the forest."

"I care nothing for little kings and their history. You say you shall protect the forest. Why should I believe you? Magpie King upon Magpie King has uttered this promise in the past, and still there is fighting, fear and death. No, I think my gift shall remain with me."

Adahy was at a loss. He had not expected claiming the flower to be easy, but similarly he had not been expecting such a wall of resistance. A task, a riddle, a challenge, maybe, but not a flat out refusal. "Is there anything I can offer you to change your mind?"

"An offer? A trade, perhaps? I do so like trades. But what have you got to offer me?"

Adahy searched his mind. He had come here without anything of value, not expecting to need it. He had nothing except the cloak on his back. Perhaps... "I offer you this cloak, sown from the gathered feathers of Magpies throughout our great forest. Such a garment takes years-"

"Pah." At this exclamation the voice in his ear turned more guttural, and his paranoia told him that there was more anger in the Pale Lady's words than there had been before. "What would I want with a bird man's cloak? Will it let me fly like a bird? Do not tell me it shall keep me warm. No clothing in the forest exists that could perform such a task. Do not tell me how fetching I shall look draped in it. I above all others know of where that path ultimately leads. Pah to your cloak."

Adahy searched his mind. The stories of the Pale Lady were so sparse, he could not gleam any details from them that could aid him now. Tales such as hers normally involved unusual prices such as a first-born child, a traveller's Knack or one's very soul. He was unsure about which of those prices he would be willing to pay.

"Great Lady, I struggle to think of anything I have with me that would match the value of this flower. Please, aid our negotiations by telling me the currency that would interest you."

"Why, young Adahy, the only currency that is worth trading in. Blood."

As if she had uttered the final lines of a spell, at the close of that sentence the window exploded, shattering inwards in a hail of glass and fur. Adahy was too late. The Wolves had found him.

The prince made a desperate leap for the source of his father's power. Unfortunately, one-on-one, he was no match for the beast in speed or size. The lone Wolf easily intercepted the boy mid-air, sending him spiralling back across the room, sending cracks up the wooden wall where Adahy impacted upon it. Despite the death that was moving towards him, Adahy's look of fear was saved for the Pale Lady, terrified of her reaction to the violation of her home. She simply hung in the air beside the fireplace, watching events unfold before her.

"Will you not help me?" Adahy pleaded. As if in response, the Wolf darted forward to rake a claw across Adahy's chest, leaving a deliberately shallow wound, but one still deep enough to cause the prince to cry out in pain and fall to his knees. His assailant gave him a backhanded blow that sent him to the floor. Only when his cheek was lying flat on the wood did he see a new figure silently skulking in through the now-exposed wall. It was Maedoc, his trembling showing how absolutely terrified he was. Like Adahy, his remaining eye was fixed on the Pale Lady, completely ignoring the Wolf when faced with her presence.

Then Maedoc nodded his head, gaze still fixed on the floating apparition.

Is he communicating with her somehow?

Almost against his own will, Maedoc painfully made his way up to the fireplace, extended his hand to the flower, and picked a single black petal from it. He faced the Wolf, which by now had one of its hind paws placed firmly on Adahy's head, beginning to push it into the floor. Maedoc placed the petal on his tongue. Adahy stared at the whipping boy as the boy with the mauled face chewed, and then charged at the Wolf.

The creature went careening off through the wall into the hallway, with Maedoc soaring after it, screaming while he pounded his enemy with his bare fists. Adahy picked himself up, wincing through the pain. His heart fell when he looked at the gap in the house where the window used to be. Three pairs of eyes stared back at him. His head turned again to the flower sitting atop the mantelpiece. The Pale Lady moved aside, raising her hand in a welcoming gesture. He sprinted across the room to grab the bloom. As one, the Wolves leapt through the gap in the wall towards their prey. In the hallway, Maedoc's tortured screams were accompanied by wet impacts as his punches broke his enemy's bones and jellied its flesh. Adahy opened his mouth and tasted the sweet tang of the black flower's nectar. The three Wolves arrived at their target, their necks already broken as they sailed past him and fell in a heap to the floor. It took seconds for Adahy to realise he was the one who had, by instinct, committed their murder. Already, the power of the Magpie King flowed through his veins.

Maedoc stumbled through the opening he had created mere moments earlier, giving a soft moan as he stepped. He raised his hands to hold his head, blood mixed with torn flesh and hair dripping down his face. Adahy ran to his friend to help him stand.

"Ah, the mayfly hero and the Magpie King. My Lords." The Pale Lady bowed to the pair and then left the room.

"Did you see me?" Maedoc gasped, wheezing as he breathed. "I killed it. Took it apart with my bare hands." The whipping boy's breathing was getting rougher now, and his pupil was a tiny pinprick inside of his deep brown eye. The flower's poison was already working on him.

"Yes," was Adahy's reply. "Now we have a chance."

He slung his friend's arm over his back and helped him move outside, through the window. The night remained as black as ever but Adahy could not help but be assaulted by a sense of discovery as he looked upon it with new eyes. He could hear a family of thrushes sheltering in a nearby oak. Across the clearing, he could spot the broken leaves and twigs that signified the path the attacking Wolves had taken to reach the Lonely House.

"What's the plan now, then?" Maedoc gasped.

Adahy's feet were picking up vibrations in the ground, caused by heavy animals pounding in the dirt several miles away. More Wolves heading towards them.

"Revenge," was the simple answer the Magpie King gave as he leapt into the night towards his prey.

THE
MAGPIE KING'S
BRIDE

An extract from the teachings of the High Corvae.

This is a tale of the early days of the forest, before the outsiders came. The Magpie King had already performed many of his great acts, such as raising the Eyrie with his bare hands over twelve nights, ridding the forest of the last bear in revenge for their insistent singing, and freeing the river from the red otters. He had made many friends and enemies in his short reign. The Leone, the lion people, had proven to be strong allies against the Serpents to the south. The Muridae were inquisitive, if not yet helpful. And the Wolves were already beginning to infect the dark heart of the forest. But what weighed most on the Magpie king's mind at this time was the presence of the Tytonidae, the owl people, in the hills to the north.

It was King Reoric of the Leone that had first brought their existence to the attention of the Magpie King, making them more than just the bedtime cautionary tales the Corvae gave their young.

"Eerie is what they are," the gruff warrior had said. "Only ever seen 'em alone, just one at a time. Always at night too." The large man had taken a swig of ale at this point, to calm his nerves. "But the Owls shine in the moon, so you can see 'em from miles off. Never let you get close enough though. Just a jump and then they're gone, poof." The last part had been meant to startle the Magpie King, but the wise ruler had sensed the rise in the Lion's heart rate before the attempt, and had merely smiled in response.

He met one of the Owls not long after this conversation, during another of his great adventures. She did not spot him, at least not at first. It was night, as King Reoric had forewarned, and she was invading his forest. The Magpie King was perched high in the trees, scouring the land before him for food when a ghostly white shape floated through the bare winter branches to a lake, and there cupped her hands to drink. As strong as it was, the Magpie King's heart laboured heavily at this sight. He thought at first that this emotion was fear, stoked by the Lion's tale and the rumours of his own people. His eyes took in her mane of thick white hair, expecting a pruned hag's face when she turned her head. Instead, he was treated with smooth skin, radiant in the moonlight, and purple eyes opened wide as she scanned the treetops. Their eyes locked for a brief moment, she leapt, and then was gone.

The Magpie King had more pressing matters to attend to and did not pursue on that night, despite a most urgent curiosity to do so. In a time when peace returned to his land, his mind turned again to the white-haired maiden that haunted his waking thoughts. Wise as the Magpie King was, it took him many turns of the moon before he would finally admit why this figure remained close to his mind's surface. When he realised that this was the woman he wanted for his wife, he resolved to do all in his power to claim her.

The Owls were figures of great superstition for the Corvae. The Magpie King's people believed that the Great Magpie comes at the moment of their deaths to carry their souls to their final reward. However, the White Owl was another figure of death, one with many unknowns attached to it. Legend had it that if an owl arrived to claim one's soul instead of a magpie, the soul of that departed person shall never join those of his ancestors. Because of this fear, and despite the fierce loyalty of his people, the Magpie King could find no volunteers from his warriors to accompany him to the hills to the north, not even from his personal guard. He was, however, visited by an old peddler woman with some sage advice for him.

"We are frightened of them, m'lord, but they fear us too, else why run off? Do not let her know who you are. Disguise yourself as one of their own."

The Magpie King, never one to dismiss the wisdom of his elders, pondered her words deeply. Not able to find any further companions or any more advice for his quest, the Magpie King headed north to find his bride.

After many months of searching he finally happened upon one of the palaces of the Tytonidae, a tall stone building built around an ancient oak that stood alone on the hilltops. Climbing to the top of the structure, his heart skipped a beat when he peered inside to see the white-haired woman that haunted his dreams sitting at a banquet table, breaking bread with a large company. Obsessed, the Magpie King spent many hours listening to the conversation. It transpired that it was the princess of the Tytonidae that his heart had chosen, and that her father was sick to death of her constant rejection of fine suitors.

The Magpie King heard the old man exclaim, "Finding a husband for my daughter is impossible. Let he who can complete an impossible task take her hand. Listen well - any man who can spit upon the fire of my hearth and ignite it may have my daughter as his wife."

At this proclamation, the banquet hall doors burst open and a tall man walked in. He was dressed in the white fabrics of the Tytonidae, but whereas most owls were fair of face and hair, this man was dark and mysterious. Silently, the dark man strode to the hearth of the owl king and spat into the dying embers there. Immediately the fireplace burst into life with tall flames spouting to the high ceiling. The owl princess gasped, but could not refuse a promise made by her father to the court. The couple were quickly wed in a ceremony involving a silver cord joining their forearms together, and the princess retired to her bedchamber with her new husband.

The dark man was, of course, the Magpie King. Upon hearing this opportunity, he had quickly clothed himself in a disguise he had fashioned and had filled his mouth with a poison that was deadly if consumed, but ignited with anger at a naked flame. He was a gentle and courteous lover to his new wife, but as he slept, his disguise slipped away and the princess could see that this man who had bedded her was not of her people. Her scream woke the Magpie King and the rest of the castle, and in a panic, he fled from the building.

Despite his victory that night, the Magpie King was not yet satisfied for he wanted the princess's heart, not just her bed.

Some months later, word reached the palace of a newcomer to the area, a rich man from one of the furthest Tytonidae settlements who had established a new lodge close by and had invited all in the palace to a great feast. All chose to attend, servants, nobles, king and princess. The hunting lodge was vast, and on this night all manner of game and greens were served to the welcome guests. Their host, a man of fair complexion but unusual mannerisms, was gracious to all, but paid especial attention to the young princess.

As night began to turn into morning, their host called for stories, beginning the round with a tale about a black squirrel eating the sun like a nut. Guests took it in turn, until only the princess was left. She smiled, and then said in her honeyed voice, "I have a tale, but this one must be whispered. Come close, my wonderful host, so I may whisper into your ear."

With great excitement, the host, who was of course the Magpie King in disguise, pushed his way to the princess's side. She leaned forward as if to speak softly to him, but then grabbed his disguise and tugged it off to the great shock and disgust of all onlookers. The Magpie King shot the princess a look of fury, and she responded with, "You shall not fool me twice, crow."

Consumed with frustration, the Magpie King fled back to the borders of his forest, and there fell into an uncomfortable sleep. In his dreams, he was visited by a great white owl who demanded of him, "Why do you continue to pursue me?"

Knowing this was only a dream, and that here he could speak his true mind without betraying his weakness to anyone, the Magpie King responded in a whisper choked with sadness, "Because I am overcome with you. You are in every thought that invades my mind. Even if you forced me to chase you until the ends of my days, growing to hate me as I hate death itself, I would still continue to pursue you."

At these raw emotions, the haughtiness of the owl softened, and a smile formed across the human face that it sported just before the dream faded.

He awoke on the edge of the forest, greeted by the sight of his white-haired wife staring back at him.

"Why now?" was the only phrase that he could bring himself to mutter.

"Because I am no longer afraid," was his wife's response. "Because you were a gentle lover. And because the thought of a life with you excites me."

Together, they flew hand in hand back to the Magpie King's forest home, to rule over our dark land.

CHAPTER FIVE

Lonan was the first to wake, probably because he had had so much sleep the day before. The cellar door was still closed and the lack of light creeping through the joins in the planks of wood suggested it remained dark outside.

Dammit. Why'd I have to leave the dream, just as things were starting to look up?

Despite his disappointment at waking so early, he could not help himself smiling. There was a new Magpie King. The power Lonan had felt from Adahy in those few moments before he awoke was unlike any sensations he had ever experienced in his life.

Artemis protect them, and please do not let that be my last dream of the prince. Of the king, now.

In his bunk, Harlow gave a grunt of unrest. Lonan expected it to wake Inteus or Mother Ogma, but neither appeared to stir. It must have been earlier than Lonan had thought for Mother Ogma to miss one of Harlow's infrequent noises.

He pondered the still figure of the visiting courtier, fully convinced the man was not who he claimed to be. Lonan's dreams had shown him the fall of the Eyrie, and yet this man claimed to have travelled from it only a day ago. He could not be a complete charlatan - he did have details of the villagers and their Knacks, after all. *Well, most of them,* Lonan thought, grinning again. *Mother Ogma said last night that my Knack was my dreams, and I'm inclined to agree with her. How else could I explain this ongoing tale of events that marries up so well with events in the village?*

Perhaps Inteus had fled the Eyrie on the night of the attack, looking to use information from its libraries to milk the village of its resources in the name of a king he now assumed to be dead. The villagers were also vaguely aware of peoples throughout the world who were not Corvae. Perhaps this man was sent to gather information for a foreign power, in preparation for an attack. With the Eyrie occupied, the forest would be an easy target for an outside force.

He studied the sleeping figure, lightly snoring in his purple robe and thin sandals, ill fit for a working man's life. Lonan's eyes rested on the parchment lying by the liar's bed. Taking a peek at the words would do Lonan no good for like most in the village he was unable to read. Still...

Aping the movements of the wild cats that he shadowed when out foraging, Lonan hunkered down on all fours and slowly crept across the room towards the man's bed. The floor of the cellar had originally been a thick clay, but decades of movement across it had beaten it into a flat, almost polished surface. Lonan's fingers stabbed into this clay due to the tension in his body. He moved forward within reaching distance of the parchment. His hand stretched out, planning to take only one sheet from the mess of writing that had been abandoned by the bedside. His fingers closed on the paper and Lonan's eyes moved upwards, expecting Inteus to wake now and catch him in the act. As the sleeping man remained undisturbed, Lonan slowly pulled the parchment away from its brothers. He clenched his teeth as the dry material cracked free of the folds of the roll, but still Inteus remained unmoving. With a wicked grin on his face Lonan turned around and walked straight into Mother Ogma.

"Gods, but you are loud," the old woman chided him, grabbing the paperwork. "And what do you think you are doing with this?"

"He's lying, Mother. I know you believe in my dreams now. The Eyrie has fallen. This man could not have come from there."

Mother Ogma nodded grudgingly at Lonan. "Still, he definitely has the air of the Eyrie about him, and he has all of our information too."

"Well, now I have it, don't I? If it was easy enough for me to lift, why not him?"

"This?" Mother Ogma looked at the parchment she had taken from Lonan. "No, this isn't a list of village Knacks. This..." Her brow wrinkled as she studied the parchment further.

"Mother Ogma?"

"This is a suspect list. All of the villagers are named on it. Many old names too, long since passed. See, your father is right here." She pointed at a scrawl with a line through it.

`"That's because he's dead, right? The line? No, wait..." At first Lonan thought all of the names had been scored through, but he spotted two that remained unmarked. "Who are they?"

"This one is Branwen. Branwen Dripper, as she is named here. And this? This is you, Lonan." It was not his own name's inclusion on the list that caused his heart to fill with dread, but hearing Branwen named first set Lonan's teeth on edge.

"What's it for? What else does it say?" Lonan's aggressive tone caused the visitor to stir in his sleep.

"There is nothing of detail here," Mother Ogma spoke as she scanned the page, moving her head from left to right in an exaggerated motion in her hurry to be done with the task. "A note here to the man's master? Employer? Just stating that you are both equally viable choices, and perhaps both should be looked into for thoroughness. Nothing of detail. Lonan, this document is important - it will be missed."

As if on cue, Inteus yawned, stretched his arms and turned to face the talking pair. As the stranger performed this movement, Lonan grabbed the paper from Mother Ogma and dived over his own bed, straight into the pile of parchments belonging to Inteus.

"You complete fool," Inteus spluttered, jumping from his bed with a start. "One sheet of that parchment is worth more than your miserable life." He pushed Lonan roughly to the side and busied himself checking the paperwork, looking to ascertain the damage.

"Wha- what happened?" Lonan stammered.

"Another nightmare dear, nothing unusual. You just gave Mister Inteus a fright, that's all."

Inteus turned to look at Lonan with narrow eyes. "Nightmares? This is a common problem?"

"Among villagers, yes," Mother Ogma interjected before Lonan had a chance to respond. "Up in the Eyrie, you have to deal with attacks regularly, I'm sure, but down here, things can be a bit more immediate. It can have a lasting effect on impressionable minds."

"You might have warned me before walling me up in this hole with such problems."

"I'm sorry, dearie, I wasn't aware you had other options. Oh look, daylight. I think it's time we opened the doors, don't you?"

With Inteus watching on, Lonan and Mother Ogma worked together to push open the cellar doors. Upon exiting the cottage, Inteus found himself assailed by a small group of villagers who had had a sleepless night mulling over the debts he had presented them with.

"So," Lonan began as he sweetened his porridge with honey, "What do you think then?"

"What's that, dearie?"

"What I'm suspected of?"

Mother Ogma looked at him, trying to read how he was taking the information. "Not just you, dearie. Branwen too."

Lonan pulled a face. This was where his real concern lay. He could not help himself. All of the recent encounters with Branwen, especially the look on her face after he had saved her life, had rekindled emotions he had spent the last eight years trying to hide from. He cared about this woman. He was more concerned about her safety than his own.

Mother Ogma waved her ladle at him, distracting Lonan from his thoughts. "And that is where your clue lies. If he came here to find someone, what is it the two of you share?"

Lonan could not stop himself from bursting out laughing. "You're joking, aren't you? Branwen has hardly spoken to me for years, and when she has I'd rather she hadn't. We haven't been in a position to share anything for the best part of a decade."

"I like that brave front that you are putting up, dearie, but you can't fool me. Find out what he sees in you and her. If you are interested in looking out for her. And yourself, of course."

Lonan looked up, chewing on a mouthful of porridge, thinking about what she had said. "And just how do you think I could get her to speak to me?"

"Catch," she responded. Lonan caught the carefully wrapped vial she threw to him. "She had a baby a few weeks ago. It takes a woman some time to recover from that."

Lonan looked at the vial for a moment. "Well, I can't keep the lady waiting then, can I?"

Outside of the cottage, avoiding the throng gathering around Inteus, Lonan finally felt his nerves falter. It had seemed so easy to approach Branwen again while he sat at Mother Ogma's table, but the reality of actually doing it was a different matter altogether. Lonan had managed to put up a shell around himself to deal with the dirty looks and jibes from the rest of the village, often responding by giving as good as he got, but Branwen could break through his defences with a single steely glare. He had dealt with this mostly by avoiding her as much as possible, so the thought that he would have to go against these instincts terrified him.

He walked past the Quarry house without stopping, quickly glancing through the window and door, but could see nothing. Eventually he gathered up the courage to knock on the door but received no answer. Jarleth was busy fawning over Inteus, so thankfully took no heed of Lonan's enquiries. If Branwen was not at home, Lonan was sure he knew where she was.

Branwen's Knack was for cleaning. Specifically, it was for washing clothes. Not a terribly exciting Knack, but this tended to be the norm for village women - Knacks to do with the upkeep of the household. A comely girl with a Knack for cooking was a fine catch. Seamstress and healing Knacks were also favourable, but tended to require someone experienced to help them to develop. When Branwen and Lonan were young they would often discuss what life would be like when their Knacks developed. Lonan had been fully convinced he would inherit his father's, but Branwen's desires were many and exciting. She wanted Knacks that traditionally belonged to men - woodwork, smithing, even fighting - and many that Lonan was sure did not exist - exploring, playing, climbing. When these conversations first began, Lonan had teased Branwen by suggesting that she would develop a housework Knack like the rest of the women. He quickly learnt that continuing that line of thinking would lose him a friendship, and possibly some teeth. Also, as a child he had thought Branwen would be different. She had been so unlike the other women of the village. Where they were dutiful, she was playful and ambitious. The attack took all of that fire away from her.

When Lonan had heard of Branwen's Knack developing he had been saddened, but by that stage it was not shocking. Since losing her mother and her face, Branwen had become withdraw, sullen, and all of the energy that had previously drawn him to her had fled. Jarleth's marriage to her simply came about because they were the only two eligible partners of their generation. She was not a catch for him, and Lonan was convinced she was not particularly enamoured of her husband. But, there were no other choices.

Whilst pondering these thoughts Lonan had wandered through the thin patch of forest before the river that ran close to the village. It was from here that drinking water was fetched, and where household items were washed, including clothes. Sure enough, Branwen was here, babe swaddled and sleeping nearby. Branwen was singing a lullaby as she worked, taking clothing from her washing basket and beating it against her washboard, expertly dealing with any particularly difficult stains. It was a beautiful song that Branwen was crooning to her child, one Lonan did not remember hearing before, about Artemis returning to the Eyrie in disguise to seduce a noble lady. In the Artemis tales he was used to, this act would normally be one of revenge or deviousness, with Artemis looking to punish the lady's husband or the lady herself through the seduction. In Branwen's tune, however, the noblewoman was caught in a loveless marriage, and Artemis was risking his life to try to be with the woman who had captured his heart.

As Branwen sang, she gazed at her surroundings, the clouded sky and green trees. Watching her work, Lonan suspected the reason that Branwen's Knack had developed was because coming here to wash was a way to get herself out of the village. She was in the forest, alone. A small glimpse of her previous adventurous nature. He watched her while she finished the song, and at that point decided he should approach her now or risk being rightly accused of spying on her.

He coughed as he moved away from his hiding place among the trees. Catching sight of him, Branwen instinctively dropped the tunic she was working at and grabbed her child.

"What do you want, Anvil?"

Lonan's heart sank. His rescue had not changed her gut reaction on seeing him. Perhaps Jarleth had had time to work his Knack on her.

"I just wanted to see if things were all right. Everything was better last night?"

She looked around suspiciously, clutching her baby close. "What is this about? Why're you really here? We're close enough to the village that they will hear me scream."

Lonan did his best to fight the anger rising from his gut. "Any particular reason you felt like mentioning that? Or is this how dinner table conversations in the Quarry household tend to start?" He had not quite achieved the calm response he had been trying for.

"I don't need this now, Anvil. Too much has been going on over the past few days. Don't add to my worries - you'll find I have a breaking point you don't want to cross."

"Oh, I remember. I crossed it plenty of times back in the day and learnt to regret it."

"Back when we were children. Do not even compare me to that silly little girl. I will kill you if you take another step towards me and my daughter." At that, she pulled out a small fisherman's knife from up her sleeve and brandished it at Lonan.

He had had enough.

"Gods, forgive me for trying to have a conversation. Or for expecting some kind of gratitude for saving your life the other night. Taken too many blows to the face recently to be able to think straight, I reckon." He instantly regretted that last comment as soon as it passed his lips.

"You bastard," came the hurt response.

Lonan pinched the bridge of his nose and screwed up his eyes. "Yeah, you're right, that was horrible of me. I'll leave - this is not how I wanted it to go." Lonan turned to leave.

"Wait." He turned back to see Branwen standing there, knife still held high. "Why did you come here?"

He looked around, giving a gesture of openness and then repeated, "To see if you're all right."

She studied him for a moment and then decided, "You're lying, Anvil." There was no threat in her voice this time though. She was speaking as if just stating a plain fact.

He thought for a moment. "No, not lying. I'm not telling you everything, but that wasn't a lie. I want to know if you're all right."

"So, why have you really come?"

A pause again, and then, "I'm not going to tell you."

"Why?"

"A couple of reasons, really. First, you won't believe me.

92

Second, as you mentioned before, you don't need anyone adding to your worries."

She raised her eyebrows. "This is you trying not to worry me? You always were an idiot, Anvil."

He nodded, and allowed himself a smile. "True. Perhaps you're worried enough to answer my question?" The knife remained raised. "I know you think ill of me. You know I've always denied what people have said about me. You also know, I think, that I risked my life to save you all the other night. I guess I'd hoped that would buy me a little bit of trust, and if I can help you, I'd be helping her as well." He indicated the babe, now stretching out her arms to signal to her mother that it was time to feed.

Branwen lowered the knife.

"Now, how have things been the last few days?"

"Terrible. Is that supposed to be a stupid question? Terrible. The worst days of my life since..." Branwen's hand subconsciously raised to touch her face. "You know a lot of it - the attack on the cellar and stuff like that. But Jarleth, he doesn't do well in these situations. And you being the hero, that was the last straw for him. He's been pretty angry. Not a fan of Mother Ogma either."

"Has he done anything to you?"

Branwen shook her head, but her hand moved to clutch her side protectively.

"Go on."

"We had to stay with my father last night. You can imagine how that made him feel. Jarleth spent a good bit of time after dark raging about you. I thought my father was going to box his ears in."

Lonan's eyebrows raised. "Your father stood up for me?"

"Well, you did save his only daughter and grandchild from certain death, so that does redeem you a little in most people's eyes. Also," and she lowered her eyes from him at this, "he did suggest that maybe we'd gotten things wrong about you when mother died. He changed his mind about that pretty quickly though."

"Anything in particular make him change his mind?"

"Yeah, Jarleth explained things to him. Funny thing is, he didn't say anything particularly special to him. It was more..."

"...the way he said it?" Lonan finished.

Branwen looked at him again with shock. "Yes. You... you've seen it too?"

"The Knack? It's been haunting me since the night I lost my father."

This was too much for Branwen. She brought her hand up to her face and started sobbing into it. "Oh no, no..."

Instinctively, Lonan rushed forward to comfort her by holding her to him. He was surprised by her willingness to allow the embrace, and as she sobbed into his tunic the touch of her body close to his sent him spiralling back through the years.

He remembered a time that they were on the hills above the village. Although the monsters, the Wolves as Lonan could now call them, did not come out during the day, the forest still had its dangers and both children fully expected a beating when they finally traipsed home. This price was not unknown to them, however, and they had been fully prepared to pay it in return for a day of freedom and adventure.

"Comon, smithy," Branwen had shouted after the young boy, racing through the trees ahead and losing him. Little Lonan, shorter than the girl despite being four months older than her, had tears of frustration in his eyes as he peeled after her.

"Look out!" had been the warning, but it had registered in Lonan's mind moments too late. His feet were not prepared to stop at the sharp drop that appeared before him, and he tumbled over the edge. He could not remember the passage of time at that point, but he was assured since then that he had spent a good five minutes without moving. More than enough time for Branwen to scramble safely down after him and worry at his side. Although his head was screaming at him when he had finally awoke, his enduring memory of that moment had been the desperate, loving grasp of Branwen as she cried for him to come back. At that moment, Lonan had realised the reality of what every other villager told the pair when they saw them running around together. They would be married, and Lonan had known that nothing would make him happier.

"It should have been you."

Branwen's voice brought Lonan's mind back to the present. He dared not release the embrace he now held her in, for fear she would never let him hold her again. Instead, Lonan allowed Branwen to continue uninterrupted.

"It should have been you I married."

Lonan stopped breathing, stood deathly still, not wanting to do anything to change what Branwen was saying.

"I mean, I never loved him. It was you. I think I knew, even back then, it was you I was supposed to marry."

Releasing the tightness of his hold on Branwen was the hardest thing Lonan had ever done, but he did so to look deep into her eyes. Tears ran down the unblemished skin on the right side of her face, and Lonan tentatively brought his hand up to stroke the rough, scarred skin where she had been mauled.

"Yes," he said simply, eyes wide in wonder at finally being able to speak to Branwen like this. "We both knew it back then."

Branwen pulled away from him at this, shirking from his touch. "I thought you ruined my life."

"That was someone else. He ruined both our lives."

Their eyes met again, and Lonan was surprised to see how frightened Branwen looked now. She reached up to touch his cheek this time with a shaking hand.

"Lonan, I'm so sorry. I…"

She was interrupted by the rising cries of her child. Branwen hurriedly manoeuvred her clothing to feed the babe, thankful for the distraction from her emotions.

"I know it's still far too early, but any thoughts on a name yet?" Lonan questioned, breaking the increasingly uncomfortable silence.

"We're thinking of Clare."

"Your mother's name? I've got to say, I thought Jarleth would have insisted on his mother."

"No, he… He was disappointed we didn't have a boy. He hasn't… sometimes it can take a while for the father to find affection for a baby, they say."

Branwen looked at the child, hungrily feeding at her breast, thin wisps of red hair dancing in the soft breeze.

"She's beautiful," Lonan said softly. "Just like her mother."

Branwen's head whipped around in anger, hand instinctively raising to her mauled face. "You ass."

"Just what in the hells is going on here?" Jarleth's bellow echoed down the trail the river cut through the forest.

Lonan whirled around to see the blond bastard bearing down on him, leather apron flapping in the wind and face bright red with anger and exertion. The sight of Branwen's bare breast and tear-streaked face stopped Jarleth from listening to any further conversation from the other two, not allowing his rage to be satisfied until he planted a right hook firmly on Lonan's jaw, sending him straight to the river's edge, face and hands splashing into the water.

"I'll give you one thing," Lonan spluttered as he began to raise himself from the ground, "all that ineffectual flailing around with my father's hammer has certainly done wonders for your punches."

This further enraged the man, causing him to knock Lonan to the ground again, this time following his attack with a kick to Lonan's chest that was rewarded by a large internal crack.

"Jarleth, no!"

Branwen's scream shot through the pain that was wracking Lonan's body as he doubled over to clutch his broken rib.

"We were just talking, nothing happened."

Jarleth ignored his wife, continuing to beat on the fallen man with his feet. "Assault my wife will you? Harm my child? Take what is mine?" Another kick sent Lonan's face into some sharp rocks, opening up a multitude of cuts. "Take what is mine?"

"I was just feeding the baby and we were talking," Branwen shouted again, forcing her way between her husband and Lonan. "He didn't do anything. Damn it, Jarleth, he saved our lives."

"No," Jarleth grabbed Branwen's wrist, pointed his finger at her and looked deep into her eyes. "No, he was trying to rape you. He ripped open your blouse, was taking the baby from you and-"

"No." Branwen slapped her husband as she said this, stopping Jarleth's Knack in its tracks. "Don't do that to me again. Haven't you ruined enough lives with that evil talent?"

Jarleth looked at Branwen with brief shock before punching her directly in the face. There was a wet crunch and Branwen fell. The baby dropped onto the rocks, emitting a shrill scream that died as it rolled into the water.

Branwen's horror was voiced in an uncannily low wail that bubbled from her throat as the blood from her nose threatened to flow down it. She slipped her way across the wet boulders to throw herself into the running river. Lonan attempted to pick himself up from the ground to help but the pain in his chest forced him to the ground again. Jarleth stood and watched his wife frantically make her way downstream, his face white. For the first time, Lonan saw Jarleth as something other than a demon who had haunted his life for the last ten years. This lost face belonged to the sickly boy who had hidden behind his mother's skirts when the other children played their rough and tumble games.

With a primal cry of success Branwen plucked a bundle of rags up from the water. A good bit downstream now, she stumbled from the river back to the leafy forest floor, and then stopped to spare a glance at Lonan lying vulnerable in front of the blacksmith.

"Go," Lonan shouted as loud as he could. "Get her help."

Like a distant rag doll, the figure that was Branwen nodded and ran into the forest.

There was a horrible pause in which Jarleth continued to stare at the river. Lonan painfully shifted himself up so he was leaning on his right elbow. The blacksmith turned to look at him, and Lonan's blood ran cold. Jarleth's eyes were red, with twin streams running down his pale face from them, joining the line of wet snot running from his nose to his mouth. He was breathing heavily, his face damp with sweat.

"Look what you made me do," he whispered.

Calm down Jarleth, was what Lonan should have said.

"Is that what you tell Branwen before you beat her at night?" was his actual retort.

"Look what you made me do." It was a scream this time, a bellow from the lungs of a lost soul.

Lonan should have been scared. He should have realised how desperate someone like Jarleth would be when he came close to losing everything. Instead, he was giddy with pain and euphoric fulfilment at seeing the man who had poisoned every aspect of his life finally being brought low.

"Don't give me any credit. You did your best to murder that baby all by yourself."

Jarleth bent down to pick up a large rock. He hefted it high above his head. It took all of the blacksmith's strength to do so, and Lonan realised that he himself would not have been able to attempt to lift something that heavy.

"Now, even you aren't that stupid," he attempted to convince the bastard, only now becoming aware to his danger. "The baby was a mistake. You don't want to deliberately kill anyone, do you?"

Jarleth smashed the rock down onto Lonan. In the last seconds, Lonan rolled and raised his arm to ward off the blow. The pain of the impact was unbearable. It felt as though his arm had just been shoved into his father's forge. The boulder dropped with a splintering thud, and Lonan cried out in pain. This was overshadowed, however, by the maddened, incomprehensible cry coming from Jarleth. The cry continued as the blacksmith bent to pick up the stone again. Lonan's arm was limp and useless now. He scrambled to get to his feet and move away, but the loss of use of his limb and the pain from his chest made this a pointless task.

Through the haze of pain Lonan saw Jarleth, still shouting nonsense, raising the rock again.

"You stupid bastard," was all Lonan had time to whisper before the boulder came down on his head.

The wind whispered to the Magpie King. Perched atop an emergent elm, Adahy sniffed the wind. It carried the smell of blood, death and fresh stool. It told him the Eyrie was still occupied, that his home required cleansing.

As the sun hung low in the sky, the Magpie King's ears picked out the noise of shuffling bodies, curled up together for warmth but beginning to grow restless at the threat of nightfall. He strained his newfound senses to hear more, doing his best to drown out the whimpering of his poisoned companion that he had left in a secluded cave. His father had warned him that his own bloodline had built up a resistance to the flower's poison - only time would tell how Maedoc's mind and body would react to the poison without that protection.

There. A growl, deeper than the others. Commanding. She is still there, the den mother. The leader of the Wolves, the murderer of my father. If she falls the Wolves will break apart, leaderless and lost. This was the victory my father had hoped for all his life, to free the forest. I must succeed at this.

The Eyrie was a couple of miles away, the tree tops between his perch and his home illuminated by the dye of the setting sun. Adahy started to move towards his home, remaining above the trees. His movement was effortless, the iron coils within his legs propelling him across fields of green, his hands reaching instinctively for a safe branch that had not even been visible to him when he had started his jump. Within minutes, he stood upon the Eyrie roof, and quickly navigated his way across it to the rooftop above the throne room.

He peered down again into that dark pit and was met with the smell of rotting flesh. Half-eaten bodies lingering in the corners of the room now fed maggots instead of Wolves. None of those feral animals rested in this room, it was too exposed to the daylight that they hated. Of his father, only a splattered patch of red remained. The new Magpie King dropped down from the ceiling, his feet brushing against the floor as a falling leaf kisses the grass. The large double doors to the throne room were now shut, so he walked forward to open them and stepped into the blackness inside.

Although it was daytime, in their effort to make the Eyrie into their new den, the Wolves had extinguished or blocked up all potential sources of light. A day ago this would have meant that Adahy would have had to stumble along blind, tripping up over every loose stone and using his hands to feel his way. Now the corridors were as clear to his eyes as if sunlight streamed through them. Physically they were empty, but to the Magpie King they were occupied by sounds and smells that were all leading him in the same direction as the wet stains on the flagstones beneath his feet. At the bottom of the Eyrie, below his feet was a whole floor devoted to housing and homing the palace's servants. These rooms were considerably less windowed than those designed for the nobles. Perfect for avoiding the sun. He moved onwards, ignoring the restless sounds of the animals in the rooms all about him, moving towards the heart of the evil that occupied his home. It was only at the hint of a familiar, metallic scent that he stopped in his tracks.

The smell led him to a regular-sized doorway not far from the main corridor he had been walking down. He pushed the portal open. Five pairs of eyes greeted his arrival with a loud, purring growl. The Magpie King moved first. He ran inside, grabbing at the jaws of the closest Wolf as it opened them to howl in anger. The King helped the jaws to open, pulling them apart with his bare hands. The second Wolf did not even get fully up from its sleeping position on the floor before the Magpie King's foot caught its neck and pushed it down to the stone again with a crack. The other three had more of a chance to react, with two of them rushing at him as the third slid around the walls to take him from behind. The Magpie King grabbed each of his attacker's heads and brought them both together with a wet crumple. The final monster, realising it had underestimated its prey, turned and ran for the exit, sprinting down the long corridors whilst alerting its brethren with its howls.

The Magpie King cursed under his breath, but was more concerned with the prize he had located. This room contained a number of human bodies that had been moved for the animals to gnaw on while they slept, and one of them wore familiar ceremonial garments. The thick feathered cloak was torn, many of the feathers shredded, but still when Adahy removed it from his father's corpse and clasped it around his own neck, it seemed to take on a life of its own, shrouding its new owner in darkness. He pulled twin black sickles from the multitude of weapons that had been gathered in one of the corners of this room. Finally, the Magpie King rolled aside a nobleman's corpse to reveal his father's helm, battered but unbroken. The metal helm seemed unreasonably large, as if his head would feel completely unbalanced once it was fitted to him. Instead, it made him feel whole. Weapons held effortlessly in both hands he strode from the abattoir to avenge his people.

The howls of the wakened Wolves now rang freely throughout the corridors. However, the confined space of the passageways coupled with the Magpie King's rediscovered sense of self meant doom for any attackers. Scores of Wolves were expertly cut down as the Magpie King moved closer to his prey. He could hear her below, frantically bellowing orders to her pack to intercept the intruder.

The Wolves continued to fall, batted to the side and sliced open in a single motion from the warrior, until finally he arrived at the servant's mess hall. A mound of meaty bodies told the Magpie King he had found his target. A wall of Wolves greeted him, but they did not press their attack from the shadows of the hall, and when he stepped forward and growled at them they visibly shrank back.

"Who will challenge me?" he yelled at the frightened murderers. "Who will challenge me?"

The wall of monsters parted to reveal the reluctant figure of the den mother, uncurling from her hiding position to reveal her true size and strength.

For the first time since his empowerment at the Lonely House, Adahy felt the sting of doubt. This creature was almost twice his size with years of experience of slaughter and combat. It had quickly dispatched his father before his eyes. What made Adahy think he had a chance against this monster?

Because I have to.

The den mother sneered at him, beckoning for him to make the first move. The Magpie King responded by leaping to his side towards some of the cowering onlookers, efficiently dispatching a score of them with some quick flashes of his sickles. A few of the horde moved to intercept him, but he dealt with these as well, all the while keeping his eyes on the mother.

"Is this how you protect them?" He leapt again at some more huddled monsters, ending their wretched lives without mercy. "Is this how you look after your babies?"

The horde of Wolves howled again, but this time it was not directed at the Magpie King. They were screaming at the den mother, urging her into action.

It took one more fatal leap from the Magpie King to goad the mother into an attack. She moved forward with death-like speed, taking him completely by surprise. Adahy only survived that first attack because of the thickness of his father's cloak, moving it to intercept the oncoming blow. Despite his protective garb and the speed of his own reflexes, her claws still bit deep, flaying skin and muscle. The pack of Wolves shrieked as Adahy cried out in pain, and they pushed in closer to the combat, sensing the kill. Their celebration turned to horror, however, when their leader fell to the floor, a jet-black blade embedded into the back of her skull. The Magpie King stepped forward to wrench his weapon free, using another flick of his wrist to remove her head completely from her body. He turned slowly to eye the multitude of onlookers.

"Scatter," he commanded.

The pack broke and fled. He did not grant them safe passage, but neither did he exert himself to hunt down every single monster that had occupied his home.

Hours later, after ensuring that the last of the creatures had fled from the palace, the Magpie King stood on the roof of his home in a spot he once saw his father occupy, surveying his kingdom. He could sense the animals moving through the forest, but no longer as a pack. As a people, they were broken now, the loss of the den mother removing any leadership from them. They continued to run, moving past the Corvae villages, towards the forest borders.

In his cave in the forest, miles away, Maedoc began to whimper. The Magpie King leapt down from his perch to reclaim his subject.

Morning was not far away, and he had a kingdom to rebuild.

ARTEMIS
AND
MOTHER WEB

A tale from the fireplaces of the Low Corvae.

This is a tale that takes place after the Great Theft, when Artemis was on the run from the Magpie Guard. Day and night they hounded him, fixed on finding their quarry and reclaiming the kingdom's lost treasure. At their head was the Magpie King himself, dark and unrelenting, filled with passion and fury at Artemis' crime. But Artemis was hidden from the Magpie King's unnatural senses - a pricey bargain that he had struck with the head priestess of the Snake people had ensured he was cloaked in her magic until his task was complete.

Despite this arcane protection, crafty Artemis was still vulnerable to detection from the normal senses of sight and sound, and the Guard's continued dogging of him from village to village was weighing greatly on the thief. Where once a sly smile was permanently etched, now the man sported a tight grimace. His clothing, normally the most extravagant nobleman's washing he could find, was hanging off him in ribbons as unchecked movement through bush and thorn took their toll. Anytime Artemis thought he had found solace in a lonely barn or vacant cave, the sounds of pursuit would strike up again and he would be forced to push on.

Finally, in his desperation, Artemis turned to the dark heart of the forest where even the Magpie King would think twice about entering. This was a part of the woodland that the sun refused to visit, and greenery was merely a rumour on the wind. The trees here were barren, twisted and searching, and the bile in Artemis' gut rose to his mouth as he felt true fear for the first time in his life.

Just as sly Artemis had decided to take his chances with the pursuers in more friendly surroundings, he heard her speak.

"I can smell you, little one," came a chiding voice from somewhere in the woods ahead of Artemis. It was a sound like the fresh crinkle of leaves, followed by the plunging of one's foot into mud and shit hidden below them. "I can smell you and shall soon find you. Lay still, little one, and make things easy on mother after such a long, dreary day."

Artemis froze, wide eyed, searching for the source of the voice.

He heard a tutting, this time closer still. "It shall be dark soon, dearie, and my little ones will need fed. Why not be a good boy and come and say hello to them?"

Artemis exhaled slightly and heard a rustling coming from somewhere before him. His eyes raised slowly to the tops of the trees.

"I am not as young as I used to be," the rustling voice continued, "and have not the patience nor the heart for such a chase. I shall find you eventually, you know. And then catch you, and then eat you. Why not save each other the distress of a chase and give yourself to me now?"

It was then that Artemis saw her. High in the tree canopy, suspended upside down was a grotesquely fat-bodied spider, her once-black abdomen littered with pox marks and boils. In contrast, her thin spindly legs worked themselves methodically through the treetops, taking it in turn to support their owner's weight whilst probing for the next suitable branch to grip to. From the spider's head grew a length of bushy grey hair that trailed towards the ground like a curtain of filth.

Artemis stood perfectly still as the creature moved directly overhead, twisting back and forwards in the canopy to seek out the prey she knew was nearby.

"Strange," the creature mused in frustration. "I could hear you tramp into my black forest, I can still smell the fear on your breath. But I cannot find you."

Artemis gave a silent offering of thanks to the serpent witch. Her magics that clouded the Magpie King's senses also worked on this foul creature. Then he prayed she did not choose that time to remove her spell from him.

They say that familiarity breeds confidence, and this truth works doubly quick for a mind as cunning as Artemis'. Not permitting himself to give in to fear, Artemis studied his would-be killer and began to learn from her. In the hours that she stalked him unsuccessfully, he learnt her weak spots, and found the courage to make small movements when the creature above was distracted. Eventually, he was able to move confidently about the forest floor again, and began to make plans for his escape.

"Now dearie," the voice came again, the creature's frustration causing her to end each word spoken with a snap of her jaws, "this is enough. I am tired, I am hungry, and you shall be in my belly before long. Show yourself to me now and I shall make your end painless. Force me to continue searching and you shall be begging me to consume your heart and end your suffering before I let you slip behind the veil."

Cunning Artemis found the courage to finally shout out to his pursuer. "Mother Web, are you not enjoying our dance? It has been far too many years since I have had such an able partner, and it would pain me to end our festivities so soon."

At the sound of the trickster's voice, the ancient creature dropped from the trees, scuttling like a wounded rabbit to the tree root that Artemis had been behind. Artemis was already gone from that spot, a sly grin on his face as he watched her vent her frustration from afar.

"Curse you, root dweller," Mother Web roared to the forest. "My babies are calling to me, and I shall fill my larder before they hatch. Fie on you who taunts me so."

Once again, Mother Web took to the treetops, clambering through them with an increased urgency. Artemis, now, was always two steps ahead of his dancing partner. She would fancy she heard some movement in the darkness below and would dive down to seek it out, and then Artemis would move on further.

"You win, little mouse," Mother Web eventually admitted, her voice soaked in defeat. "I return to my children empty-handed. Think about their lifeless shells on the floor of my den when you walk free in the sunlight."

Not believing the creature would give up chase so easily, Artemis called out, "It was a fine dance, yes, like no other I have had. How good it is to part as friends after an evening of mirth."

Mother Web was on his hiding place in a breath, her front legs impaling the brown bush that Artemis had called from. However, she found only leaf and wood, for Artemis had moved on once again. The creature screamed and Artemis could not stifle his chuckle this time, which was almost the end for him, for it led Mother Web on another dash through the bracken towards his new hiding spot, which he had to vacate much quicker than anticipated.

More hours of searching followed, and it became obvious that Mother Web was becoming more and more weary. Her sudden leaps from the treetops were occurring less often now, and became slower and also less purposeful. When she called out for her prey, her sentences were shorter, and eventually pleading. Artemis noticed she was pursuing him in a circular fashion, spiralling ever inwards until eventually she reached her dark nest, a deep hole in the forest floor that sheltered the bones of her previous dinners and the white eggs that held her unborn children. With one final movement from the treetop, Mother Web dropped to the entrance to her nest and slowly pulled herself inside.

Artemis smiled to himself at evading such a foe, but his gaze lingered on the spider's nest and he pursed his lips. After a moment's brief thought, he strode forward and entered the dark domain of Mother Web.

On all fours, he crawled through her round passageway, the earthen walls of the tube covered with pus from the boils on her abdomen that had burst as she had squeezed her large body through that narrow opening. Eventually, the smaller tunnel opened into a larger cavern. There, on the far wall, was a hive of white eggs, writhing and squirming as the unborn lives within them sensed the arrival of something that they would eventually call food. In the middle of the cavern, collapsed on a pile of bones, lay the exhausted Mother Web.

Artemis stepped forward into the chamber, and the only response he received from his foe was a brief movement of her head as she shifted it to regard him. She had exhausted her ancient body chasing nimble Artemis through the black forest, and had no energy left to pounce.

Confident he was safe from further attacks, devious Artemis drew his dagger and stepped towards the trembling egg sacs.

"No..." was all Mother Web could muster as Artemis took his blade and slid it across the thin skin of the eggs, sending their malformed contents to the floor of the cavern. Artemis watched the white spiders struggle briefly, coming to terms with the world outside of the safety of their mother's purse before he crushed them underfoot. The thief performed the same act with the remaining eggs until none were left alive. Satisfied his work was complete, Artemis cleaned his blade and made to leave.

"Why?" came the tortured question from Mother Web as she lay weeping and powerless to avenge her offspring.

Artemis turned to his defeated foe, thought briefly, then gave her a gentle smile.

"The man who escapes from the spider is lucky. The man who defeats the spider is a legend. Otherwise, they would never tell this tale."

And from that day on, Mother Web forever cursed his name.

CHAPTER
SIX

Lonan drifted in and out of consciousness. Through half-open eyes he was able to discern that he was in a cottage, although it was difficult to say which one. There were many voices around him - he recognised the busy tones of Mother Ogma barking sharp orders at everyone else, as she did when her Knack was under great strain. Every now and again Lonan was able to make out a baby crying, and his sister's voice rang loud and clear when she visited his bed. His hand and brow were handled constantly, and he came to recognise the sensation of someone else's tears on his skin.

When he gave his first moan, many voices, mostly female, called for aid and ordered each other about. He blacked out again shortly thereafter. This routine continued for a number of days - slipping back to his sick bed in the cottage to cause a few minutes of excitement, with Mother Ogma or Branwen desperately trying to hold a conversation with him, and then back to blackness. Often blackness would be all that he would experience, but now and again he drifted back to Adahy for long enough to get an idea of how the new Magpie King was faring. Although Maedoc remained ill, the liberation of the Eyrie spurred hiding nobles back into the open, from their shelters among the trees or local villages. The Eyrie began to fill again, with pockets of guards returning as well, but more strong men were recruited from the closest Corvae villages. Adahy seemed driven, saddened beyond belief by the death of his father and so many others close to him, but determined to rebuild what had been lost. Of Inteus Lonan saw no sign, but the name Smithsdown did pop up in conversation now and again, and there was much talk of sending tax collectors out to the villages again to reestablish connections. Unfortunately, in his ill state Lonan could not piece all of this information together to make much sense of it.

It took five days for Lonan to speak again.

"The... baby?" was all he could manage, addressing the shuffling figure in the darkness beyond the candle by his bedside. The concerned wrinkled features of Mother Ogma drifted into his view.

"Now there, dearie, don't stress yourself. You've still got a lot of work to do."

Summing up all of his strength, Lonan feebly grabbed the healer's tunic and repeated his question, "The baby?"

She smiled at this. "Well, I am glad to see he didn't manage to beat your stubbornness out of you. Yes, the babe is fine, now. It needed a good bit of warming up and both she and her mother were in a decent state of shock, but unlike some people a few days were all it took for her to be as good as new again." Concern bloomed on her face as she checked the bandages that were wound around Lonan's head. "Some wounds are easily mended."

"If you're trying to tell me that I'll never go courting again, I think I'll survive," he attempted to croak out from between cracked lips.

Mother Ogma did her best to smile as his comment. "Now, you rest up, dearie. I imagine Branwen shall be here soon, and she'll not be happy with me if I use up all of your energy."

"Branwen? Where are we?"

"You're at my house, in your usual bed. Branwen and Clare have been staying with us for the past few nights. It seemed necessary given the... unusual situation in the village right now."

Lonan fell back asleep at this point, and spent a lot of time with Adahy in a boring meeting with an emissary from outside of the forest, from the owl people. He faded back into reality at the sound of Branwen's voice.

"...what was he saying? Is he going to be all right? You said too much may have been broken..."

"Now shush, dearie, I have been wrong many times before, and look - your patient is stirring."

Branwen's face faded into the candlelight, tears forming as she looked into Lonan's opening eyes. "Please don't hit me," Lonan croaked with a smile, "if I say that this is the prettiest sight I could have hoped for."

The familiar anger touched Branwen's ruined face for a moment, but then tears leapt forth instead and she kissed his hand. "Look, Clare," she managed, raising her daughter to Lonan's eye level, "this is the man who saved your life."

"In fairness, I remember you doing most of the swimming."

The baby stared at Lonan for a few moments, but then its lips curled into a wail.

"Yes, I imagine I do look fairly horrific at the moment. I don't suppose there's any chance I can get up?"

"Not in the slightest, dearie."

Despite Mother Ogma's protests, Lonan fought to shift himself into a sitting position. This proved to be impossible. He was able to move his right arm, the arm that had been crushed by the boulder, but it was agony to do so.

"Dislocated, that was really the worst that it got, other than cuts and severe bruising, obviously. A miracle all the bones didn't just shatter on impact. He must have just managed a glancing blow," Mother Ogma explained. "It should heal up nicely, although I daresay it's going to pop loose any time you take any bad knocks."

His torso was in worse shape. He had correctly surmised that the kicking had cracked some ribs. There was not really much that could be done for them except to ignore the pain until they healed, hopefully back in place. One of the boulder blows after he had been knocked out had, however, punctured one of his lungs and his weak breathing had been a concern for a long while.

It was very clear that Mother Ogma had been dodging the subject of Lonan's head injuries, however.

"Just give it to me straight," he ordered. "It can't be all that bad if I'm sitting here, talking to you both."

She looked away from him. "I have to be honest, I was shocked when you spoke to me. I've seen people with head injuries like yours never able to interact with the world again. Poor old Harlow, for instance. Lonan, your head was broken. That evil man had cracked your skull before the Tumulty brothers made it to him. Any sensible person could see you were as good as dead, dearie."

"Well, that explains it," Lonan muttered, now very aware of the sharp pains all along his scalp, "nobody ever accused me of being sensible. So, I beat the odds, right? Because here I am, walking and talking. Well," he continued, wiggling his toes under the bed sheets, "it certainly looks like walking shouldn't be an issue when the time comes."

"Yes," she responded, uncertainly, "it looks like a true miracle. Still," and at this she looked Lonan straight into the eyes, "let's not assume you've gotten off without repercussions. You may find that headaches come more easily now, and there might be memory issues too."

Lonan let everything sink in for a moment, now clutching Branwen's hand. "I've one piece of good news, though. The dreams haven't stopped."

"Dreams?" Branwen queried, looking at Mother Ogma to clarify. "What dreams?"

"Ah, perhaps this can wait until later-" Mother Ogma began, but Lonan cut her off.

"No, I want her to know. I shouldn't have to hide it anymore. Branwen, my Knack has appeared."

Branwen shook her head in disbelief, smiling. "Your...?"

"I'm not sure if we ever confirmed that it is a Knack," Mother Ogma intercepted.

"It must be. How else can you explain it? You were the first to say it, and it makes sense."

"What in the Great Spirit's name are you both talking about?"

"Branwen, I see things in my dreams."

At this, Branwen turned to look at Mother Ogma in concern.

Recognising Branwen's fear he continued, "No, this started before the attack. In my dreams, I follow the life of a prince up at the Eyrie, Adahy." Then he directed his attention to Mother Ogma. "Except now, he's the Magpie King. He found the flower that gives them their power, and used it to tear apart countless Wolves and their leader. The Wolves have fled the forest now. We're all safe."

Branwen clasped Lonan's hand tighter, but looked silently to Mother Ogma with tears in her eyes.

"I think you should rest now, Lonan," Mother Ogma said, rising from her seat to usher Branwen out of the cellar. "It seems we all have a lot to chat about when you are back on your feet."

Lonan laughed. "I know what you're thinking, Branwen, but it is true. There haven't been any more attacks in the night, have there? Nobody has heard anything, have they?"

Mother Ogma smiled at him. "No, dearie, they have not. But you still need to rest. This will have taken a lot out of you."

Lonan looked at her sternly. After Branwen left, but before the healer took her leave too, he ventured, "How is she doing?"

"Her husband tried to kill their child, and she thinks the man who she is falling in love with is a raving lunatic. She has had better weeks," came the chiding response.

"Haven't we all?" Lonan countered, arranging the bandages on his head into a more comfortable position to allow him to get back to sleep.

He was not comfortable in these clothes anymore. Adahy pulled at his velvet tunic. Weeks ago, he would have been proud to have such a fine garment. They were even rarer now during this time of rebuilding. However, Adahy's life had taken dramatic turns since the night his father had found him crying up on the ridge. He was king now, with all the responsibilities the title entailed.

It had been up to Adahy to piece together any remains of his father's court, and to press the villages close to the Eyrie to supply young men and women to make up the low numbers at the palace. Most had been happy to come to join him. Life at court, even in a serving position, held considerably more promise for most villagers than anything their homes could offer. Even the thought of not having to hole themselves up in the ground every night was a huge draw. The Eyrie had done their best to convince the villages that this custom did not need to be followed through with anymore, but very few of them chose to experiment with different sleeping arrangements. There were still a number of villages that word had not spread to yet, but Adahy did not currently have the manpower to reach out to them, especially with other matters that had arisen since the Eyrie had come to life again.

He arrived at the door to his destination. Adahy stood there for a moment, using his other senses to put together the scene beyond the oak. His quarry was still there, although this was to be expected, as Adahy had locked him in this prison himself. The room also stank of neglect and blood, telling Adahy that matters had not improved in the days since his last visit. He knocked.

"Maedoc?"

There was no answer, again as usual, but some shuffling beyond the portal told Adahy that he had been heard and that Maedoc had prepared himself accordingly. He opened the door.

The room was dark, as Maedoc seemed to prefer now. It was also littered with various odds and ends that the young man had chosen to interact with and later discard. Copious amounts of clothing lay shredded, food was half eaten and rotten, furniture was overturned at best, but mostly broken. Maedoc himself was sitting hunched over on the windowsill, leaning against the windows Adahy had had barred for his friend's own good. Maedoc remained in the black tunic he had been wearing on that fateful night at the Lonely House. In his hands he held a haunch of meat, lamb, which he was gnawing at while he eyed his visitor. Red liquid ran down his chin as he did so. Maedoc preferred his meat raw now.

Adahy's father had warned him that the black flower was only for those of royal blood. Only someone from the line of the Magpie King could consume it and remain sane. The signs of madness had been apparent from the first night Maedoc had received his powers. When the whipping boy had emerged from beating the Wolf into a bloody pulp, Adahy had assumed he had been physically injured in the fight, or possibly overcome with the gravity of the changes that had taken place in his life in those few short moments. As they had leapt through the trees together, Adahy guiding his friend's actions as Maedoc moaned and groaned, he had already begun to consider the fact that he would never have to be alone when going into battle, that his friend and servant would always be able to be by his side, providing companionship and backup. These thoughts had quickly subsided when he realised Maedoc was breaking into an extreme fever. This did not break until days after the reclaiming of the Eyrie when Adahy's duties had led him elsewhere. Maedoc's response to his minders had been violent and mindless, stealing the eye of one and crushing another's wrist. The new Magpie Guard had managed to confine him to this room, where Adahy had discovered him overwhelmed with remorse for his actions.

Since then the whipping boy's emotions had been in complete flux - sometimes violently aggressive, sometimes inconsolable, and rarely completely coherent. Most dangerously, Maedoc's physical attributes remained, making him almost as powerful as Adahy when pushed. Both of them had agreed that Maedoc was to remain confined to this cell until the madness passed, but Adahy secretly mourned the loss of his friend's support. The challenges of the last few weeks had involved wrestling through layers of bureaucracy and diplomacy, instead of actual physical wrestling which Adahy would have infinitely preferred. Ofttimes he would find himself feeling like a stranger in his own home, walking through the corridors and experiencing a multitude of unknown faces.

"How fare you today, old friend?"

Maedoc bared his teeth at Adahy, the harsh contrast of red blood on white startling even the Magpie King. It was going to be one of those days then.

"I'm tired too," Adahy responded. "They arrived today, the Owls. With my bride."

Prior to his death, Adahy's father had come to an arrangement with the head of the Tytonidae clan, the owl worshippers, who lived in the hills to the north of the forest. A union, to quell any thoughts of invasion from other tribes that may be pressing on their borders. Adahy had not had much education on foreign relations beyond the forest borders, and the previous Magpie King had not spent much of his time attending to such matters, focussing more on local issues. However, Adahy was aware that other tribes existed. The Mice he knew better, and the Owls. He had also heard talk of Lions and Snakes, although had much less information about them. He had overheard his father speaking to advisers about the Wolves as well, alluding to the fact that they may have been similar to the Corvae at one point too. Adahy could not fathom how anything could have changed humans into those monsters, but this thought alone warned him to be mindful of dealings with other tribes. Indeed, if any outside force chose to take action against the forest in its present state then they would find little significant resistance. There was only so much that one man could achieve, even one empowered as the Magpie King. When his court began to piece itself together again, one of Adahy's first acts was to send a messenger to the Tytonidae to hasten his betrothal.

"Get a peek at her then?" The growl from Maedoc was unexpected, but welcome.

Adahy shook his head. "Not really, and the same can be said for her of me. Tradition dictates we must greet each other in our ceremonial garb, so instead of a potential husband, she was greeted today by the Magpie King." He smiled at his friend. "Can you imagine any woman who would fancy a lifetime of that?"

Maedoc sneered at him. "You'd be surprised. Late at night, after a bit of wine, the kitchen staff would often debate about what your father would be capable of in the bedroom. Probably thinking of you like that now."

Adahy turned red. "Any lady then. She must have been terrified."

"You worried she's a hag then?"

Adahy shrugged off his friend's crudeness. "No, she was comely enough, from what I could tell. Dressed in white, soft feathers. Her headdress showed her mouth and her chin. They seemed ... delicate? Firm? I don't know. I certainly get the impression she is attractive."

"What's your problem then? Fair play to you - most men go through a lifetime not getting to touch anything like that, let alone play with it every night. With a face like this, I'll have to content myself with waiting for the scullery maids to get drunk and lonely."

Adahy shuffled uneasily. *What is my problem with the match? She is clearly attractive, that much is certain, so why was that not enough? The meeting had been so... formal. Andromeda's father had done all the speaking for her, and so very few words passed between the two of us at all.*

"I want to know what she's like. What kind of person she is. If she's really interested in this marriage at all. You could help me with that, if you would sort yourself out and pull yourself out of this state."

At this, Maedoc began a low, manic laugh. Adahy rolled his eyes. He was clearly going to get nowhere with the man - when he started like this the laughing could go on for hours at a time.

"Forget it," he whispered, and got up to leave.

"No," Maedoc waved at him, gesturing for him to sit back down again. "Tell me how I could help. I'd very much like to hear this."

Adahy sat again and leaned forward to get closer to his friend. "She has not seen me yet. There is a feast tonight. If I was to wait at her table and serve her, I might be able to get what I want."

"And I?"

"The Magpie King must be there. Her father would not approve if I spoke to her unchaperoned before our marriage. Only you could pull off wearing the garb. You wouldn't really even have to speak, I will make it brief, and we could arrange for you to be given an urgent message needing your skills. Give a little show of your abilities as you leave and nobody will be the wiser."

Maedoc dropped the meat, looking seriously at the king. "You want me to be the Magpie King?"

Adahy smiled. "I hadn't really thought of it like that, but-"

"Yes." Maedoc was intense now, remaining eye narrow. "I'll do it."

Maedoc's clear hunger for this made Adahy regret his decision, but it would be worth it if it would return his friend to the world and give Adahy more information about his bride.

"Well then, let's find something to put you into for the feast. Do you fancy something in black?"

A few hours later and the feast was in full flow. The Tytonidae were keeping to themselves, choosing to sit at separate tables from the Corvae. Normally on an occasion such as this there would be a head table consisting of a mix between the two families, but relations remained strained between the two peoples. There was a small head table, but this mainly consisted of the Magpie King, the chief of the Owls and his spouse. Andromeda was seated separately, which suited Adahy just fine. His serving people were informed by Maedoc masquerading as the Magpie King that Adahy was to wait on the princess. Adahy himself was dressed in a simple serving tunic, liberated from Maedoc's own wardrobe. As Adahy navigated the busy aisles, he cast a glance over to the head table. The Magpie King was sitting stoically beside the chief of the Owls, giving very little in the way of conversation.

As planned.

Adahy focussed his attention on his own task.

Funny how nervous I feel at approaching her. The last female in my life I had no problems approaching. And had no issues ripping her to pieces in front of her bloodthirsty offspring. But this simple girl has me quivering like a wreck.

He looked at her, sitting alone in a sea of people. The individuals who should be close to her were sitting at a different table, doing their best to engage Maedoc in everyday chat.

Andromeda sat between servants and noble ladies uninterested in her thoughts or feelings. Adahy leaned over to speak to her.

"Carrots?"

She had not realised that she was being spoken to.

"My lady, carrots?"

As if a spell was being broken, she slowly turned her head to regard him. "I'm sorry?"

"Would you like some carrots? On your plate, my lady?"

She waved her acceptance to him and returned to her rigid position. She was going to be more difficult to crack than Adahy had imagined.

He returned with a bottle of wine. "How does my lady feel about Rutherweave?"

Annoyed confusion crossed her face as she was distracted from her brooding. "Again, I am sorry. I do not understand what you are talking about."

So, she has little time for servants then. Not exactly the attitude I am looking for in a future bride.

"Rutherweave, my lady. The Corvae vineyard. The only village around here that produces anything worth drinking at the Eyrie, or so they say. I thought we supplied some to the Tytonidae regularly?"

"Hmm?" she responded, distracted. "Yes, fine, yes."

"I think a sample is in order. They do say that someone not accustomed to its bitterness should not drink an entire glass."

"Hmm, yes." She had not made eye contact with him since he started this conversation. Adahy had almost made up his mind about his future wife by this point.

She took a sip of the drop in her glass. "Oh, good gods." She looked at Adahy in disgust. "Just what in the name of the Spirit have you given me?" Her violent reaction got the attention of the nobles sitting close to her. Adahy suspected it would not be long before he was vacated from his own feast hall. It did not matter - he had got what he had come for.

"My lady, is something bothering you? We shall remove this boy at once."

"No, no," she commanded, and for the first time she smiled. "That was my own fault, I suppose. This fine young gentleman had given me plenty of warning, but I was too wrapped up in my own thoughts to pay attention to good advice."

Adahy shrugged. "It was just wine I was talking about, m'lady. Important to me, in my job, but I can't expect a fine noble lady like yourself to put the same importance on such things."

She smiled again, and whispered conspiratorially to him, "My grandmother had always told me that only a fool did not take care of what was going on under her nose first before thinking about future hopes and dreams. Fool I am today, it seems."

She held the glass to her face to have a look at the remains at the bottom of it. "Yes, too bitter for me, I'm afraid. So, my dear expert, what should your future queen sample instead?"

"My queen?" Adahy feigned wide eyed ignorance. "Oh, my lady, I did not know. My apologies, I should not be talking-"

"Nonsense. Send away the one friendly face I've seen since I arrived here? My grandmother didn't have a saying about that one, but I don't need her advice to recognise foolishness when I contemplate it. Another vintage, my dear-heart expert. Nothing too strong, if you please. One must at least keep up the pretence of decorum."

This shift in attitude changed things considerably. "Just a pretence, my lady?" he queried whilst pouring a glass from the Eyrie's own vineyards.

She looked at him from the corners of her eyes. "Well, one does have natural reactions at being brought to marry a monster."

"Sorry, my lady?"

She nodded towards the main table. "Over there. Your monster. Your protector." She was indicating the Magpie King.

It was Adahy's turn for his brow to crumple. "He - he is just a man, my lady. Like me."

She laughed at this. Not a mean laugh, at a servant's expense. More, Adahy realised, because he had probably just echoed what she had been repeating to herself since he got here.

"Fine, a man then. But a man unlike any I have ever seen."

Adahy looked over to Maedoc, the Magpie King. Perched upon his throne, his metal helm watching them all like a dark gargoyle standing in judgement. Maedoc turned his head slightly to hear what Andromeda's father was saying to him, and even that brief movement seemed alien.

"I... have met him, my lady. When he is not dressed like that. He is a man, nothing more, and he does not seem too bad, at that."

She smiled again. "I appreciate the words of comfort. I hope you understand, however, my heart will not fully believe them until I discover that for myself, and that journey will be terrifying for me, I feel."

As if on cue, Maedoc's arm thumped to the table. Adahy rose his head sharply to see a messenger at the Magpie King's ear. The dark figure overturned the table he was sitting at, and in one leap thrust himself to the windows high above the audience, disappearing into the night.

The audience was silent for a brief moment, and then erupted into conversation. Andromeda sat alone in the bustle - she had turned a pale white. Instinctively, Adahy took her hands.

"You dare?" she began, but he interrupted her.

"My princess, allow me to speak. I know you feel fear at the thought of this union, and looking from the outside now, I can understand it fully. However, let me make you a promise. You can find love with this man. And safety. He is the kind of man who will put his people first, and his wife. He may be able to leap across the forest as if on wings, but he carries a heavy load and looks for a soul to share it with him as an equal. He is also not the sort of man to send an ordinary servant to wait on his future bride."

Her face first displayed shock, then confusion, and then, just before Adahy was escorted out of the feast hall for laying his hands on the royal consort, she gave him a curiously cheeky smile.

That is the woman for me. Adahy grinned as he made his way to find Maedoc.

THE MAGPIE KING
AND THE
PIES

A tale from the fireplaces of the Low Corvae.

It was after the great battle between the Magpies, the Lions, and the Serpents of whom we speak no longer. The Corvae and Leone had been victorious, and the Magpie King himself had cast down the Serpent's chief from the mountains to the forest floor, snapping the betrayer's spine in seven different places.

But the Serpent's fangs had found their mark just before that final fall, and the toll it had taken on the Magpie King was great. Venom scurried through his veins, turning his breath purple and his tears the colour of fire. While the Lions raised their cups in celebration, the Corvae turned to their leader and could not find him. He was lost.

Long did our King wander alone in the forest, fevered and mad. We do not know much of this time. Some say that he visited the trees, taking pains to ensure he touched every tall trunk in his domain. Others claim to have come across a dark, bearded man who said he was a mushroom, ordering all who came close to depart else he turn them into a dandelion. What we do know is that his powers allowed his body to survive an ordeal that would have broken lesser men. And that when he awoke from his madness, he was hungry.

We cannot fathom how a being such as the Magpie King perceives the world. It is known he can sense a mouse move from half way across the forest. He knows when a man is lying by the irregular beating of the deceiver's heart, and by the stench of distrust from the sinner's sweat. Who knows exactly what his heightened senses were experiencing when he arose from the dirt, mind finally free of the Serpent's poison, but we do know that the overriding smell which assaulted him was that of pies.

Free from the Serpent's madness, but with hunger threatening to serve as a replacement for the poison, the Magpie King scrambled across the forest floor, his usual grace and strength replaced by the desperation in his gut. Finally, he came to a ledge that overlooked a small Corvae village, and he caught sight of the source of his desire - a small cottage, removed from the rest of the settlement, had its shutters open, and resting upon the windowsill to cool were three blueberry pies.

With a hunger we cannot comprehend tearing at his insides the Magpie King half-ran, half-tumbled down the slope to the cottage window. Hand now shaking, he reached out to grab one of the pastries.

"Shoo, shoo," came the cries of the cottage's sole resident as she ran out of the front door, wooden broom in hand, and proceeded to beat her king about his head with it. For you see, those weeks or months lost in the forest had stolen much of the Magpie King's majesty. His cloak and cowl were gone, leaving only the rags that remained of his underclothing. His normally clean-shaven features were now covered in a bushy, unkempt beard.

"Away with you," she ordered her king, shaking her broom at him. "I did not slave all day over these pies to have them eaten by the likes of you. One is for myself, a bit of sweetness to stave off the end of days. Another is for my son, a reward for him taking the time to visit me if he bothers to. The final one I shall barter to find someone to do some tasks about my home." She stood stern between the Magpie King and the food.

Now, weakened as he was, it was still well within the Magpie King's power to push the old woman aside and claim her pies for himself. But the Magpie King was good and just in all things, and he did not want to see one of his people suffer just to sate his own hunger.

"Goodwife, your pies are the most glorious foods that I have ever smelt, and I would perform any tasks you request to have one. I am strong, and can work hard - what must I do to earn my prize?"

A sly smile crept across the old woman's face. "Yes, I have need of a strong back. The thatch of my cottage has worn away, and it leaks in the spring rains. Head up there and patch it together to earn my thanks."

"Without delay, Goodwife," the Magpie King replied. "Beforehand, might I impose on your kind nature to let me sample some of your wares before I begin?" he suggested, reaching a hand out yet again towards his prize.

"No," she barked in response, rewarding her king with a slap on his arm. "Do not misplace my age for stupidity - there shall be no rewards until your task is complete."

So the Magpie King spent all of that morning on the roof of the woman's cottage, skin and eyes pricked by the thorny straw of her roof, the emptiness of his belly weighing on him like an illness.

"The task is complete," he finally announced as the sun was at the highest point in the sky. "That roof shall not leak again in your lifetime. Now, my pie please," he requested, hand outstretched.

The sly grin appeared again. "Pie? I do not believe we had agreed on the pie as payment," the crafty woman smirked. "In fact, I clearly remember offering you my thanks for thatching my roof, and my thanks you have earned - you have made a fine job."

The Magpie King was annoyed, but could not argue with the old woman's logic, and was amused by her cunning. He nodded in agreement. "That was well done, and I fit the role of fool well. But I am reaching desperation and the smell of that pie is making a madness within my mind. What must I do to earn the pie?"

"Last winter, the apple tree in my garden died," the old woman explained. "I wish it removed so I may plant cabbages instead, as they agree much more with my innards than the bitter fruit that the tree once gave. Do this for me."

"I shall, in return for one of those blueberry pies," the Magpie King stated clearly, and the woman nodded in response, sealing the deal.

The apple tree had been old, and the roots had burrowed deep. The sun was beginning to set by the time he had removed all trace of it from the woman's garden.

"It is done," he stated with exhaustion, entering the cottage again to report his success. "My pie, please."

"Well now," the woman began, the sly smile appearing yet again, "the task is done, but I am not sure the price is at all fair. This is, apparently, the most glorious pie ever produced, and you have made it very clear how desperate you are. I believe that changes the price I must ask."

The Magpie King grew angry. "We had a clear deal," he stated, with menace, "and you have already cheated me once. Surely you shall not do so again?"

The woman simply gave him that sly smile in response.

Now, weakened as he was after his day of toil, it was still well within the Magpie King's power to beat the hag for her insolence and to take all three of her pies, yet he did not believe any of these actions were worthy of a king.

"What must I do for one of your pies?" he questioned through gritted teeth. "Do not cheat me again."

"My pigs," she said. "They need mucking out. I hate the task."

The Magpie King spent his evening shovelling the shit from the small pigsty attached to the cottage, his bare feet squelching through the swine's waste as he worked to gather it all up.

It was dark when his task was finally complete. Wordlessly, he entered the cottage, took his cold pie from the windowsill and shovelled it into his empty belly. The bitterness of his ordeal melted away as his hunger was finally sated. The woman's son did not come to visit, so the old woman graciously split the remaining pie between the two of them and they ate it silently in front of the fire. Both of them drifted off, she on her chair and he on the cold floor. When she woke in the morning, the Magpie King was already gone.

Weeks passed, and the woman was eventually disturbed by a knocking at her door. She answered it to find two black-cloaked guards who took her roughly from her home and brought her to a fine tent pitched in the middle of the village green. There she came face-to-face with the Magpie King, and immediately recognised him as the raggedy man she had cheated. With a wail, she threw herself at his feet, begging forgiveness.

At this sight, the Magpie King's stern face gave way to a kind smile. "I have not come here to punish you, Goodwife, although you were indeed wicked to me," he explained. "Since I have sampled your wares, I have been haunted by their taste. I have come to demand that you bake me another pie."

This time, no service was asked of the king, and the old woman silently worked at her stove to recreate the blueberry pie that had helped his strength to return. Upon presenting it to him with shaking hands, the old woman was thankful to hear it met the expectations of the king's memory.

"Now, we must address your punishment," the king stated.

"But," the old woman responded in panic, blood draining from her face, "you said you were not here to punish me."

At this, a sly smile crept across the Magpie King's face.

And so it was that the old woman was tasked to bake a new pie every day, just in case the king was happening by and took a fancy to sampling her wares again. The old goodwife was thankful that her baking was good, and that her king was a just one who had a sweet tooth.

CHAPTER
SEVEN

It was the day of Jarleth's execution. Mother Ogma had made it very clear that Lonan was not to rise to the occasion, so of course he ignored her orders completely. He made his way to the village green supported by Niall Tumulty, and stood by Mother Ogma at the back of the crowd. Everyone was there, with Branwen and Clare taking centre stage. Inteus the tax collector had long since vanished, apparently leaving with much haste after Jarleth had attacked Lonan. His presence at the execution was not missed.

Most had recognised that the incident with the baby and the river had been an accident, but an accident born out of Jarleth's anger. However, the beating Jarleth had given Lonan was clearly intended to kill him, and in this small community, that was unforgivable. Worse still for Jarleth had been the revelations of his unusual Knack and how he had employed it throughout the years. Once these facts had come out into the open, many within the village jumped onto the bandwagon of claiming Jarleth's atrocities against them. Old Man Tumulty claimed that Jarleth had constantly cheated him when trading grain for metal work. Widow Weaver suggested that Jarleth had seduced and bedded her against her will. However, all were unanimous in their contempt for how Jarleth had employed his talents against Lonan and his family, and for that there could be no more fitting punishment than death.

The rain was torrential this morning, but Lonan could not help but have a light heart on such an eventful day. A quiet voice inside his head suggested he should be ashamed at taking pleasure in the loss of someone else's life, but Lonan took little notice of this. He hated Jarleth. He hated what the man had done to him, what he had taken from him. There was no doubt in his mind that removing Jarleth from the world would improve everyone's lives.

Old Man Tumulty stood beside the condemned. There was a wooden tree stump on the ground before Jarleth. Another of the Tumulty boys stood beside him with a sharp axe in his hands. Nobody had offered Lonan the task himself, but he gladly would have taken it if he had thought his weak arm could have managed the weapon.

Jarleth himself looked terrible. He remained clothed in the tunic he had been wearing when beating Lonan to unconsciousness, still stained dark brown with Lonan's blood. He was unkempt, unshaved. The Corvae did not believe in giving condemned men access to amenities such as fresh water, unless anyone wished to volunteer to fetch it in their own free time. His head was hung low, and he was weeping openly.

Branwen stepped forward, ushered to do so by Old Man Tumulty. She was clearly reluctant to speak to her husband, but listened to Jarleth, not responding to him in any way. Jarleth soon became frustrated with her stoicism and began shouting. Eventually Tumulty ended the conversation by beating Jarleth roughly across his face. The condemned had tried to employ his Knack one last time.

Branwen stepped back, reclaiming Clare from her father. Old Man Tumulty gave the signal for Jarleth to be lowered to the stump. Two Tumulty boys held him down while the third got ready to swing the axe.

"Wait." The volume from his own throat surprised even Lonan. "Wait. I would like to speak to him."

Old Man Tumulty stared at Lonan for just a brief second, and then shrugged. The execution could wait for a few moments. Artemis knew that Lonan of all people deserved this.

He hobbled forward and knelt before the condemned man.

"I suppose you've come to gloat then."

Lonan thought for a moment. "No." He surprised himself with this reply. "I thought that… I was going to, yes, but now that I see you here…" Lonan's brow crumpled. "This gives me no joy."

Jarleth lifted his head, jaw resting on the tree stump, to stare at Lonan with a terror-stained face. "That was never really your style though, was it? You tended to run and hide from your fights instead of facing me. Only at the end do you have the guts to confront me, with the rest of the village behind you as backup." Jarleth's eyes were wide and erratic now, not fixing themselves on Lonan as he spoke but darting wildly around the village green.

Lonan thought again. "You see, I know how I should feel. I should be angry with myself for letting you ruin my life. For taking my father from me, my career, and Branwen. Perhaps I should be ashamed that in all these years I've never tried to do anything about it. But really, here at the end, I am sorry. Sorry that you ruined my life, Branwen's life. But dammit, Jarleth, some stupid part of me is sorry for you too."

Jarleth spat at him. "You can't get any of it back, you know. You'll never get your Knack now, and they'll never really trust you, even after what they know about me. And Branwen? Oh, I imagine she'll find her way into your bed eventually, but believe me - I have ruined her for you. She'll never let you do the things to her that I did. I guess you don't have the… charisma I do."

Jarleth nodded his head towards Branwen and the baby. "And that is my child you'll bring up. Every time you look at it, you will remember that I put it in your woman's belly."

Lonan shook his head. "That's where you're wrong. That girl will be my daughter. She'll grow up with the love and devotion from a father that she deserves, that you never would have given her."

He wrinkled his nose, looking at Jarleth's head on the tree stump, realising that in seconds this man who he had hated for so long would be gone. "This gives me no joy."

Without giving Jarleth time to respond, Lonan turned and walked away, lowering his head in confusion and sadness.

Old Man Tumulty nodded to his son. A minute later, the green was empty, with everyone going back to their usual business.

"Well, dearie," Mother Ogma opened conversation again as she pottered about in her cottage, "that's that then." Harlow drooled away in his chair as usual, the only resident of Smithsdown to not attend the event.

"Hrm," Lonan murmured, not entirely in agreement. "Do you know, I think I fancy a short walk before we close up for the evening."

Mother Ogma frowned at him. "I don't know why I'm bothering to say this, but I really do not feel that would be wise in your condition. Do I have to remind you you're lucky to be alive right now?"

"You certainly don't have to, as I believe you reminded me of that fact not thirty minutes ago. Then, as now, I was very gracious for the attentions of your Knack, but I really must insist that I stretch my legs."

"I thought as much," she muttered, moving to pull her shawl on again, "let's make it quick then."

"Ah, this wasn't the type of walk that I was hoping to take accompanied."

She raised an eyebrow at this. "Heading to Branwen's? Don't you find that a little bit distasteful today? I think she'd prefer you to wait a few days, or weeks even, before calling on her."

"Now," he grunted, raising himself from his chair, "you're thinking of her as someone who's mourning her dead husband, but I suspect she isn't far away from feeling the complete opposite of that."

Mother Ogma wrinkled her nose up at this, but waved him her permission. A few aching steps later and Lonan was at Branwen's door, waiting on a reply.

"Lonan?" she answered finally, in hushed tones. "Clare is already down for the night, I was going to join her shortly."

"Yeah, sure. I guess… I guess I just wanted to come and see how you were doing."

Branwen let out a sigh. "Bored. Frustrated. Exhausted. When anyone has come up to me today, they haven't known whether to console me or celebrate with me. To be honest, I don't know which reaction I prefer."

"But… surely you're happy he's gone?"

"It's not that easy, Lonan."

"Of course it is. The man was a monster. He killed your mother, Branwen. Almost killed Clare. And let's not forget he tried his damned best to kill me after almost ruining my life for the last eight years. I don't get the impression your life with him has been a piece of cake either."

Her face turned red in anger, and she barked back, "No, but he was a man, Lonan. He had a place in this village. He put food on our plates. That's my job now. Clare and I have to look out for ourselves, and that's going to be bloody hard."

Lonan's cockiness dissipated. "But... that's my job now, isn't it? I thought that we..."

The look of shock on Branwen's face clearly told Lonan that he had read the situation all wrong. He had just assumed that their relationship would pick up from where they had left off eight years ago. *What an idiot.* Her face told him that the notion had never even occurred to her.

"Ah, sorry, I've been a complete fool, haven't I? You'd better lock up." Lonan turned to walk away.

"Wait." Branwen was still at the door, face white. "Lonan, you don't want me. Not now. I'm another man's wife. A murderer and a liar. I've had his child." She laughed, indicating her face. "By Artemis, just look at me. You should aim higher."

Lonan did not join in her humour. "You know, I hated walking past this house. This forge. The fact that he had taken my father's job and home from me stung. I felt ill coming close to this place. I would go into the forest to scream at the world in frustration at how nobody else would believe I was innocent of your mother's death. But Branwen, nothing hurt me more than the looks you gave me each day. That what we had as children so quickly turned to hate. And when he married you..."

At this, Lonan spat to the ground. "His biggest crime against me was taking you."

Branwen paused, looking at the man before her with new eyes. Casting a glance to the horizon, she ran out of her home, threw her arms around Lonan's neck and kissed him. Her lips were rough, the cheek of her ruined face felt alien and ragged against his own, but at that point, Lonan knew he was the happiest man in the forest.

"I love you," he whispered finally, into her ear. "I always have."

She pulled away from him, smiling through her tears, and opened her mouth to speak.

The evening bell rang.

Branwen pulled reluctantly away. "You should head back now.

We can talk about this in the morning." The smile she gave him made his heart sing.

Lonan chuckled. "You know, there's no reason to wall ourselves up anymore. Don't you fancy spending a few hours looking at the stars in the night sky?"

Branwen drew back in fear at the very suggestion. "You can't be serious?"

"I told you about my dreams, didn't I? The Magpie King has won, Branwen. The Wolves have gone. Night is safe for us now."

Her uncertainty was plain to read. "Lonan, promise me you won't do anything silly tonight. You haven't been well..."

Annoyed, he responded, "They're real, Branwen. I've been having the dreams for a while now, before the accident."

"Promise me, Lonan."

He threw up his arms in mock frustration. "Fine. You win this one, our first argument. But I'll get you out in the night soon enough," he added with an evil glint in his eye.

"Goodnight, Lonan." She smiled and then was gone.

He could not stop himself from grinning. Everything was coming together now. With Jarleth out of the way, Branwen's affections were returning to him. His own status in the village was already well repaired. Lonan was convinced the forge would default to him soon. He knew Knacks did not normally come after the age of eighteen, but if he pushed himself hard enough...

A selection of thuds signalled the closing of cellar doors. One ahead of him alerted Lonan to the fact that Mother Ogma had closed her door without him.

That cheeky little minx. She had assumed he would be staying the night with Branwen. What secrets did that suggest about the old healer? He always thought Old Tumulty gave her strange looks when her back was turned. Ogma's door was shut, but it would not be too much of a bother for her to open it for him again.

Except, why should she have to?

He knew he had promised Branwen he would not stay outside in the night, but it had been a foolish promise to make. Lonan knew fine well the danger of the Wolves had disappeared from the forest. In his dreams, Adahy leapt from village to village, desperately seeking physical combat to distract him from the rigours of diplomacy, but there was nothing to be found any more. No movement had been reported by anyone in Smithsdown since

Lonan's dream showed the den mother's fall.

And Lonan wanted to see the stars again.

They had never been completely foreign to him, of course. In a cloudless sky in the late evening, the brightest stars were often visible. Lonan had also spent a lot of the past few weeks looking through the eyes of the Magpie King, who walked beneath the stars regularly. However, it was another thing entirely to lie on your back on the village green and stare into a wealth of sparks on a dark canvas. Lonan began by counting them, but quickly realised he had not the numbers in his head to complete the task. *By Artemis, I did not expect there to be so many - where do they all hide when the brightest pop out in the evenings? Another mystery I'll gladly investigate in the future.*

The young man shivered. *Hadn't expected it to be so cold, but I guess winter isn't far from the forest now. Perhaps, for that reason only, it might be best to find shelter indoors tonight.*

Lonan picked himself up off the ground and froze. There was movement, over by the forge. Something shifting in the shadows.

Lonan could feel his heart rate ramping up, his mind whirring through the possibilities. A Wolf? But Adahy had been so sure they were gone now. What about Adahy himself? That made no sense either. Why would the Magpie King feel the need to hide himself from a villager?

The shadow by the wall shifted slightly, tilting itself in Lonan's direction. It was clear that whoever or whatever was sheltering over there had seen him now.

It would still not be impossible for Lonan to get to safety. Mother Ogma's cottage was within his reach, and he was convinced she would not have fallen asleep yet. However, Lonan's morbid curiosity was fighting that notion. Also, the dark shape was closest to Branwen's cottage...

Lonan shifted closer to the forge. Something moved in the darkness again. Definitely too large to be a woodland animal. Unless it was a bear, of course, but Lonan was not foolish enough to believe in such a beast. The way this shape was hiding, he was convinced it was just as scared of him as he was of it.

"Hello?" he whispered gently.

Then it leapt at him.

The blackness was swifter than anything Lonan had seen before. He did not have a chance to even make a move, and when it hit him it did so with the force of one of the Tumulty brothers driving a fence post into the dirt. Lonan hit the ground with a violent thump, sending needles into the fresh wounds of his head, arm and chest.

He screamed at this, and the shape screamed back at him. It was unnerving, inhuman. Lonan's bowels released, reminding him of Adahy all those weeks ago on the ridge over Smithsdown. The black shape screamed again, and he realised his initial assumption that it was inhuman was incorrect. The thing standing over him was clearly human, or at least was at one point. Its skin was a burnt black, like the end of a log left in a fire. Despite its strength the thing had no meat on its bones, its powerful arms were no more than ruined skin stretched over a thin frame.

Most distinctive, however, was its face. A metal mask covered its eyes and nose, drawing attention to its face's black chin and yellow teeth, which were filed to a point. Lonan should have been most horrified by its eyes. They were clearly human, but the whites had been turned a deep red as if they were constantly, deeply irritated. However, Lonan was transfixed by the nose of the mask. Or perhaps *beak* would be a better word, for the mask's nose stuck out and then bent downwards into a point. That and the black feathered cloak that the creature wore could not help but draw attention to its similarities to the Magpie King.

"What in the hell are you?" Lonan gasped.

In response the creature screamed at him again, took his right hand in its mouth and bit off his ring finger.

It took Lonan a moment to realise he was now screaming too. The figure continued to shout, yet now there was a sinister mirth in its bellows. It was making fun of him.

"No, no," Lonan struggled underneath his attacker, but it was no use. Its strength dwarfed anything that he could muster even if he had been uninjured. In all of his fear, in what he now assumed were his last moments alive, he marvelled at how unfair this was. Everything had just started to go right. After years of misfortune and being plotted against, this was supposed to be his time.

"Adahy! Adahy, help me!" It was a last ditch attempt before he said goodbye to his life.

He was almost as surprised as his attacker when it worked.

From the black sky, as if leaping straight down from the moon, the Magpie King fell. He was exactly as Lonan had seen him in his dreams. The black and white feathers poured over his body, concealing it in a mist-like embrace, but most significant was the helm. The black metal beak, dwarfing the tiny mask of Lonan's attacker, pointed accusingly at the duo grappling on the ground.

"Adahy, my king - get it off, get it off me!"

The Magpie King rose to his full height and the attacking figure sank back from him, but remained hunched over Lonan. The Magpie King stepped forward.

"What did you call me?" His deep voice contained a wounded rasp that Lonan had not expected. It also took him a long second to realise that the Magpie King was addressing him.

"Adahy? I know it's you. I - I have these dreams. For Artemis' sake, get this thing off me."

The Magpie King reached out and grabbed Lonan roughly by the chin. The first creature did not shy away from the Magpie King's closeness.

Something was horribly wrong.

"You dream of the Magpie King?"

"Adahy? You are Adahy, aren't you? You're here to help me?"

The Magpie King was silent for a moment, staring at Lonan with his blank mask.

"Do not leave any remains."

And with that, he was gone.

"Wait, Adahy, wait-"

Pain shot up Lonan's arm again as he lost another digit. This time, the creature brought its pointed teeth close to Lonan's face as it chomped joyfully on his flesh, allowing his own blood to fall into his mouth as he screamed mindlessly.

He was going to die.

A rage-filled female voice pierced the pain. "Get off him."

A thick amber liquid sprayed over the creature and Lonan, blinding the young man's attacker.

"Lonan, roll."

Released by the attacking shape as it brought its hands to its face, Lonan squirmed out from under the creature and rolled off to the side, clutching his injured hand as he did so. This gave Mother Ogma all the space that she needed to throw her lantern at the oil-covered monster. Flames enveloped it, and black feathers, now alight, rose to the sky as it shrieked.

"Quick," she gasped, pulling Lonan across the green as the creature burned out to a dead husk, "Back to the cellar. Harlow is flailing around like a madman - I don't know what to do with him."

Lonan was going to be very little help, however. As he lost consciousness, his enduring question was: *why, Adahy, why?*

Adahy eventually found Maedoc on the Eyrie's roof. As Magpie Kings were wont to do, he was perched on the roof edge, still in full ceremonial garb, peering out to the forest.

"There you are, my friend. Your task was performed well, and it bore tasteful fruit."

Maedoc did not turn to look at his king, but answered in a gravelly voice. "I take it you liked what you saw then?"

"Yes, I did. She is terrified, poor girl, and very alone. But she has a good wit about her, and a keen mind."

"Quite the looker too, I imagine."

Adahy could not help but give an embarrassed grin. "Well, it was hard to say with all that gear on her, but I did fancy the look of those lips."

"Her father is very proud of her, you know. Says he has had suitors from all five peoples chasing after her to be their new queen. None of them have a Magpie King though. None that can do this." With that, Maedoc threw himself up into the air, feathered cloak whistling softly in the wind. Anyone with lesser eyes would have lost sight of him as he disappeared into the night, but Adahy could spy him in the air high above, eventually descending to the roof slightly behind him.

"Now there are two of us, my friend. Think of what this could mean for the future of our people. Two with the power of the Magpie Spirit, now that you have become accustomed to your condition. We shall talk about this later. Now I should return to the gathering, in your place."

Maedoc cocked his head at this. "And what for me? Should I return in your place, and serve the princess some more wine?"

Adahy looked uncomfortable. "I think rest would be the best option for you, my friend. You have taken quite a large step today."

"No, I suppose that would be a bad idea. Pretty princesses do not want to look at faces such as mine, do they? In fact, would I have been able to get into your party without this mask? It would turn people's stomachs just to look at me."

"Not so," Adahy reprimanded. "Many of the Corvae serving tonight carry marks of conflict, and bare them with pride. We have won a great victory against an old enemy, but it has not been without a price."

"So, it is to be a servant again then."

"I am sorry, my friend?"

"A servant. I am still a servant to you."

Adahy looked lost. "You... Maedoc, we have always been close friends, you and I. My closest, and that is no secret. My friends shall be rewarded."

"But still a servant. Despite powers such as these," and with that he tore a slate off the roof and threw it into the distance. "I remain a servant to the king and his nobles."

"Maedoc, this is how it has always been. Mine is a line traced deep into history. We are the true Corvae, the nobles of our people. We were of the forest long before the villagers came, escaping the disintegration of the world outside. This is not something you can earn, despite your new gifts."

Maedoc was silent for a while, and then spoke again. "What do you know of my parents?"

Adahy paused. "Little. Nothing, if I am honest. You have never spoken of them."

"That is because I've nothing to tell. I never knew them, you see. I've always lived here at the Eyrie, at the whim of your father."

"Yes..." Adahy was not sure where any of this was going, and was beginning to regret encouraging Maedoc to leave his cell. Clearly the young man's mind still had some paths to walk on the journey to recovery.

"But I heard of them. Not from your father, however. Not from a noble. It was a kitchen maid. I had spent the evening trying to seduce her, and her final excuse was she didn't want a traitor's son putting a babe in her belly."

"I don't understand."

"My parents, you see, they were traitors. Involved in a village uprising not long after we would have been born. I don't know what exactly was involved, but I do know my family's lives were the price. My parents lost theirs, and I was to give mine to the Eyrie."

"I had no idea, Maedoc. I am sorry."

"So you see, I'm not really a servant. I haven't really been your friend all of these years. I'm a slave. Brought into this noble house to be beaten when the young prince was bad."

"Think about what you are saying, Maedoc. To claim that we are not friends is madness."

"When I saw you tonight, with that princess, it made me realise I'll never have a woman like that. Despite how close we have been in our lives. Despite the power we both share. My place in life and my face mean I shall be taking the scrapings of the barrel from the palace servants, if I am lucky."

"I'm sorry, what? This is about the princess now?" Adahy was losing track of the flow of conversation.

"Did she like the look of your face?"

"I - I have no idea. How would I even-"

"Did she know it was you?"

"No. I mean, I don't think-"

"What about her father? Does he approve of your looks? Your face?"

"Maedoc. By the Great Spirit. What I look like has nothing to do with this."

"Does he approve?"

"He has not seen me, Maedoc, you know that. Tradition. Now-"

"Nobody?"

"What are you talking about?"

"None of the Owls have seen your face? To approve what their princess is looking forward to?"

"No, I-"

"Excellent." With a flick of his wrist, Maedoc buried one of his sickles into Adahy's right eye, splitting the skin across his face.

The young king, motionless, remaining eye open wide in shock as the functions of his brain died, was drawn close to his attacker with a fist tightly gripping the servant's tunic he still wore.

"Long live the King," the Magpie King whispered, and then threw Adahy's thoughtless body off the roof, down the cliff face to be wrecked on the forest floor far below.

THE COMING
OF THE
OUTSIDERS

An extract from the teachings of the High Corvae.

Under the rule of the Magpie King, the forest flourished. The darkness of the spider and the Wolves was kept at bay. Allies were made with the Lions and Owls. Others were kept under control, either through fear or military force. All remained good under the powerful gaze of the Magpie King, good and unchanging, until the outsiders arrived.

They came in small groups at first. Sometimes a couple, sometimes an individual, once or twice an entire family. They would be found hunting game or gathering fruit, often doing their best to piece together some kind of dwelling in the depths of the woods. Each time the sight of the Magpie King would send the outsiders fleeing to the forest borders, but each time the king grew more disturbed at the sight of these new people. They were unlike the Corvae in so many ways. Most importantly, they clearly had no comprehension of how to live in the forest. The largest groups in particular used their resources wastefully, felling dozens of trees for lumber that could have been provided by just a handful, or by allowing some fruits to rot on the vine instead of taking the time to gather them when they had ripened.

The Leone and Muridae experienced these incursions too, but paid them less heed than the Magpie King did. The Muridae worried them away from their lands, deceiving them or frightening them until they were pushed from the grassland borders. The Lions were more direct in the expulsion of the strangers from the mountains.

"They fear us now, and are right to do so," Reoric had boasted to the Magpie King when last they met. "You should do the same, my friend. They are a desperate people. Some disaster befell them, an empire crumbled, and their people no longer have the strength they once possessed. There is nobody now to protect them from the world, and they seek to hide from those who would take advantage of their plight. Best to send them a message, set them running, before you invite their troubles to your doorstep."

But this added knowledge of the outsiders' woes weighed heavily on the Magpie King's mind. Although the strangers continued to flee at the sight of him, this was no longer his purpose. He merely wished to observe, as he came to a decision.

Then it came to be that the outsiders grouped themselves together and forced their way into the forest as one. They numbered the size of a great army, although there were just as many children and elderly among them as there were fit women and men. Few warriors walked with them, and although most of the adults were armed, many of those weapons took the form of crude clubs or sharpened farming equipment. However, the sheer weight of their numbers was enough to allow them to push further into the heart of the forest than they had before. They burned fires to protect themselves and thought little of the danger this could pose in the dry woodland. The Magpie King watched their progress with great interest, intervening to protect the forest from their flames or to protect the outsiders from any threats that were naturally drawn towards the din they created.

Their march ended upon reaching the shrine of the Great Magpie. The host of outsiders stood in awe of that great structure so deep in the forest, and looked with fear upon the Magpie Guard sentries that remained silent and unmoving at their posts outside of the temple. It was when the bravest of the outsiders stepped forth to challenge the guards that the Magpie King took it upon himself to intervene, dropping to the forest floor to stand between his people and the invaders.

The one who had stepped forward was a tall woman, who hefted a large iron blade before her. "Stay back, monster. We shall harm you if you approach any further."

"I am no monster," the Magpie King replied. "I mean you no harm."

Another stepped from the crowd, this time a handsome man with no weapons of note, simply a backpack slung over his shoulder. He wore a sly grin, and his quick mind was working hard to turn this situation in his own favour. "There are many of us, and we have nowhere left to turn. Leave this land now, for we claim it as our own."

"That I cannot do," came the Magpie King's response. "This land, this forest, was gifted to us by the Great Magpie. I watch over it and protect it for our people."

"Us?" came the question from the clever stranger's lips. As if on cue, the branches rustled above the heads of the assembled outsiders, betraying the host of Magpie Guard that lay perched above them, armed and ready to pounce.

Overcome with exhaustion, the woman threw herself at the feet of the Magpie King, much to the disgust of her companion. "Spare us, please," she pleaded. "We have nowhere left to go. We cannot stay in the lands of our fathers - they are overrun with bandits and raiders which we have no power to protect ourselves from. Everywhere we turn, we are forced out or killed by all manner of beasts - snakes, owls, wolves, lions, even mice. We simply wish for, simply need somewhere to call our own again. Somewhere to live in safety."

The Magpie King put a sympathetic hand on the woman's shoulder, feeling her shudder in fear at his gentle touch. "I am afraid the forest has not been your best choice for sanctuary. This is a dangerous place, as dangerous a place as there must be on this world. It will not allow you to stay here in peace. Dark things will seek to feed on you and force you from its borders. You will find no rest here."

The woman looked up at the Magpie King and met his dark eyes with hers, so filled with desperation and hope. "Then protect us, please. Let us join with you, become your people. Rule over us and keep us safe. Let us live again."

The handsome man, some steps behind, scowled at her words, but like all others gathered there he held his tongue, awaiting the king's response.

The Magpie King did not speak for some time. He stood, hand on the woman's shoulder, thinking. "I could accept you," he finally announced, "but my charge was made very clear to me by the Great Magpie. I have these gifts to protect my people, the Corvae, from life in the forest. It is not my acceptance you seek, but that of the Great Magpie."

The handsome man laughed at the announcement, but the woman remained serious.

"How may I do that?" she queried forcefully. "Show me this Magpie so I may entreat him as well."

The Magpie King gestured behind him, to the silent temple with its half-open door.

The woman stood and made to walk towards the building, but found herself stopped by her companion.

"It is a trap," the clever man warned her. "A giant magpie? There is no such thing. We do not have to dance to this tune. We must outnumber them greatly."

"Even if that were true, what cost would come with those actions?" she retorted. "I am tired, we all are, and peace could finally be in our grasp."

Ignoring her companion's unceasing scowls, she pulled from his grasp and entered the dark portal of the temple.

Both parties restlessly awaited her return. The outsiders stood in agitation, sharpening their blades and moving their weak and young away from any overhead rustling. The Magpie King and his guard stood in silence. After an hour of night had passed, a white figure glided to the king's side, causing a new commotion to rise from the ranks of the strangers.

"I do not trust them," spoke the Magpie King's wife. "There is anger and deceit here. We do not want this in our forest."

The King stood with his bride and surveyed the outsiders. "Yes, they bring much ill with them, but strength and selflessness as well. Look at the large families huddled together. Most of those children do not share the same parents, but yet they are cared for. How could I be the one to send them back out into the world?"

His wife did not reply, but her eyes saw not only the goodness of the people. She also spied the pickpockets, the liars, the adulterers. She felt fear.

Finally, the tall woman exited the temple, exhausted and gasping for breath.

"What took you so long?" the handsome outsider barked at her. "What happened in there?"

She did not answer him, but instead turned to speak with the king. "It spoke to me," she began, in a voice saturated with awe. "It will have us, despite our flaws, if we pass three tests. One of strength, one of trust, and one of love."

The Magpie King nodded. "Will you attempt these tests for your people?"

The woman met his eyes with a look of pure fear, but then hardened herself and nodded her acceptance.

The following day was the day of strength. As the sun peered over the horizon, it illuminated a tall cliff that stood behind the temple. From their make-shift tents the most eagle-eyed outsiders could just make out a castle at the top of the cliff.

"The test of strength," the Magpie King directed the outsider woman. "You must climb this cliff, and arrive at my home before nightfall. Otherwise, you all must depart this forest."

"It is a trick," the sly stranger warned her. "Look at the size of that rock - this is an impossible task. Come away now. There are other ways to win this forest."

But the tall woman ignored her companion and steeled herself for the climb ahead. When the sunlight finally made its way to the forest floor, she threw herself at the rock face and began to climb. At first, it seemed as if the man had spoken truthfully - this climb did indeed appear to be impossible. However, fingers and feet found previously untouched crevices, and by mid day, she had climbed higher than the majority of the outsiders could see.

A small party of the Corvae and outsiders made their way to the top of a winding path that was the main route to the Magpie King's castle. There they waited, but the woman did not arrive. Afternoon came and went, and evening began to fall, the yellow orb of the sun sheltering beneath the treetops. The outsiders began to despair, and the Magpie King took it upon himself to scale down the cliff to locate the stranger.

He found her, eventually, sheltered beneath an overhang that blocked her path. She was rigid with fear, and exhausted from her exertion. "I have failed," she moaned, softly. "I have failed them."

"You have not failed, sister," the Magpie King assured her, brushing a lock of hair out of her eyes and guiding the mouth of his water skin to her lips. "Your companions are not far above us now, but evening threatens to fall. Retreat a few paces, and then begin your ascent in a new direction. You will be in their arms again soon."

She gave a nod of thanks, and followed his instructions. As the last light of the day fell, her hand came over the edge of the cliff to grasp that of the Magpie King. The trial of strength had been passed.

The next day was the day of trust. The Magpie King brought

the woman to a wild part of the forest, where thick bushes with needles the size of knives grew in great thickets.

"The razor-trees are as sharp as any sword," the Magpie King explained, "and any brush up against them will mark you for life." To demonstrate, he gently rubbed a green apple along one of the nearby protrusions. The fruit fell apart in his hands.

"However," he warned, "this is not the greatest threat. The thorns also carry a deadly poison that will give you a swift, if not agonising, death." All outsiders recoiled from the plants at this information.

"Your challenge," the Magpie King continued, "is to travel from one end of this thicket to the other. Blindfolded."

The woman took a few moments to digest this information before looking to the Magpie King in confusion. "But then, how?"

"There is a safe path through this part of the woods, known to all Corvae." At this, the Magpie King nodded and his people spread out before him, amongst the deadly thorns, awaiting the beginning of the trial. "They shall be your eyes for this task. They shall instruct you on how to move through the forest unharmed."

The cunning man laughed again at the presentation of this challenge. "Another ploy," he counselled his companion. "They could not lose you on the cliff, so they seek to kill you here and blame it on your own fumbling. What will the rest of us do once you, the greatest of us, have fallen? They will force us to leave these lands."

But the strong woman remembered the kind words of the Magpie King on the cliff on the previous day, and she accepted the blindfold gladly. The soft cloth blocked her vision and she took tentative steps forward.

"Hold, sister," came a voice to her right. "The way forward is not safe," came her instructions by the unseen Corvae. "Instead, walk towards my voice, and continue on that path until you reach my son."

Taking a deep breath, she turned to the speaker and walked towards him, and continued to do so until a new voice instructed her to do otherwise.

This continued for many hours. The strong woman was passed from father to brother, from wife to grandmother, a long chain of forest people guiding her to safety. All went well, and her confidence began to grow. As it did so, her pace quickened, eager as she was to regain her sight.

"Sister, no," came a shout to her left. She felt a small shove to her side that caused her to side-step slightly, and she then stood rigid with fear. Beside her, she could feel the earth tremble as a body collapsed, frantic convulsions and pain-wracked gurgles signalling the end of a life.

Panicking, the woman lifted a hand to her blindfold.

"No, sister."

She recognised the deep tone straight away.

"Your task is almost complete, but all would be forfeit if you stole back your vision now. A Corvae has fallen here, but in doing so she has saved your life and the fate of your people. Honour her - turn towards me and walk, slowly."

The strong woman turned to the Magpie King and began to walk. She rejoined the chain of voices, which eventually led her to the edge of the thicket. She was greeted by the cheers of her people, but this time her sense of victory was muted by the sadness surrounding the Corvae at the loss of one of their own.

The day of the final trial arrived. This was held back at the temple, in front of the assembled outsiders and a host of Corvae larger than any the outsiders had yet seen. The Magpie King stood at the head of the gathering with his wife at his side, a look of stoic sadness on both of their faces.

"The trial of love," the Magpie King began. "This is the most difficult of all tasks, yet can be completed by any assembled here." His voice rose at this, allowing all to hear. "Think hard about everything this woman has done for you," he counselled them. "She is not the only one who can provide for her people."

He allowed a pause for this to register with all assembled, and then continued. "For the trial of love, the Great Magpie demands a sacrifice. For countless generations, the Corvae have lived here without malice towards each other. Yes, we have had arguments, but we never forget that we are one people. If you are to become Corvae, the Great Magpie demands a sign that your people are capable of this too." He scanned the audience now, his gaze resting on nobody specific, although all felt that his speech was intended for them and them alone.

"The Magpie demands that one of you sacrifice your bonds with the Corvae. The rest of the people assembled here will join us with our arms stretched open in welcome. They shall become Corvae, they shall live and find peace in the forest."

"But one shall be cast out, exiled from the forest. Your knowledge that this sacrifice will save every other outsider here is the only balm you shall be offered."

"Preposterous," the handsome outsider shouted in response. "Do you really think that any of us would be foolish enough to give up so much and never benefit ourselves? My people, listen to me. Do not be taken in by these false promises. We have the ability to force our way into this forest without any sacrifices needing to be made."

A great murmuring broke out among the gathered outsiders. Although many of them were in agreement with the cunning man, many more were raising their voices to address the Magpie King. They were looking to save their friends, their family.

The strong woman turned to the Magpie King, and for the third day in a row a look of fear was etched on her face. "Do not let them volunteer first. Let me take this final burden."

She then stood up and shouted above the rising noises from the crowd. "It is me. I am to be exiled." She turned in desperation to look at the Magpie King.

After a pause for consideration he nodded his approval.

Within the hour the Magpie King stood atop his castle, his sharp eyes picking out the forlorn figure making her way to the forest border. Below him, two peoples mingled, becoming one. The sites for new villages to house the outsiders - no, the new Corvae - were already being planned.

And as he watched a handsome, tall man slink around the borders of the campsites below, a bitter scowl on his features, the Magpie King wondered what exactly he had invited into his domain.

✦CHAPTER✦
EIGHT

His gentle sobbing told Mother Ogma that Lonan was awake. She waddled over to his bed and rested her hand on his head.

"Now, dearie, nothing too much to worry about. A couple of fingers is a small price to pay for how unbelievably stupid you were last night."

Lonan shrugged her off him, sat up and eyed his ruined hand. Sniffing he replied, "He's dead, Mother Ogma."

"Yes, I have to say I'm rather proud of myself. Who would have thought I had it in me, at my age?"

"No, not that monster. Adahy. He was killed."

Mother Ogma's brow creased. "Now, dearie. Surely last night's events have helped you to see that all this dream nonsense has been leading you astray? That wasn't even a Wolf out there last night."

"No!" He half-screamed his answer, causing Harlow to jump up in response.

To Lonan's surprise, the old man continued to move, flailing around on his bedsit. Mother Ogma moved over to him again to calm him down.

"No, Mother Ogma," Lonan continued in a lower tone when

Harlow had settled again. "He was there last night. The Magpie King, exactly as I told you."

She clearly did not believe him. "Then why did he not stop that thing from hurting you?"

"That's just it. He told it to kill me. It was working with him. You must have got a good glimpse of that thing that ate my fingers - it even looked like how I described the Magpie King. Almost."

"I don't understand then. If this Adahy is who you say he is, why would he want that to happen to you?"

"He wouldn't. That isn't the kind of man he is. Was. He was a good king, Mother Ogma. He was going to make us safe..."

"Perhaps it was the other one then? Maedoc?"

"Seems more like him, but that couldn't be right. They were at the palace in my dream last night, the party was still happening..." Lonan slipped into silence.

"What is it, dearie?"

"My dream last night. The party was still going on. The party that began the night before."

"That seems unusual, dearie."

Lonan cupped his head in his hands and gave out a groan. "I've been a fool. They don't mean anything, the dreams, do they?"

"Perhaps. But I've heard the dreams of madmen before, and very rarely do they remain so consistent. The Magpie King last night - are you sure it was him? He was the same as in your dreams?

"Every last feather, yes."

"Well then, there must be truth there. None of our stories describe him in such detail."

"Yeah. Yes, that's right. That part still makes sense. But everything else is so different. No Wolves outside, but instead those... birds?" Lonan shuddered, clutching his bandages again. "And the timing of last night's dream, that was all wrong. It should have been a day on from when I last saw Adahy, not just an hour or so."

He raised his eyes to look at Mother Ogma. "I thought my dreams were showing me events as they happened. I was wrong."

Mother Ogma sat on her bed, letting everything fit into place. "That was Maedoc last night, then. As the Magpie King."

"Adahy did save us from the Wolves, but now there's

something else out there, attacking the villages. Something to do with the Magpie King. Something that dresses like him, answers to him."

"Is there any way this Maedoc could have been hiding something like this from the prince, hiding that bird monster, and maybe more like it?"

"No. Not a chance. There would've been nowhere to hide a secret this big. There was nothing like them at the Eyrie, Mother Ogma, not when I've seen it at night. This is something new."

At that moment, they heard a commotion out on the green.

"They've probably found the body by now," Mother Ogma muttered. "Stay down here, dearie. I'll go and see what's happening." The old healer opened the cellar door to the daylight and went upstairs. Seconds later, she ran back down again.

"He's back, Lonan. The tax collector is back."

Lonan quickly wrapped himself and his wounded hand in a blanket and ran upstairs and outside to the village green to join in the throng surrounding the purple-robed man.

"I have been sent back to support you in this distressing time," Inteus was addressing the people, "and to help to make funeral arrangements for the family."

There were shouts of confusion with families asking the tax man to explain himself.

He raised his hand for silence, then continued. "The Magpie King has told me that one of your number was attacked and killed last night. I have been sent to help you deal with this."

"Who?" This bellow came from Old Man Tumulty. "Was anyone breached?"

"It was the young man known as Lonan Anvil," Inteus announced in a consoling voice. "Alas, he chose to not confine himself to the cellars last night, and our lord reports he has paid the price."

At this, there were shouts throughout the village, and Lonan could pick out Branwen's high pitched wail at the news. However, a few heads close by were beginning to turn in his direction.

"Can you lead me to the body?" Inteus asked the crowd. A murmur spread through the gathered villagers, and they began to part, exposing a stern faced Lonan to the tax collector's searching gaze.

"Well," Lonan addressed him, eyes full of anger, "it looks like someone's lord hasn't quite got their facts straight, doesn't it?"

"I-I don't understand," the outsider stammered, stooping down to gather his belongings. "I must consult-"

"Oh, I think you must, but your consultations will be taking place a bit closer to home." Lonan ran the last few feet towards the man and grabbed his robes at the chest. Inteus buckled in fear and confusion.

"Now wait just a moment-" Old Man Tumulty began to challenge, but Lonan interrupted by holding up his bandaged hand, the blood from last night's wound staining the white linen red.

"I'm still alive, but something had a pretty good go at me last night. This man knows more than he's telling us. I reckon my fingers have bought me the right to ask a few questions, so who is going to help this mess to the healer's cottage?" At that final sentence, Lonan's eyes fell on Branwen's, and he knew this time he had earned the anger she shot at him. He turned away, not wanting to let his emotions cloud his judgement.

The Tumulty boys, always game for helping roughhouse a deserving soul, took Inteus from Lonan and helped to bind him to a chair in Mother Ogma's house.

Lonan stood and watched as they did so, losing his thoughts in the gentle rocking of Harlow's chair. He glanced at the old man and the hairs on the back of his neck stood on end. Harlow was looking straight at him. The invalid had never before registered Lonan's existence in the years they had spent under the same roof, but now his accusing eye tracked Lonan as he moved from one side of the room to the other. This uncanny gaze added to the volatile mix of emotions currently assaulting Lonan, his insides pumping a heady mix of adrenaline as his survival instincts kicked in. *If the Magpie King, whoever wears the helm, wants me dead, he's not going to rest until the job is done. How am I, a Knackless villager, going to be able to stop him? This man must have some information I can use.*

"He's all yours, Lonan," Niall Tumulty told him, breaking Lonan's train of thought.

"Thanks, guys. Best that you leave, though. If this waste of space knows the Magpie King, and I think he does, the less you all know, the better."

The men left with a little protest, leaving only the inhabitants of the cottage and Inteus behind.

The visitor appeared to have regained some of his composure, despite his now uncomfortable position. "Well, Master Anvil, we are all very pleased you have survived. I am sure my lord will feel so too when I tell him."

Lonan responded by punching the tax collector across the face. "Now, this is going to be slow and painful if we don't understand each other, so listen closely. You remember your friend, Jarleth Quarry?"

Inteus nodded, silently, shocked at the sudden violence. This was a man who had never experienced a good punch in the face before.

"Didn't see him outside there, did you?"

Inteus thought and shook his head.

Lonan leaned in close to him. "That's because we executed him yesterday. For doing this to me," Lonan indicated the bandages on his head. "You see, Mister Inteus, people in Smithsdown take each other's safety very seriously. And after this?" He held up his hand to display the stumps that remained of his two eaten digits. "Well, let's just say that this means you are going to have to work very hard to try and stay alive."

"Now listen, young forager, you really cannot be serious-"

Lonan rolled his eyes and hit the man again.

"Knife," Lonan requested, and Mother Ogma handed him a large chopping knife. "Now," he said in a matter of fact tone, "there are people in this village I want to protect. I will not hesitate to use this knife to get what I need from you. So, answer my question: why does the Magpie King want me dead?"

Inteus looked in panic at the weapon. "But... he'll kill me..."

"You do know I'm not planning on tickling you with this, don't you?"

Inteus stared directly at the knife, refusing to answer. Taking a deep breath, Lonan stuck the knife into the skin on Inteus' forehead and began to draw a red line down the right side of the man's face.

"Your dreams, your dreams," the man screamed, and Lonan removed the blade. "He does not like that you dream about him."

"Why not?"

"He would not tell me. He is worried about something you might have seen."

Lonan nodded his head. "How did he know about them, the dreams?"

"He didn't know it was you. He just knew someone in this village had had them."

"How? How could he know something like that?"

"It was his wife. She has sight, a gift of her people, she knows things. Queen Andromeda told him."

A shriek came up from the other side of the room. Harlow lifted himself out of his chair, and then crumpled onto the wooden floor, flopping about like a dying fish, continuing with his moans.

"Is he all right?" Lonan questioned as Mother Ogma ran to him. "What the hell got into him? He's madder than–"

Then Lonan froze, another piece of the mystery sliding into place.

"What is it?" Inteus questioned, straining against his bonds to see behind him. "Is that the old man? He wasn't on my records - who is he?"

"It's just Harlow," Mother Ogma shouted back as she hauled the old man back to his seat. "He's been with me for years."

Lonan remained unmoving. *No. That's not Harlow. Harlow the simpleton has no part to play in this drama. Harlow the invalid wouldn't react in such a frenzy at hearing the name of the Magpie King's wife.*

But Adahy would.

For the last ten years, Lonan had been helping to wipe up the dribbles and clean the bedpan of the Magpie King.

Mother Ogma caught Lonan's shocked gaze, looked back at Harlow, and Lonan could tell that her mind was not too far behind his in putting the puzzle pieces together.

Lonan directed his attention back to Inteus to distract him from Mother Ogma. "The queen knew I was dreaming? I must see her then. Where is she?"

"The Eyrie."

Lonan shook his head. "No good. We both know I wouldn't last a second at those gates. She must leave the castle sometimes."

Inteus shrugged and then Lonan pressed the knife close again.

"The temple. She has permission to visit the temple to pray. She does so regularly, under guard."

Lonan raised his eyebrow at that last comment. *Why the guard - to keep her safe, or to keep her under control?*

"Is she happy?" he asked, instinctively.

"Sorry?"

"The queen. Would you say she's happy?"

149

"I- it must be a great honour to be consort to the Magpie King." Lonan raised his eyebrow at the tax collector. "But... no. No, I do not think so. The Eyrie is... tense. It is not an easy life, to be so close to the crown. For any of us."

No, Lonan thought, remembering his journey through Adahy's life. *But I bet it's a damned sight different now from back in the prince's day.* He looked over at Mother Ogma who was now patting Harlow's - no, Adahy's - hand reverently.

"I have to go," he stated bluntly. "To see the queen. Keep this one under lock and key until I'm gone."

At this, Adahy stood up. It was a shock to see him do so, to see him so in control of his actions. It was like watching a piece of furniture come to life.

"...Harlow?" Lonan questioned, not wishing to give away the true Magpie King's identity.

"I think," Mother Ogma decided, "that our old friend wishes to come with you." Adahy stood, fixing his eye on Lonan, but otherwise not responding.

Lonan shook his head with incredulity at the idea. "Not a chance. He hasn't been out of his chair in decades. He can't even think for himself - he'd get himself killed out there."

At this, Adahy grunted and remained staring at Lonan.

"Dearie," Mother Ogma interceded, "do you really think you should be refusing our friend's command?"

To refuse the command of the king is high treason.

"Fine," Lonan relented, "but I've a bad feeling about this."

"Let me get this straight," Inteus sneered, "you escaped almost certain death last night, just to walk back into it now? My lord was wrong to be concerned about you. Such a fool is no threat to the crown."

This insult earned Inteus a slap on the back of his head, which only served to spur the bureaucrat on further.

"And you think this foolishness will save the life of your family and friends? He knows where you live now, and expects to hear from me within two days. Where do you think he will look first for answers when I do not arrive back? His questioning is not kind."

Lonan pointed the knife at Inteus' face, giving him a steely glare. "I shall not be back here, not while the Magpie King lives. You tell him that if you see him. Mother Ogma, set this fool free after two days. He can go and deliver his message, to keep the village safe."

"But," and as Lonan uttered this last sentence he lowered his hand so the knife point tickled the end of Inteus' nose, "you'd better pray he doesn't find me. Because if he does then your name and the information you gave me will be the first thing that I mention to him."

Inteus paled, and was silent.

"Come on then," Lonan motioned to Adahy. The old man continued to stare. Lonan rolled his eyes. "Artemis' beard," he muttered, and took the king's arm to help him totter out of the cottage door.

Mother Ogma came outside with them, bringing travelling cloaks and bags she had hastily prepared with bread and dried meat. "Good gods, the king," she was finally able to whisper to Lonan, free from prying ears. "I've been living with the Magpie King for all this time and didn't know it."

Lonan smiled sadly at her. "I suspect Adahy doesn't know it either. The wound was bad - I can't imagine there's much of him left in there."

"I hope not, dearie. A lot of what he has heard and seen under my roof were not fit for a king to weather."

He caught the twinkle in her eye and smiled with her.

Then she frowned. "But dearie, the monsters. Your dreams showed you the Wolves attacking us, and you were able to find their tracks in the morning.

Lonan shrugged. "We always knew monsters roamed the village at night. Of course I was able to find some kind of evidence that something had been there. Not the Wolves though - I reckon there hasn't been a Wolf in the forest since before I was born, probably since you were young. The thing that got me last night, those are the monsters we hide ourselves from."

Ogma smiled again. "One less for us to worry about now though."

Lonan nodded, and then thought for a moment. "So, the temple then?"

Mother Ogma pointed north. Lonan gave her a brief hug and she attempted to do so to Adahy, but received no physical response. With that, Lonan and Adahy trotted out of Smithsdown towards the Eyrie.

The town's northern border was marked by a river which the pair crossed by way of an old log that had been placed across the current. As he helped Adahy make his way across it, Lonan instinctively looked upstream. There in the distance was the tiny figure of a young woman washing clothing, a baby girl sleeping close by. For a brief moment Lonan considered leaving her alone. She would still be angry with him for breaking his promise last night, and there was no point in making up with her now, only to break her heart all over again by dying. Time enough to heal those wounds if he survived. The sensible, selfless thing would be for Lonan to walk away now.

"Wait here a moment," he said to Adahy, and made his way down the river towards Branwen.

Her face was a mix of emotions when she eventually caught sight of him. Lonan could tell she was thankful to see him, thankful he had not died as the tax collector had suggested. However, the relief on her face lasted only a moment, and was replaced by the angry scowl that Lonan had looked at for most of his life.

"Go away," she said simply. "I'm not ready to speak with you yet."

Lonan nodded his head. "Yeah, I get that. Really, I understand - I was stupid."

"You lied to me," she said, the anger working its way to the surface. "Do you know what I need less of in my life right now? Lies."

Lonan winced. Her whole life with Jarleth had been built on lies, and Lonan was not doing any better at this early point in their relationship. He looked away in shame.

"I know, it was really bad. I'm really sorry. I just wanted to see you before-"

"Where're you going?" He looked back at her, but Branwen's gaze was now directed downstream. She had spotted Adahy, waiting silently for him.

Lonan winced again, unsure about how much he should explain. "I have to leave for a while." He showed her his bandaged hand. "It's to do with all of this. I'm going to stop this from happening again."

Branwen looked puzzled. "Whoever did that, are they coming back to finish the job?"

Caught by a sudden burst of inspiration, Lonan stepped forward and took Branwen by the shoulders. "They come back every night, Branwen. They always do, they're always out there, but

I'm going to do what I can to stop it from happening ever again."

She shook her head, eyes darting between each of his. "You're mad. The blow to the head, and then last night - you aren't in your right mind."

He smiled wearily. "I wish that was the case, truly. I want nothing more than to win back your trust, settle down with you and raise Clare together. But this has to be sorted first. What kind of man would I be if I brought danger to your door? I've no idea if the thing that did this will let our buried cellars stop it." He drew himself closer to Branwen and lowered his voice. "I want to show you I can protect you, protect Clare, the village, maybe the whole damned forest."

Then he kissed her. This was not like before. This was not a chaste kiss between two strangers unsure of how to show their love to each other, unsure of how much affection they were allowed to give at this early stage. This was a full embrace, two people baring all, showing each other how deeply and how long they had cared and wanted to be together. As he held Branwen in his arms, his lips joined with hers, Lonan saw them together. He saw them walking hand in hand along the village green. Clare was there too, older now, having inherited her mother's brown locks, running around them both and laughing. Another child was being carried - a boy, his face just beyond Lonan's ability to picture in detail. His own son, a possibility if he stayed here with Branwen.

He felt her hands grip him, pulling him closer, and the image in Lonan's mind changed again. This time it was him and Branwen, much older, sitting with each other in a dark cottage, smiling together beside a roaring fire.

They pulled apart from each other and both had streaks of tears down their faces.

"I have to go," he said reluctantly, "we're racing against nightfall."

"Promise you'll come back to me," Branwen said.

Lonan smiled at her sadly. "I don't want to lie to you again."

"Just promise me."

Lonan looked down at his feet and then raised his head to smile at her one last time. "I love you, Branwen Dripper." Then he turned and walked away to rejoin Adahy. Once they had entered the forest again, away from the sight of the river, Lonan finally allowed himself some lonely sobs while he walked with the mute.

As they plodded through the forest, those last words echoed through Lonan's mind. *I don't want to lie to you again.* He had faced death last night, and in those terrible minutes had been sure that he was about to meet his end. The sense of dread had not disappeared with his rescue, and as the information mounted up he had become increasingly aware he had unwittingly fallen into the centre of events that had been in play before he was born. Maedoc was the Magpie King now, and had been for longer than Lonan's lifetime. Adahy's bride-to-be had lived a life of fear in the mad king's clutches for decades. Now new monsters had come to the forest to replace the good that Adahy had done in his short reign.

The pair were walking along an old path, one that Lonan assumed had been used much more frequently in the days of Adahy's father when there had been more contact between the Eyrie and the villages. It was still possible to make out the route it had carved through the greenery, but lack of use made it more difficult to travel, especially if you were an old man not used to walking. Adahy tripped and stumbled on the clumps of ferns and shrub roots that now littered the path, causing Lonan to spend longer guiding him along and thus slowing their progress significantly.

"I suppose those dreams were all to do with you?" Lonan queried Adahy, not expecting an answer.

"It meant a lot to me, when I first thought I was special," Lonan continued, "when I thought I had a Knack nobody else had. But it makes sense now that it had something to do with you being close by. Some sort of Magpie King power, or kingly Knack? Your mother was an Owl, wasn't she? I heard they have dream powers - could have been something you inherited from her."

Lonan allowed a sad smile to play across his face at the continued silence of his walking partner. He turned to look at the man's face as he guided Adahy through a pair of particularly dense gorse bushes that had taken root on either side of the unused path. Lonan found it so difficult to think of this old, ruined man as the young prince whose mind he had shared so much over the past few weeks.

"I could've done it at one point, you know. Developed a Knack. I could feel it coming when I first started living with Mother Ogma. I liked it there. She was the only person in the village to keep treating me like a normal child. So, I wanted to keep her happy. As a healer, she needed herbs and flowers, and I wanted to be the one to do that for her."

"I spent weeks running around the forest and the cliffs nearby, and I got really good at it. Then one day, I realised I was getting too good. I was starting to spot where a flower would grow because of other vegetation nearby. I was recognising herbs by their scent instead of sight." Lonan spat as they continued to walk. "I was damned if I was going to trade a blacksmith's Knack for one of a forager, so I stopped being useful."

They walked together in silence for a while. "Something we both had in common for her, I guess."

Lonan whittled on now and again about more trivial matters, but generally the two walked in silence. Mother Ogma had told Lonan that the temple was a day's journey from Smithsdown, but with Adahy travelling with him there was no chance that Lonan could keep the necessary pace. When the sun was lower in the sky than Lonan was comfortable with, he found a tree that he was able to heft Adahy into the branches of, and secured them both with rope from Mother Ogma's backpack. Lonan planned to stay awake to look out for Wolves or bird-monsters, but exhaustion from last night's events overcame him and he drifted off to sleep.

For the first night in a long time, Lonan did not dream.

They awoke with sunrise the following morning. Lonan untied them both and they continued on their way. Sometime after midday they arrived at the shrine. It had clearly undergone some repairs since Lonan had last viewed it through Adahy's eyes, as the broken door had been replaced and windows were now repaired, but the holy building did not hold the air of reverence it once had. The doors to the shrine appeared to be unguarded and the gardens were overgrown and untended. For the first time since leaving Smithsdown, Lonan felt at a loss for what to do.

"Any ideas, big guy?" Lonan asked Adahy. No response. "Keep quiet then, not a bad idea."

Aiming to look like curious pilgrims instead of wanted criminals, Lonan and Adahy walked through the clearing to the building and stepped inside. They need not have been worried about discovery, as the shrine was unoccupied. The interior was also much changed. It remained dark, but most of the building walls were now bare, with no sign of the former storytelling wood carvings. The magpie totem pole had been repaired without care, stretching again to the building rafters, but now containing many incomplete, crippled animals.

"Well, we're a bit stuck now, aren't we?"

There was nothing for them to do but wait. Their entire plan consisted of intercepting the queen as she visited the shrine. They idled away many hours until people arrived at the building in the late afternoon.

A black caped figure emerged from the daylight into the gloom of the shrine. For a split second Lonan thought it was another creature like the one that had attacked him last night, but he quickly came to realise that this was one of the Magpie Guard.

The guardsman seemed surprised to spy anyone inside. "You there, what are you doing?" The man drew his sword and marched over to Lonan and Adahy, with two more soldiers following after him.

Lonan decided to play it dumb, remaining speechless as he was surrounded by armed men.

"State your name and your business or we shall cut you down here and now."

"I- I am Jarleth Dripper. The Dripper family from Gallowglass. This is my father, Callum. We - we are here for the shrine. Pilgrims." Lonan was quite pleased with his trout impression, doing his best to convey complete hopelessness to the guards.

"Why have you come here?" Lonan received a boot on his back with the question, pushing him to the flagstones and causing his broken ribs to argue violently within his chest.

"My-my father. He's dying. He wanted to come on pilgrimage one last time."

"Is this true?" The guard addressed Adahy, who remained motionless as usual. He received a fist in his gut for such insolence, causing the old man to double over.

"No, sire, do not hurt him. He cannot speak, or even see or hear us really. His illness is in its final stages."

"If this is so, then how do you know he wanted to come here?"

"He always spoke of this shrine, of his journeys here as a boy. Made me promise when I was younger to take him here one last time. This is my only chance to live up to that promise."

The guards looked at each other, clearly irritated by the presence of the villagers. "You are not worried about sundown?" they asked, suspiciously.

"Of course," Lonan replied. "We've walked hard since early morning to get here on time. We assumed there would be protection for us here…" He let his voice trail off.

"Villagers do not come to the shrine anymore," the guard informed Lonan brusquely. "They are not welcome here. You must leave."

"But," Lonan replied with feigned horror on his face, "where shall we find shelter?"

"Not our problem-"

"Let them stay," a commanding female voice ordered the guards, just before they laid their hands on the two villagers to escort them outside. "The least we can do is offer some shade of safety to these men of faith." The owner of the voice stepped through the door.

She was female, but the gravelly tone in her words betrayed her age. This was kept hidden from sight, however, by the light grey hooded cloak that the woman kept furled around herself, hood pulled low to cast shadows on her face. Only a few wisps of white hair falling from the darkness of her hood betrayed her identity, although Lonan had guessed it already. Andromeda, his queen.

Lonan quickly bent his knee, struggling to get Adahy to do the same. He realised that a single tear was running down the old man's face, and did his best to brush it away in the confusion. "My-my lady," Lonan stammered, "I had not known. We shall leave here at once."

"Nonsense," she commanded, waving a wrinkled hand at Lonan to stop him from removing himself from the building. "For too long have I prayed to my husband's god in solitude in this hall. It would be refreshing to have some company for once."

"But, my lady," the head guardsman objected, "my orders-"

"Your orders are to keep me safe," the queen snapped back at him, "and to keep me within sight at all times. Unless you view these two men as a serious threat, I think your duties can be performed most admirably from the shrine doorway. Or should I have a word with my husband about the capabilities of my personal guard?"

The guard shifted uneasily. "No, my lady. Apologies, my lady."

The guardsmen set up post at the doorway, and Andromeda beckoned for Lonan to bring Adahy and join her kneeling at the foot of the totem.

"What a curious stare your father has," she remarked in humour as they knelt staring at the butchered wooden birds. Sure enough, Adahy's eyes had not left the shadow of the queen's face since she had entered the room, even as they knelt now side by side together.

"Yes, he's been doing a good bit of that lately," Lonan muttered under his breath.

This is exactly where I wanted to be, to have the ear of the queen.

"Actually, your majesty, I've a confession to make."

"Well, young man, I am afraid there are no priests here to take your confession. Ghosts and wooden pigeons are all the ears you will find here now."

Lonan smiled. "Yes. And yours, your majesty."

The queen turned to look at him and for the first time, Lonan caught a glimpse of her face. When he had seen her in his dream a few nights ago she had been young, beautiful and with a life full of possibility. What Lonan saw now was an old woman, drained of vitality and spirit, and a face in which happiness no longer lived.

"Now, young man, what on earth would you have to confess to my ears?"

Lonan took a deep breath. "Well, for a start, your majesty, this man is not my father."

The queen's face was rigid, tensed for danger.

"In fact, your majesty, you've met him before. A long time ago."

The queen's eyes darted to Adahy's face, widened, and then her head turned back to a praying pose, regarding the totem pole before her.

Lonan decided to continue his confession. "He served you wine at a feast, but I think that even then you knew he wasn't a normal servant."

In a different voice now, one that choked out from her withered throat, she stated, "You are the dreamer."

"Actually, m'lady, I suspect he is. I was just along for the ride, it seems. This is no ordinary man. This is Adahy, the true Magpie King. The man who should have been your husband."

The queen remained praying, but her hands were shaking. "And what do you have to say to me, Adahy? Why have you abandoned me for all of this time?"

"He cannot respond, my lady. He was… well, he was as good as murdered on the night that you met. He hasn't spoken a word since, or even really had any kind of interaction with the outside world until he heard your name yesterday. These tears, even, are new to me though I've known him my entire life."

Andromeda turned to look at Adahy again, and both of them shared tears on their cheeks. She looked away. "I do not need to ask you who has been sharing my marriage bed for the past forty years. I have learnt much in recent nights. I have a gift, you see. It runs in my bloodline, much like the gift of the Magpie King runs through the Corvae. I can walk in dreams, and have been walking through yours." Still staring forward, she slipped a thin silver dagger from her wrist.

At the sight of the weapon, Lonan flinched backwards.

"This was for me. Tonight. I imagine I would have used it already if you had not appeared." Lonan did not know how to reply to this so allowed her to continue. "After all that has been revealed to me, I see no further reason to remain in this life."

"We need your help," Lonan stated bluntly.

She laughed at this. "And I should care about two insignificant lives? When so many have suffered already, none more so than me?"

"The Andromeda that the Magpie King met all those years ago would have cared."

"Ah, well, that is your problem, then. She died years ago, at the hands of another Magpie King. The one your friend Adahy allowed to have me."

"He hardly allowed it. The man was his friend. He had no clue until it was too late."

The queen sighed. "This too, I know. Forgive my abruptness. I had come here tonight in search of a simple end, which you have stolen away from me. When you told me that the serving boy had returned, I had hoped it was in some way to save me. If he had truly felt that he was falling in love with me, would he not have come back from the dead all those years ago?"

"Look at him," Lonan suggested firmly.

The queen turned again to look into the old man's eye.

"This man has come back from the dead. As much as his body was able to live, he kept it going after all the damage it had sustained. It was your name that brought him to life again, that caused him to make sounds and move again. He has come back for you, as much as he is able to."

Tears fell and Queen Andromeda moved her hand to touch that of the man who would have loved her. Adahy let out a low moan at the feel of her skin against his.

"But," Lonan continued, "all of this may be coming to an end anyway. He knows who I am now, Maedoc. I don't think it will be long before he discovers Adahy. I was attacked by a… monster last night, and was lucky to escape with only this." Lonan held up the stumps on his hand to show his wound.

The queen grew pale. "What did that to you?"

"A monster. Like a person, but with jet black skin and sharp teeth. He was there, the Magpie King, commanding it. It was dressed like him."

Andromeda began to shake. "What became of your attacker?"

"Dead, thank Artemis. I was saved by another who set it on fire."

The queen's face disappeared back into her hood. Then, to his surprise, Lonan heard her give out a sharp sob.

"My lady?"

She held out a hand to command him to stop his questioning, but his curiosity was too strong.

"What attacked me on that night?"

It was the queen's turn to inhale deeply. "My son. Or daughter, possibly. I do not know which have survived."

She looked to Lonan again. He could only kneel there with his mouth open, aghast.

"I always thought it was me," she explained. "When they came out wrong, twisted, he claimed it was my fault. I was a bad mother, poor breeding ground. Then he took them away from me, to raise as his offspring. And put a new monster in my belly as quickly as he could."

Adahy's hand, still in hers, trembled.

"Since stealing into your dreams, I now know the truth, however. It was him, his blood, poisoned by the black flower of the Magpie King. Blood that he passed on to our children." She looked Lonan deep into his eyes. "That thing you killed was mine, but it would not know me if it saw me. I did tell you I have suffered."

Lonan left the silence to breed for a while, and then continued, "He wants to find me."

"Yes. Yes, he does. He wants the information you have in your head."

"I don't understand?"

"The Lonely House. The black flower. He wants it, for our children."

"But, he was there. Why does he need me to tell him?"

"You underestimate the effects the drug has had on his mind. It is riddled with holes and inaccuracies now. He does not mount the night in any strategic pattern. He could not travel to a specific village in the forest if he wanted to. I doubt he even knows all of their names. He roams at wild, taking what he wants. But he wants that flower again, and will take the knowledge from you if he can. That is why he has been sending his agents to your village, both at day and night, to find the person who had been dreaming about his past. The attacks on your village have been much worse recently, have they not? Did you not wonder why this had happened?"

No, because I thought it was happening in my dreams. Because I thought what was happening to young Adahy was affecting my village. "What about you? You know too, do you not? Where the flower is?"

She laughed. "Oh, I dare not tell him that I know. He would torture the information from me and then kill me for fear it fell into other hands. It was dangerous enough when I let slip that I had started to see these dreams in the first place - that is not a mistake I shall repeat twice."

"Could I not just tell him? Would he let me live if I showed him the way?"

Lonan's voice faded at the stare that he earned from the Owl Queen. *Yes, that had been a foolish thing to say. If the queen's life was at stake, then a lowly villager with no Knack had no chance.*

"What would happen if he got the flower? What difference would it make for him?"

"For the Magpie King?" The queen shrugged. "Nothing, I expect. For his children? They possess power already, yes, but nothing like him. My husband is old now, his body ruined by neglect. I daresay it shall not be long before the forest is rid of him. In a generation or two, it could be that the villagers will have nothing unnatural to fear in the dark anymore. But if my children all possessed the power of the Magpie King, and if they learnt how to pass it down to any offspring that may come... He is mad, completely mad. There are days when he roams the halls of the

Eyrie, screaming at Wolves that are not there, but some part of him, some primal instinct, cares for those abominations, his Children. The only time I see him show any affection is towards those creatures. He wants to provide for them before his end. He wants them all to have his power."

Lonan understood what Andromeda was saying to him, but he could not allow his mind to move past one particular thought. *You're talking about me as if I'm already dead. We aren't talking about how to save me, we are talking about how to save the future of the forest. But my life is just beginning. This isn't fair.*

In Lonan's desperation, the accusing face of Branwen came into his thoughts. *I can still make a difference for her, though. And for Aileen, our mother, and little Clare. And for the Tumulty boys and their children, for Mother Ogma and the rest of Smithsdown. My life's as good as over, but maybe with the end of it I can make some kind of difference for everyone else.*

"So… so, we have to go to the Lonely House then. That's where the flower is. We could get rid of it, get it away from him for good." *Or maybe use it to beat him?* "That's where this will all end."

"Perhaps. I cannot see the future. Or the past, most of the time. You will find what you seek there, but it would do to you as it did to him. If you use it then you will only replace one mad king with another."

Lonan's mind was whirring. "Still, that's the only course of action we have."

"You know who will be waiting there for you?"

"Yes. I saw her in the dream."

"You know it will be different this time?"

Lonan looked to the queen for clarification.

"Adahy and Maedoc visited when the moon was waxing full, when she was almost at her most content. The new moon is three days from now. She will be feeling empty and cruel."

Lonan's skin crawled. "So, the Magpie King and the Pale Lady will have to fight over who gets first shot at me. Such a conflict could work in my favour."

"You should leave. It will be dark soon, and I have a deed to perform before he arrives with the night."

"You're still going through with it?"

"What would you have me do? Suffer him again, knowing what I know?"

Lonan had no words to answer with.

162

The queen took Adahy's hands in hers, and spoke softly to him. "Avenge me, king that would have been my husband. Avenge the life we should have had together."

Lonan bowed to the totem pole, then stood to leave. "My lady, Gallowglass. Which direction is it in?"

"Head west. The paths that lead that way from the temple should take you there. Beyond the village, you will need to find your own route."

"Thank you, my lady. And... one more question?"

Andromeda nodded for him to continue.

"How many children do you have?"

Her face grew grim, and she turned away from him, forever shading her features in blackness. "You must understand, madness can be infectious. I... I'm ashamed to say I struggle to answer that question. I do not know which survived childbirth or their father. Memories of the infants blend into one. Suffice to say he bred with me until my body could gift him no more abominations. A dozen, perhaps? I truly cannot tell. Now leave an old woman with her last thoughts."

Lonan and Adahy left the temple, the last people to ever speak to the queen.

Back outside, they moved quickly. Lonan did not doubt the queen would hold off her suicide for as long as possible to give them time to clear, but when it did happen, it would be expected that the two villagers who prayed with her might have information about why she took her life. Lonan did his best to encourage Adahy to jog with him, but the old man remained as stubborn as ever with his movements. The only difference were the tears that now streamed from Adahy's face as he mourned the woman he loved.

"It's terrible, I know," Lonan attempted to convince the old man, "but she gave us a command, her last command. If we don't keep moving forward, we'll not be able to complete it for her."

His encouragement fell on deaf ears, however, as Adahy stoically plodded along the path. It did not help when the land began to rise steeply, straining their calves as they were forced to push upwards as well as forwards. As night fell, they found themselves on a narrow path that was winding up a cliff face. On one side of them was sheer rock, the other was empty space, with the trees below distancing themselves further the more the pair pushed onwards. Lonan's instinct was to find somewhere to shelter, but a lack of a place to hide and the uncertainty of what was behind them forced them to continue through the night.

It was on this cliff path they were found by the enemy.

A black shape dropped in front of them, just within the shadows cast by the fading moon. Lonan stopped cold in his tracks, frozen by fear of what was about to happen.

"Bad boys," came a manic chuckling from within the shadows. "Oh, bad booooys." The voice would sound almost child-like, if not for the menace that laced every syllable uttered by it. "Daddy will be so happy I have found you, yes he will."

The shape emerged from the blackness. It was female, this time. Much like her brother, she had obsidian skin, a beak mask and a feathered cloak. Her chest was bare, however, and long greasy hair sprouted from behind her cowl, plastering itself across her mask and face.

"Going to pick a pop of ratties, bake 'em, fry 'em, crunch for later," she sang as she moved lazily towards them on all fours. "Put 'em in a pocket holding, smack 'em if they're being bolding."

"Well," Lonan ventured, assuming there was no way he was going to escape having to tussle with this creature, "Mummy was right. You're fucking crazy."

The creature stopped and cocked her head. "Mummy?"

Sensing a glimmer of hope, Lonan continued. "Yep, that's right, the person who gave birth to you? The person who took one look at you and got rid of you? I don't suppose you were able to speak as soon as you popped out of the womb? Because if you were singing that song as you sprouted from between her legs, that would explain why she abandoned you."

The creature ignored the insults. "Lily has a mummy?"

"Well... possibly. When I last spoke to her a few hours ago, she was planning on taking her life. You have to understand, nobody in their right mind is going to be proud of producing something like you."

"No more mummy?"

"Well, I don't know. How quickly can you get to the temple?"

The creature suddenly disappeared. Lonan stood for only a second, then grabbed Adahy again and pushed forward.

"I give sunrise the best part of an hour. If we can survive for that long, we may have bought ourselves another day."

The pair pushed onwards, reaching the top of the cliff and achieving a burst of speed when their feet found a gentler gradient to follow. At every sound Lonan assumed their death had returned. A rustle in the bushes turned out to be a badger foraging for snacks. A dark shape that covered the moon was a stray cloud playing tricks on the forest below it. For the second time in Lonan's life, dawn was unexpected and welcome.

With the knowledge that they were safe from pursuit, Lonan led Adahy away from the path and they collapsed in an exhausted heap to catch a few hours' worth of sleep.

Again, there were no dreams.

THE THIEF
AND THE
LADY

A Lost Tale of the Corvae

This is one of the final tales of Artemis the sly.

Artemis first came across the Lonely House in the days immediately following his theft from the Magpie King. He saw the open glade surrounding the building. He saw the House's occupant waiting silently at the window.

Artemis uttered up a prayer of thanks to the gods his people worshipped before arriving in the forest. He gave thanks that he was not desperate enough to seek her aid, and then turned his back on her and left.

The second time he came upon the Lonely House was years later. Those years had been difficult for sly Artemis, as the Magpie King's agents continued to pursue him throughout the forest, constantly seeking that which had been stolen from their master. At this visit, Artemis stood for almost an hour, staring at the figure that waited silently for him.

Finally, he turned his back on the Pale Lady a second time, deciding he would rather face death and ruin at the hands of the Magpie King than strike a bargain with the creature awaiting him inside.

The final time that Artemis came upon the Lonely House was in his last days, when his hair had more grey in it than brown, and the treasure that he had stolen from the Magpie King weighed heavily on his old frame.

With a smile of relief, he entered the House without hesitation.

The Lady was waiting for him inside. She had taken the appearance of a faceless young woman.

"You have finally brought me the black flower of the Magpie

King," she said. Although the Lady had no mouth, Artemis could tell she was smiling.

He reached into his bag and withdrew the treasure he had stolen from the Magpie King's home.

"It has brought me no pleasure," Artemis said. "Since I stole this plant, I have been hounded across the forest, unable to stay in one place for more than a few days."

"Then why have you kept it for so long?"

Artemis scowled. "The only thing worse than living a life of being hunted would be living a life in which he gets his own way. I will die before this flower is returned to the Magpie King. Unfortunately, I fear that time is very near to hand."

The Pale Lady nodded, silently.

Artemis held up the black flower, offering it to his host. The Pale Lady leaned forward earnestly.

"I want you to take the flower. Keep it from him, continue my purpose after I am gone."

The Pale Lady paused, tutted, and then leaned back.

"I am afraid, Artemis the Thief, this I cannot do."

A look of dismay flooded across Artemis' face. "But, this is why I have come to you. You make bargains with others, you give them what they want in return for unthinkable prices. Perhaps I am not being clear enough. I want you to keep this treasure from the Magpie King. In return I offer you my life."

The Pale Lady tutted again, the smile returning to her voice. "There are two problems with your request, friend Artemis. First, what you offer me is not worth my time. Your life is now measured in days, not even weeks, and thus holds little value to me. The second problem is much greater. The black flower cannot be kept from the Magpie King."

Artemis shook his head. "You are wrong. Look at me, I have succeeded for so long. If I was younger, if age had not crept up on me..."

"No, the tale of the Magpie King and his gift from the Magpie Spirit is now etched into the very fabric of this forest - it cannot be written away that easily. The forest itself wishes to return things as they were. Just look at the troubles it has sent your way since you stole the flower from him. In my hands the flower could be kept from him for some time longer, but eventually it would be returned. Perhaps at great cost to myself."

Artemis hung his head in defeat. "I am without hope then. That bastard and his brood have stolen my people from me, and turned them all against me. I am to be denied my revenge, and his gifts will continue to pass down his line for all of history."

The Pale Lady stroked her chin. "You speak of revenge. If this is truly what you seek, then perhaps I can give you what you wish."

"You can keep the flower from him?"

"No. The Magpie King must rule the forest, and he must be able to pass his powers to his heirs, but I believe the story will suffer some small changes."

"What do you suggest?"

"The flower shall remain in my care, and future Magpie Kings must seek me out to claim their birthright."

Artemis grew angry. "Then nothing changes. The flower is the source of his hold over my people, and if he can still have it then he still controls them."

At this moment, the Pale Lady reached out one of her thin arms and trailed her twig-like fingers down Artemis' face. "Small changes, dear Artemis, and once the forest accepts this small change, more may be made. The forest must always have a Magpie King. But perhaps it may not always be one of the Corvae who claims this mantle."

"My people. That is the deal that I wish to make, that his line is broken, that his power passes to my people. And in return I offer you my life."

At this the Pale Lady laughed. "You continue to peddle that worthless commodity?" She reached out and took the black flower from Artemis. "No, this shall be my payment. With this I can write myself back into the forest's story, after being removed from it for so long."

"But his line shall be broken, and my people will rise to power?"

The Pale Lady nodded. "Yes. Given time - generations - this can be done."

Satisfied, Artemis stood, allowing himself a weary smile. "It is done then, the bargain struck. I have succeeded."

"Go now, and spend what little time you have left."

With that, Artemis left the Lonely House and spent his final days in this world.

CHAPTER NINE

After a fitful rest, they walked alongside the forest path, afraid to use it now in case the Magpie King had his daylight agents hunting them down. Mid-afternoon they came upon the village of Gallowglass.

Gallowglass was similar to Smithsdown in many respects. The style of buildings were the same, as was the layout around a central green. What was dissimilar was the sizable stream that ran through the village itself, cutting the community in two. Lonan could not fathom how anyone would be able to sleep with that babbling going on about them. Also, Gallowglass did not have a forge. Instead, it was well known for its glassworks, as suggested by its name. A thin plume of smoke floated from one of the buildings, where Lonan suspected the village glassblower was hard at work. This is where the majority of Corvae glasswork came from. However, it had been many years since any meaningful contact had been made between Gallowglass and Smithsdown.

Lonan was about to move out of the forest onto the village green, but something stopped him. *Night isn't far away, and the Gallowglass cellars would certainly be safer places to hide than in the trees again, but...*

"That is where they'll be expecting us to go." Lonan glanced again at his silent companion and then turned to gaze at the green to watch a brood of three children running under the heels of their young parents. "If we stay here, we'll be putting the village in danger."

Lonan continued to watch as the children ran up to their parents, laughing. He felt a hollow sadness well up inside him as he saw the children's father take the hand of his wife, and Lonan caught a glimpse of the life that he almost had with Branwen.

"No more rest for us now, old friend. We keep going until this ends, one way or the other."

They moved on through the forest, not stopping when night fell, despite every fibre of Lonan's being urging him to hide. At each moment he expected to hear signs of pursuit. What made their progress all the more difficult was the density of the foliage overhead and therefore the lack of moon or star light to guide them on their way. The untrodden ground they were traversing was a mixture of long grass, tree roots and patches of shrubbery, all covered with a thin layer of autumn leaf litter, resulting in slow progress and painful stumbles in the dark.

Despite how uncomfortable the dark of the forest was, Lonan felt a sense of dread in the pit of his stomach when moonlight broke through the trees ahead. This meant he had reached his destination. Sure enough, the cover of the trees broke, and there in front of him, in the centre of the clearing, was the Lonely House. It was exactly as Lonan remembered from Adahy's dream, although the front wall and window was completely intact despite the damage that had been caused to it years ago. Lonan was not at all surprised about this.

Adahy gave out a low moan, which Lonan initially assumed was due to the familiar sight of the building. He quickly realised, however, it was a reaction to the face that was waiting for them both at the window. Again, Lonan had expected to see the Pale Lady, but the differences between her silhouette now and when Adahy had been younger unnerved him. The white face remained, but it was her hair that was unusual. For Adahy, it had hung covering her face, but now it was suspended, stretched out above her head, waving like a seaweed halo under a stormy sea.

They may have lost the nerve to continue at this point if not for the inhuman bellow that echoed from the trees behind them.

"Adahy. IT IS MINE. IT IS MINE."

It was the cripple who began moving first, running from the sound of the Magpie King's pursuit towards the awaiting face. Lonan followed his king's lead, quickly overtaking him. At this point he realised that the face in the window had disappeared, but he feared the certainty of death that Maedoc offered much more than whatever the Lady held in store. His shoulder hit the door of the cottage with as much force as he could muster, and his efforts were rewarded with a painful shattering of wood as the ancient barrier gave way, swinging open.

Lonan tumbled onto the ground, his wildly flailing arms proving useless at stopping his face from coming into contact with the floor. A wet explosion and the loss of sight to his right signified that some damage had been caused by the fall, and as he raised himself up the now-familiar dripping of blood to the floor confirmed this. Knowing he did not have the time to tend to minor wounds, Lonan looked around for a possible exit. Based on his memories of the house from Adahy's dreams, he knew that no force within these woods would convince him to enter the downstairs room that contained the Pale Lady, so his only remaining choice was the stairs.

This choice was confirmed by the form of Adahy, who barrelled past Lonan, howling as if he was being yanked up those stairs by an invisible chain. Behind Adahy, the door to the cottage slammed shut, closed by an unseen force.

Lonan expected to hear the rampaging pursuit, to see the door splinter open and to look his death in the face.

But nothing happened.

In the seconds it took Lonan to realise that Maedoc was not going to appear before him, the silence of the Lonely House settled over him like a smothering sack. He slowly turned his head towards the doorway that opened to the downstairs room. The dancing shadows of candlelight and a quiet symphony of innocent creaks were the only signs that something or someone might be in that room, but Lonan's entire frame began to tremble uncontrollably at the thought of facing her now.

A whimpering noise from above him relieved Lonan of having to make a decision. Swiftly, yet taking as much care as possible to move with little noise, Lonan crept up the staircase to find Adahy perched on the mid-way landing, the king's fists white with tension as he clutched the banister, staring at nothing in particular, returned to his catatonic state after the action of the chase. Lonan tugged at the old man's sleeve, but Adahy's knuckles were white. He was not letting go, and simply moaned in response to the disturbance.

This delay gave Lonan time to take stock of the situation. He could discern no noises from outside, but was certain Maedoc had not called off his search so easily. From below, the firelight from the downstairs room trickled out to the hallway and up the stairs, but Lonan knew that he was not yet ready to make the journey to see her. That left only upstairs. He raised his head to the landing, which was illuminated only by moonlight from a single window. The landing was thick with cobwebs, all rife with arachnids marching up and down them. These unnatural drapes moved ever so slightly back and forward, but Lonan could not discern where exactly the breeze was coming from.

At that moment, the moon outside must have unveiled its strength from behind a cloud, because the landing became considerably brighter and Lonan noticed two things at the same time.

First, perched on a shelf at the back of the hallway was a small clay pot with a single black flower blooming in it.

But between the stairway and the landing stood the Pale Lady, the faded white of her dress blending with the hanging cobwebs.

Lonan was transfixed, his mauled fingers suddenly throbbing with the rush of adrenaline that surged through his veins. The Lady did not move towards them, but watched the pair, or at least as much as she could with her flat, featureless face. As it had been when Lonan had viewed her from the window only moments ago, her hair flowed in waves from her head, as if she was submerged underwater. The folds of her thin, white dress also rippled in the unnatural breeze. His eyes tried not to focus on the tree roots below her nightdress, moving like human muscles as she swayed her body. What he could not avoid, however, was the ruined condition of the Pale Lady's skin. When Adahy had met with her in Lonan's dream she had appeared as a child, her young skin rippling with snake-like movements underneath. Now she appeared to them both as an old hag, her pale skin thin and tattered, in some places completely torn, showing the movement of the tree roots. Her human mask was little more than puppetry, a child's sock pulled over a fearsome hand.

Tentatively, Lonan took one step up the staircase. "We've come for the flower," he forced himself to say. "May we have it?"

She did not answer, but cocked her head slightly and stretched a clawed hand towards Lonan, opening it expectantly.

She wants a gift.

Lonan cursed his own stupidity. They had nothing to offer her. He wracked his brains to think of anything on his person that might satisfy her. Back home in Smithsdown, he had an array of items that held value for him - a black squirrel pelt, his favourite carving knife, an old horse shoe his father had forged - but he was not sure if any of those items would satisfy her curiosity, even if he had remembered to bring them.

Maybe she'd be interested in something she can't hold. A year of my life? The memory of my father?

My love for Branwen?

Before he had sufficient time to process these thoughts, the downstairs door imploded.

The next few seconds seemed to happen so slowly for Lonan, as if all involved were wading through treacle as they performed their next actions.

Through the dark door below leapt Maedoc. The impact that burst the door open was the same impact that propelled him up the stairway, causing him to land like a spider on the thinly plastered wall. He hung there suspended for what must only have been a fraction of a second, although to Lonan it was an eternity. He could see now that the feathers of magpie cloak that was draped across Maedoc's back were ragged and old, and many bare patches littered the once-proud item of clothing. What he was wearing over the rest of his body had once been some sort of leather armour, but it too was not a complete item anymore. Gaping holes in the material exposed Maedoc's flesh to the world, yet his skin was so ill-kept and abused that in the darkness of the night, most would assume it was just a continuation of his clothing. The bespoke helm of the Magpie King was now firmly directed towards Lonan and Adahy. In Lonan's dreams of it, when it had been worn by Adahy and his father, the helm had been brightly polished and perfectly maintained, as was befitting of the most important symbol of the leader of the Corvae. Maedoc's reign had given much abuse to the helm, and it had clearly received poor repair work in response. At one point, it looked like it had been broken where the beak joins with the rest of the head, and the weld marks there stood out from the burnished-black metal work on the rest of the item.

With all of this visual information before him, what stood out most for Lonan was the eye that looked out from the helm. Positioned in such a way to reflect the firelight from the room downstairs, Maedoc's single eye was so horribly bloodshot, it no longer seemed human. That eye locked on Lonan and Adahy just before Maedoc's final leap.

Adahy reacted in time with the imposter's attack, pushing Lonan to the side with inhuman strength, sending him flying up the remaining stairs to the top of the landing. As Lonan completed his flight, suspended helpless in the air, he had a clear view of Maedoc's claws finding their mark, ripping Adahy open from chest to belly, the force of their impact throwing Adahy's ruined body towards Lonan. Desperately, Lonan did his best to stand up and hold his ground, just in time to catch Adahy as he flew at him. One hand found good purchase on the back of Adahy's neck, yet Lonan's left hand made an attempt to grab the old man around his waist but found only slippery red ribbons. Aghast, mouth open, Lonan moved his gaze from the old man's emptying eye to the dark figure on the stairs. With what Lonan recognised as a grunt of victory, Maedoc pounced again, making impact with Adahy's broken body, sending all three of them hurtling across the moonlit, cobwebbed landing.

With a howl of success, the reigning Magpie King reached a searching clawed hand out to Lonan's face, too impatient to wait until the mess of bodies had concluded their flight before killing his prey. Horror-stuck, Lonan jerked his head around, doing what he could to distance his face - specifically his eyes - from Maedoc's touch.

Suddenly all thoughts of Maedoc vanished from Lonan's mind as he saw what awaited him at the end of his flight. There, rushing towards him at an accelerated pace, stood the still figure of the Pale Lady, her arms open wide to welcome the trio as they surged towards her.

It was the roots beneath her nightdress, not her arms, that grabbed them first.

Both Lonan and Maedoc were restrained around the waist and thrown roughly to one side. Lonan found himself being held to the ground by a tree root, gripping him tightly like a rough-skinned snake, Maedoc lay not far from him. The reigning Magpie King struggled considerably more than Lonan did, ripping at the roots and threatening to break free. The Pale Lady responded in kind, sending more of her long appendages to coil around him, squeezing him into a wooden cocoon. Lonan's heart leapt for a moment, thinking the Pale Lady had chosen to remove the Magpie King from the forest forever. However, Maedoc continued to struggle beneath the roots, suggesting this was only a temporary arrangement.

It was clear that it was Adahy the Pale Lady wanted. Lonan baulked when he saw the old man suspended in front of the spectre. Blood was flowing from the wound in his gut now, and the Lady had noticed as well. She lowered her face to the trickle of red, the old man uncharacteristically moaning in pain.

Then, to Lonan's horror, more of the tree roots reached up to the stream of blood that came from Adahy's chest. At first they touched it tentatively, but then one by one a trio of tree roots forced their way into the old man's chest.

Lonan screamed in protest and was rewarded by another root reaching tightly across his mouth, gagging him.

Adahy began to convulse. Lonan's eyes widened as he saw movement under the old man's skin. The tree roots continued to surge into his chest, widening the hole but also stemming the flow of blood. His limbs jerked wildly and his head was thrown from side to side. The Pale Lady was learning how to work her new toy.

The illumination from the stars and moon faded, plunging the chamber's inhabitants into darkness. The Pale Lady appeared to expand, her huge, billowing shape engulfing the room. She peered into Adahy's face, blocking it from Lonan's view.

"Our time here grows short," she whispered.

The sound of the hag's voice - conjuring up images of maggots feeding from rotten corpses - made Lonan gag, but he forced himself to swallow the bile trying to rise in his throat.

"The tale is nearly over, Adahy of the Corvae. This final meeting between us was requested many, many seasons ago. I am to ask you to give in. Let Maedoc here take the flower, to start a new line of Magpie Kings. Let his people, the outsiders, thrive in the forest, to take it from the Corvae as the Corvae stole the forest from me in ages past."

"The boy. You will let the boy live?"

Lonan's head jerked at the sound of this voice. It was one that he had never heard before in his life, except in his dreams. Animated as he was now, in this suspended form between life and death, Adahy was speaking. Lonan could still not see the old man's face, but the voice was unmistakable.

I want to live! I've just been given back the life I thought I'd never have again. I want to go back to it. But what's the cost?

In response to Adahy's question, the Pale Lady hovered over to where Maedoc lay buried. Her white form remained attached to the mass of tree roots beneath, which guided her body around the chamber like the head of a snake.

The roots covering the Magpie King's face fell away, allowing the Pale Lady to address her captive directly.

"You will let the boy live. Is that not correct?" She indicated towards Lonan, ensuring that Maedoc knew who she was referring to. At her gesture the tree root gag fell from Lonan's mouth and he felt himself being pushed upright so Maedoc could get a better look at him.

"The flower will be yours and the boy's life will be spared."

Maedoc's gaze darted between the Pale Lady's face and the suspended form of Adahy, and then looked at Lonan. "I promise. You live. No more eating fingers."

"And what about him?" Lonan shouted. "What about Adahy?"

"Nothing can be done for him," The Lady answered. "This time we have together has been stolen from the last seconds of his life. Once I release him, he shall be dead before he hits the floor."

Lonan fixed Adahy with a remorseful glance. At this moment, the former king turned his head to look into Lonan's eyes. The old man's dying gaze contained a small smile, but also a look of determination. Then, for the first time in his life, Adahy spoke to Lonan.

"There is no 'them' and 'us'. You are Corvae. Do not let him destroy our people."

"But... but he is so strong. I'm alone. I cannot hope to..."

"Find the strength. Save our people. Think of those you love, under his rule."

Without waiting to see the effect that these words had on Lonan, Adahy turned to face the Pale Lady. Tree roots coiled in his chest, under his skin, but somehow he continued to speak.

"I visited you many moons ago, my lady, and I promised you a gift."

The Lady did not respond with words, but she appeared to reduce in size, moving her body down to meet with the former Magpie King.

"My life is yours now. This is all I can offer you, but I believe this is all that you are interested in. Blood."

Adahy held out his hand to the spectral figure. With a rush of greed, the Pale Lady grabbed at Adahy's hand, but he withdrew it quickly. The Lady hissed in anger, the branches of her hair stiffening and coiling back, almost as if they were readying themselves to pounce.

"No, not yet. This has not been a fair deal for me. You may have my life, and all of the suffering I have endured throughout it, but the amount of blood I have shed because of your actions - because you have kept the black flower from me and my people - places you firmly in my debt."

The Pale Lady hissed at Adahy again, but relaxed the tension in her posture. She was agreeing to his claim.

"You have my life, my lady, but you must give me something in return. Just one small favour. Give Lonan a chance, give him time."

The Pale Lady nodded, accepting the deal. She dove forwards, claiming Adahy's life.

ARTEMIS' LAST STAND

A Lost Tale of the Corvae

It was winter, as deep a winter as the forest had ever known. It was during this winter that the Magpie King finally closed upon Artemis the trickster after years of pursuing the man in retribution for his theft.

They met each other over a small stream, its waters struggling to maintain their flow due to the icy conditions. The snow here was knee deep, but this was of no concern to the Magpie King. His powers allowed him to effortlessly glide over the winter coat, allowed him to track the movements of his prey despite the whiteness that now covered his kingdom.

For Artemis, however, the snow was of much greater concern. The sly man had successfully evaded capture for year after year since he had stolen from the Magpie King. The king and his guardsmen would fly to a village in which Artemis had been sighted, only to find empty purses and broken hearts. They would cautiously stalk the fearsome beasts of the forest with whom Artemis had been sighted in conflict with - fearsome Mother Web or monstrous Wishpoosh - only to find the beasts vanquished, tricked by Artemis into submission.

But Artemis had discovered an enemy he could not outwit. Time had slowly eaten away at his good looks and his nimble fingers. Now, as he struggled to stand across from his enemy, cold sapping his strength from his bones, Artemis knew his life was at an end.

"It is over, Artemis. Give it back to me."

Artemis smiled. "I cannot. I do not have it."

The Magpie King's head tilted, studying the trickster, puzzled. "You do not lie."

Artemis shrugged, a weak smile on his face. "I am sorry to disappoint you with a truth, for once."

"This is your final mistake, then. I shall track down whoever you have given the flower to and shall reclaim it for my son."

Artemis shook his head. "You do not need to track her down - she has instructed me to tell you. The Pale Lady has your flower now. She awaits your son, if he dares to brave the journey himself. If he gives her a suitable gift, she will allow him to claim his birthright from the flower."

There was a deep pause, which Artemis found to be the most pleasurable experience he could possibly have imagined.

Finally, the Magpie King erupted. "You dare? She dares? That flower is my family's property, and we have possessed it for generations. She shall not hold it for long, that I promise you."

Artemis shrugged and then fell to his knees, his exhaustion causing his legs to give way beneath him. He did his best to push himself back to his feet, but found he could not. "You might be able to win it back by force, but at what cost? Two beings such as yourselves will cause a lot of commotion before one of you falls. She will give the power to your son, and to his son, and to his son, if they but prove themselves. Why destroy so much when you look to gain so little?"

The Magpie King's shoulders dropped, and Artemis' smile grew. The king could see the wisdom in Artemis' words.

"But why?" the Magpie King finally asked.

Artemis shrugged again. "She is an ancient being of the forest. Who am I to question her motives?"

"No. I do not speak of her. You, Artemis. Why have you done this to me?"

At this question, Artemis' expression soured. "Because I do not like you, Magpie King. I do not like what you have done to my people. We were once proud before you laid us low, before you forced us to kneel at your feet."

In his anger, Artemis collapsed further, now lying on his back in the snow. He knew he would not rise from it again. The old trickster's eyes grew dim, and his smile returned. "I can see my victory now, I think. A glimpse of what is to come, given to me in my final moments. Two figures, fighting over the fate of the forest. And you, Magpie King, there is not sign of you or those of your line. You have been written out of the forest's story."

At this, the Magpie King leapt silently over the frozen stream, removed his helm and rested one of his hands on the dying man's forehead.

"Yes," the Magpie King said finally, his eyes closed. "I see them also. But Artemis, you are wrong. These are my people. These two, they are both Corvae."

"No," Artemis spat back, "they are mine. My people, not yours."

The Magpie King shook his head sadly. "You have spent so long hating me and my people, you have not seen what has happened in the forest over these long years. Our two peoples are now one. The villages are made up of old and new blood mingling. The Eyrie is the same. The parents of half the men and women who pursue you as my Magpie Guard walked with you through the wilderness before you made your home in the forest. Most would agree that there is no conflict anymore, no difference between the two."

"Then I speak for the few whose eyes remain open," Artemis said, his smile and fire fading. "My act of revenge is for them, and for all the blind fools who have let themselves forget what freedom tastes like."

The Magpie King stood and looked upon Artemis with eyes full of pity. Then he put on his helm and took off into the night.

Alone, happy, Artemis faded from the forest and into legend.

CHAPTER TEN

When the Pale Lady made contact with Adahy's body, her thin, abused skin cracked open, allowing the roots underneath to burst forth over the corpse of the fallen Magpie King, creating a cocoon around him. Within seconds, both the Pale Lady and Adahy were gone, leaving only a mass of knotted roots.

Suddenly, Lonan felt his bonds begin to slacken. He saw the mess of roots in the room begin to diminish and he realised that the Pale Lady - her prize now claimed - was withdrawing from the conflict. The cocoon that held Adahy's body disappeared, pulled into a side room, and the floor began to clear of vegetation. Maedoc also realised his freedom was imminent, and began to thrash wildly on the floor.

But Lonan found himself free of his bonds well before his enemy.

Why does she favour me? This was you, wasn't it, Adahy? The deal you made with the Lady at the end was to give me time. Give me seconds to make my choice.

Maedoc's imposing figure began to rise from the floor, ripping the final remaining roots apart himself.

Am I going to stand aside and let Maedoc have the flower, or am I going to stop him? Is there anything I can even do to stop him?

The Magpie King staggered and fell, tripping himself up on his bonds in his frenzy to be free.

I could let you win. That's what you promised her, to keep me safe. Can't imagine even you would dare to go against a deal made with the Lady. I'd be free, could head back home to-

Unbidden, faces injected themselves into Lonan's mind. Mother Ogma and his own mother, both sheltering in fear in their cellars at night. Even Old Man Tumulty, his sons, the Hammer family and Mother Cutter with her dodgy gut. But especially Aileen and baby Clare, the young ones, and his Branwen.

All my life I've lived in fear, not knowing if each night in the cellar would be my last. Could I end this fear for everyone living in the forest?

From where he continued to struggle with his bonds, Maedoc blocked the stairway. That gave Lonan only one option for escape. Taking a deep breath, Lonan got to his feet and ran to the shelf that held the black flower of the Magpie King. Outside, thunder rolled in the distance, and fat raindrops began to hit the roof of the Lonely House. Lonan grabbed the flower, took a run at the window of the room, smashed straight through it and fell to the earth below.

His impact with the ground one storey below him was not pleasant. His upper body hit the ground first, and Lonan fancied he heard a small pop from his right arm. His brain registered no pain from the fall, but he assumed that he would suffer for this later, if he was lucky enough to have a later. He struggled to his feet, mind gasping in rising terror.

A ragged scream echoed from the house that loomed above him. "Mine! MIIINE!"

Lonan turned and ran for the trees. In truth, he had no plan for what to do next. To make his escape to a village - any village - would be his best course of action. There he would look for shelter in one of the cellars, in the hope that they would be strong enough to withstand the focussed strength of a mad Magpie King.

Lonan knew there was no chance that he would make it that far. He only had seconds of life left, as it would take no time at all for the Magpie King to find and catch him. As if to confirm Lonan's thoughts, a large thud from behind told him something heavy had made impact with the ground just below the Lonely House.

Lonan reached the tree line and found his way impeded by tree trunks and shrubbery. A large crunch from behind, much closer than the last noise, told Lonan that at least one tree had been uprooted in Maedoc's quest for his prize.

Another scream pierced the forest air, but this was one of triumph. The Magpie King had caught his prey.

A sharp, raking pain across Lonan's back lifted him off the ground, spinning him through the air to smash with multiple breaking bones against an old oak tree. Lonan lay in a heap, a lightning flash through the trees highlighting the silhouette of the Magpie King, holding aloft the black flower's small earthen pot in triumph.

As life threatened to leave his body, as Maedoc turned his dark head towards Lonan, Lonan thought of Branwen and her baby.

I'll never get to know that child now. She's not mine, but for a short while, I thought I'd be a father to her.

But I've got a different job now. I've got to protect that happiness, do what I can to take away the terror and threat from the people I love. I've got one last task to perform.

The Magpie King looked about in confusion. He lowered the pot, not understanding until too late why it was empty. Only at the last second did he turn towards Lonan.

The Magpie King screamed, this time in terror.

With his last available reserves of strength, Lonan raised his right hand. In it he clutched the black flower, hanging loose from any pot or soil, its white roots glowing brightly in the twilight.

Lonan stuffed the prize into his mouth, biting down hard on its bitterness.

Desperate, with claws outstretched, the Magpie King dived at his enemy.

Lonan was not there for the Magpie King to make contact with. Instead, he had leapt high into the air, his wounds not causing him any more pain.

At the height of his jump, well above the tops of the forest trees, it seemed to Lonan that he was suspended up there in the darkness, at once aware of his enemy beneath him, but also fully aware of the land all around. A family of squirrels squirmed together in a nearby hole, hiding from the noise of the forest outside. Further away, a young girl was crying in her sleep, locked in her cellar beneath a cottage. In the ground deep beneath Maedoc, an earthworm ate away at what used to be a rabbit, long since buried under generations of earth and grass.

As Lonan began his descent, he focussed on his enemy again. Maedoc, mad though he was, was also a wielder of the Magpie King's power, and had considerable more experience with it than Lonan. By the time that Lonan's feet touched the forest floor, the Magpie King had disappeared. Lonan's fist, intended for his quarry's head, instead cratered into the fragile earth. Sensing the quickly beating heart of his enemy, Lonan raised his eyes to find Maedoc in the branches of a tree some distance from him.

"Now two of us are kings," Lonan shouted at his foe, mustering as much bravado as he was able to.

"No," came the gravelly scream back to him. "It is mine. All mine."

Maedoc leapt from his branch, again darting towards the villager, claws outstretched to make contact with the soft flesh of Lonan's neck. This time, Lonan was prepared for him and did not make to escape the conflict, but instead moved quickly to the side, reaching out to grab Maedoc's wrists as he did so. He made contact, fastening a firm, tree-root grip on his enemy. As he touched Maedoc, Lonan briefly took in the information his new senses gave him about his foe. The Magpie King's bones were thin, but strong. Lonan could feel Maedoc's blood pumping around his body, the thick oozy syrup struggling to push its way past Lonan's tight grip. He was aware of the Magpie King's skin folding, creasing in innumerable places as the old man in front of him struggled against the younger hands. At this moment, Lonan realised exactly who he was facing - an old man.

He had only ever viewed Maedoc's face in Adahy's memories, but of course Maedoc would now be as old as Adahy had been after sheltering in mother Ogma's cottage for so long. Maedoc had more experience with these powers, but Lonan was younger and stronger. Lonan's heightened senses picked up another interesting detail. Maedoc's sweat stank of fear.

"I have you now, old man," Lonan growled, sporting a grin that surprised him with its wickedness.

Maedoc flinched back in response. He squirmed again, using his own incredible strength to break Lonan's grip. Then the Magpie King ran.

Adrenaline surged through Lonan's veins at the sight of a fleeing foe, and he dived after his prey, scrambling on fours through the forest floor to keep pace with Maedoc. Broken branches and smashed bark betrayed Maedoc's passage. Lonan allowed his new senses to widen out to the world around him. Birds flew away from the forest pursuit, having learnt long ago that such events in the forest were best to be avoided. A metallic taste in the air told Lonan they were close to Gallowglass, to the crying girl in the cellar. Lonan made a mental note to return here later, after his hunt, when he needed to feed.

Lonan stopped dead in his tracks, disgusted by the thought that had crept unbidden into his mind. His forehead crumpled. It was beginning already, the price he had known he would pay for taking the Magpie King's power. He was losing himself to madness, and quickly. He would have to deal with Maedoc swiftly, lest he lose control over his thoughts, as Maedoc had done so long ago. Resolved, Lonan dashed onwards, leaping up into the treetops to gain ground on his foe.

Up there in the twilight, Lonan allowed himself to revel in his new powers. He bounded from tree to tree, no longer scurrying along the forest floor, and he had the sensation of almost flying, launching himself into the starlit darkness above his home. He did not need to track Maedoc by scent or by sight now. The panicking man's flight through the undergrowth below was like a thunderstorm to Lonan, a trail of dark clouds marking his passage. It was also clear to Lonan where Maedoc was headed. Rising up out of the forest ahead of them was the steep cliff that housed the Eyrie. Lonan had to stop Maedoc before he reached it. He was not certain how much of the palace staff remained there, or how many Magpie Guard still existed to protect their ruler. Also, it was at the Eyrie that Maedoc was most likely to find any of his offspring, and Lonan's missing fingers still ached at the thought of his last encounter with them.

An ant-like shadow crawling up the distant cliff betrayed Lonan's quarry. Lonan did not slow in his approach to the cliff, smashing into that smooth rock face with brutal impact. Luckily for him, most of that impact was absorbed by Maedoc, not able to manoeuvre himself out of the way of his attacker in time.

Not used to travelling at such speed, Lonan was dazed by the abruptness of the collision. This allowed Maedoc a moment of respite, and he used this advantage to grab Lonan by the hair and threw him upwards, aiming the young man like an arrow at the cliff face. Lonan took great satisfaction in hearing Maedoc's broken bones grinding together as this feat took a toll on the old man's shattered form, but then he himself smashed into the cliff. Lonan groaned, embedded in the stone by the force of the impact. He heard Maedoc laugh as he leapt upwards past Lonan. The villager reached out just too late to catch the escaping king.

That small failure did not deter Lonan, and he plucked himself out of his hole and threw himself upwards, snatching at Maedoc's heels, gritting his teeth in pain against his body's protests.

He did not catch with Maedoc until the cliff disappeared and the Eyrie's smooth walls were the surface that they were running on. It was Maedoc's feet that Lonan was able to grip, and the old man responded by turning on Lonan and slashing downwards with his filed claws. Lonan sensed the attack just in time and withdrew his grasp, losing his prey again and allowing Maedoc to make it to the Eyrie roof.

The Magpie King gave a bark of triumph and aimed himself for a dark opening into the building. As Lonan dashed towards him he was vaguely aware that this was once Adahy's window. The memory of those dreams was already dimming, being flushed from Lonan's mind by the poison of the black flower. Lonan grabbed Maedoc by the scruff of his neck and threw him back onto the tiles of the roof with a wet crack. Maedoc made a weak effort to move himself, but Lonan was quicker and stronger. The villager landed with his knees on the Magpie King's chest, pinning down all hope the despot had for escape. With angry effort, Lonan grabbed a hold of the battered metal helmet attached to Maedoc's head, and ripped it off, breaking the leather straps and matted hair that had held it to the imposter's face.

For a moment, Lonan stood there, towering over his opponent, revelling in his success. Before him was the withering visage of Maedoc, a head that may well have been captive for decades inside that metal skull. His skin was grey and wrinkled, clammy in the places that sores had not spoilt it. The hair on his head and beard had thinned away to long, ghostly wisps that had entwined with each other to create a matted rat nest of hair. The only teeth that remained in his head were black stumps, and he now gaped at Lonan with an open mouth, dry tongue lolling out of it.

Then Maedoc began to cry. No tears were able to force their way through his tear ducts, but his body heaved with the strong sobs of someone who had forgotten how to do so properly.

"No, no, no..." was all the old man could mutter. Lonan remained unsure if whether or not this was a final repentance from a defeated man, or if Maedoc was simply in denial about what was about to happen.

The Magpie King suddenly did his best to sit upright, using the last of his strength to grasp Lonan by the collar and get as close to his face as possible. "You will not. You will spare me. You not like me. Not yet."

Lonan thought of Adahy, lying broken on the floor of the Lonely House. He thought of the queen, suffering through decades of lies and humiliation, only to take her own life after meeting the love that she had never known. He thought of Branwen and Clare and Aileen. He thought of his mother, and the bond that had been stolen from them because of a night time raid that would not have happened if not for the man lying in front of Lonan right now.

He thought of the little girl from Gallowglass crying in her cellar, and of how hungry he felt when he thought of her.

"I am like you," Lonan replied coldly, before easing Maedoc's chin upwards, allowing Lonan to sink his teeth into the weakness of the old man's throat.

Lonan gave himself a few moments to savour his victory. Then he became aware he was being watched.

His teeth still enjoying his red prize, he raised his head to see eyes peering at him from the darkness of the castle interior. Using his new heightened senses, he became aware of further movement on the castle roof. More figures were shambling towards him. The bedraggled cloaks and beak-like masks betrayed the identity of these onlookers. They were Maedoc's children.

The abominations slunk out of the shadows in the moonlight, surrounding Lonan. Lonan had the power of the Magpie King flowing through him now, but he did not think that it would be enough to stop all of these creatures - almost a dozen in total - if they decided to take revenge for their father's death.

But something was holding them back. They were looking at the broken body lying at Lonan's feet, and then at Lonan himself, inching forwards and then backwards in a circle around him.

Fear. They were scared of the man who had killed the Magpie King.

Lonan raised himself up to his full height, allowing the Children to see him in all his glory, chin and chest wet with victory. He threw away the body he had been worrying, and picked up the Magpie King's helm, holding it aloft for the Children to see.

"Done," he stated simply, and then smashed the helm once off of the Eyrie roof.

The Children stood still, unsure of how to act.

"Done," Lonan barked again, hitting the helm off the roof once more. This time the beak of the helm broke free and rolled over to the closest of Maedoc's offspring, who eyed it curiously.

"All done. Go. Go now. Now forest is mine." Lonan stated this loudly, and waited for any reactions from the Children. Some slunk back from his rage, but most remained standing, impassionate. To finally drive home his message, Lonan once again abused the helm upon the roof, this time smashing the headpiece repeatedly into the clay tiles. By the time he was finished, the helm and roof were in pieces. All of the Children had fled.

Lonan was alone.

THE HEALER
AND THE
THE BOY

A tale from the fireplaces of the Low Corvae.

This tale takes place in the spring, after a harsh winter for the village. The winter had been difficult because the villagers had lost two young men in a short space of time. This had thrown a veil of sadness over them all, and sadness was not a good mindset with which to approach the long nights. However, the village survived, sheltering in their cellars, consoling each other in the darkness.

One of the young men had been put to death because he had been evil. It was a shame to have to do so, but none could deny that his removal was a good thing. However, the second young man had disappeared. The majority of the village believed the man had been driven mad, and had wandered into the forest at night. Like many who chose to do this, he was never seen again.

Except, that last part of the story is not true.

On the first day of spring, the village bell rang to warn of night's approach. On this night, all but one chose to retire to their beds at the usual hour.

It was then, for the first time in her life, that the old woman decided to stay out for just a few moments to take a peek at the stars. She stood outside her doorway, gazing upwards at the clear sky, her fading eyes picking out the strongest lights twinkling above her. It was then that the healer encountered the young man.

He dropped to the village green in front of her, causing her to fall back and cry out in fright.

"By the Great Magpie. Lonan, dearie, is that you?"

The young man who had once been her charge did not answer straight away. His hair was long and matted now, and he hung his head low so his face was covered in shadow. She could tell from one glance that a strength existed in the boy that she had never seen before. The old woman felt a coldness on her skin, and she wondered why such a familiar presence now conjured fear in her soul.

"It is me," the man answered eventually, not raising his head. His speech was slow and stilted, as if it had been some time since he had used words.

"But, what has happened to you? And Harlow - Adahy - what happened to him? And the Magpie King?"

At the mention of the forest's protector, the man looked up at the old woman and hissed. She gasped at this, not so much because of the inhuman noise that he emitted, but because of his teeth. They had been filed to points.

The man told the woman of everything that had transpired. He told her of the true Magpie King and his end in the Lonely House. Of the false king, and how he had been defeated on the Eyrie's rooftop.

"But, if that was so long ago, where have you been?" she queried.

"The Children. They are out there, some of them. The smarter ones have fled the forest, but some stayed. I have been dealing with them." He shook his head and grunted. "How is the village?"

"Fine, fine. Difficult winter, but we endured. Your sister misses you. Seems to be developing her mother's Knack, and I know she'll be excited to show you."

The man shook his head. "No."

"But, dearie -"

"There was another. A woman." The young man seemed agitated as he spoke, pacing in anger now. "I have trouble with my memories. Her name?"

The healer paused before answering softly, "Her name is Branwen, dearie."

"Branwen. How is Branwen?"

The healer looked away from him at this. "She... She is fine, dearie. Her and Clare. She is being looked after well."

The man raised his head and was silent for a moment as he sniffed the air. "Callum Tumulty. He is with her."

The woman's eyebrows raised. "Has looked after them both all winter, he has. Nothing funny, mind. There's a bit of an age gap there and she's been in mourning, but I dare say if you gave them time..."

The man nodded, but said nothing more.

"Dearie. You're not coming back?"

He shook his head again. "No. Much to do. The Children are almost gone now, but there are other dangers."

"They're gone? So it's true then, the night really is safe?"

"Yes." The young man looked away from her now and smiled sadly. Catching a glimpse of this look, and without the moonlight highlighting his teeth, she found herself finally able to remember what he had looked like before all of his misfortune. "Most of the evil in the woods is gone, and as for the rest..."

He turned back to look at her again. "I can protect you now, you see. And Aileen. And Branwen." He whispered her name, then raised his hand and flexed his fist. "The power in me, I can keep everyone from harm." He tightened his fist, his hand shaking in concentration.

She looked back at him again, forehead wrinkling in confusion. The boy's eyes were darkening, the mask of humanity that he had briefly worn for her was slipping. He caught her look of confusion and relaxed himself.

"But these abilities have a price. The madness, I cannot control it. Sometimes I think I do not know what is real and what is not." He looked at the healer again, and studied her face, puzzled. "He ate people, you know. Maedoc. I was disgusted when I found their remains. But now? Now I find myself thinking, why not? We are all meat, are we not?"

The boy looked at the old woman for a while, taking in her shock and disgust, then shook his head.

"Take back the Eyrie. It is empty, and our people need each other." As the man muttered this to her, he backed away from the light of her doorway. "And relight my father's forge. None have the Knack for it, not yet, but it might be rediscovered given time. I wish I... It should have been me."

He paused for a moment, and the healer was aware of a thick sadness that weighed down on the young man's heart, a product of everything that had been promised to him and then taken away. If not for the rising fear in her belly at the young man's words she would have hurried across the green and wrapped him in a comforting embrace.

Then he smiled for a final time. "You are safe now. She is safe. As long as I keep my distance, she can have some of the happiness she is long overdue."

The figure who should have been a blacksmith melted into the night, and the healer hurried to close her cottage door and descend into the cellar.

"The Magpie King protects you," he whispered softly, before returning to the forest to hunt.

A WORD FROM THE AUTHOR

A Tinker's Tale.

That was the original working title for *They Mostly Come Out At Night*, back when the story was so very different. Despite how different it was, some key elements still remained. It was set in a dark, almost borderless forest. Wolves haunted trade routes between villages, making travel dangerous. The Magpie King hadn't arrived in the tale yet, but something more important was already front and centre – it was a world of stories.

Most of the Corvae stories are inspired by real-world traditional tales and folklore. You might have spotted that a lot of the tales the Low Corvae tell each other have strong ties to the Brothers Grimm and their research in central Europe, all the way down to my choice of wolves as one of the big enemies in the book. I'll always miss the scene in which I had a Wolf dress up as Mother Ogma.

That might be a lie.

The High Corvae have much stronger ties to Native American culture, which provided the Magpie King and his people with a very different background to the villagers.

Of course, with such a rich tapestry of storytelling to draw upon, not everything made its way into the finished novel. So, I have a few extra tales from the Corvae for your reading pleasure, two of which were referenced in *They Mostly Come Out At Night*. The first is *Stone Soup*, which is a straight up retelling of the famous folktale, but with my favourite trickster taking the lead. The second is *Artemis and Wishpoosh*. The name of the monster beaver from Native American culture is so perfect, I couldn't bring myself to change it.

And the third tale? Well, that's *The Pale Lady*. If I'm being honest, I'm not very sure where she came from. She wasn't inspired by other stories out there. She never even appeared in any of my outlines for the book. The Pale Lady just seemed to creep into the novel during the writing process, with every redraft making herself more and more essential to the overall plot. *The Pale Lady* is also a direct sequel to *The Coming Of the Outsiders*, one of the most popular tales of the Corvae with early readers of the novel.

I'm giving these stories away to everyone who signs up to receive my author newsletter. As a nervous and excited debut indie author, being able to get in touch with you through this newsletter is my lifesblood, and knowing that you want to stay in touch is the inspiration I need to keep telling more stories. These extra tales from the Magpie King's forest are my small 'thank you' for showing your interest in future novels from the Yarnsworld.

Head to <u>www.benedictpatrick.com</u> to get your free stories and to stay in touch.

Looking forward to talking to you soon – hearing from readers makes all the tears, sweat and lack of sleep worthwhile.

Benedict

Made in the USA
Monee, IL
15 October 2020

45240086R00118